Paul Doherty was born in M... History at Liverpool and Oxfor... a doctorate for his thesis on Ed... Paul is now headmaster of a school in north-east London, and has been awarded an OBE for his services to education. He lives with his family in Essex. Paul's first novel, *The Death of a King*, was published in 1985. Since then he has gone on to write over one hundred books, covering a wealth of historical periods from Ancient Egypt to the Middle Ages and beyond.

To find out more, visit www.paulcdoherty.com.

Praise for Paul Doherty's historical novels:

'Teems with colour, energy and spills'   *Time Out*

'Deliciously suspenseful, gorgeously written and atmospheric'   *Historical Novels Review*

'Supremely evocative, scrupulously researched'
          Publishers Weekly

'An opulent banquet to satisfy the most murderous appetite'
          Northern Echo

'Extensive and penetrating research coupled with a strong plot and bold characterisation. Loads of adventure and a dazzling evocation of the past'
          Herald Sun, Melbourne

'A well-written historical novel with a fast-paced, action-driven plot. Highly recommended'
          www.historicalnovelsociety.org

By Paul Doherty
The Author of Over One Hundred Novels

Visit www.headline.co.uk or www.paulcdoherty.com
to find out full details of all his publications

IMMORTAL MURDER

Paul Doherty

HEADLINE

First published in 2025 by Headline Publishing Group Limited

First published in paperback in 2025 by Headline Publishing Group Limited

1

Cataloguing in Publication Data is available from the British Library

Paperback ISBN 978 1 0354 0739 2

Typeset in Sabon LT Std by CC Book Production

Printed and bound in Great Britain by Clays Ltd, Elcograf S.p.A.

MIX
Paper | Supporting
responsible forestry
FSC
www.fsc.org
FSC® C104740

Headline's policy is to use papers that are natural, renewable and
recyclable products and made from wood grown in sustainable forests.
The logging and manufacturing processes are expected to conform
to the environmental regulations of the country of origin.

HEADLINE PUBLISHING GROUP
An Hachette UK Company
Carmelite House
50 Victoria Embankment
London EC4Y 0DZ

The authorised representative in the EEA is Hachette Ireland,
8 Castlecourt Centre, Dublin 15, D15 XTP3, Ireland
(email: info@hbgi.ie)

www.headline.co.uk
www.hachette.co.uk

To my beloved grandson
Harrison Patrick Doherty

CHARACTER LIST

The Court of England

Edward I	King of England 1272–1307
Edward II	Son and heir of the above, King of England 1307–27
Isabella	Queen of England (d. 1358), wife of Edward II, only daughter of Philip IV of France
Peter Gaveston	Edward II's Gascon favourite, created Earl of Cornwall
Thomas, Earl of Lancaster	Cousin to Edward II and his most inveterate opponent

The Royal Clerks

Sir Hugh Corbett	Keeper of the King's Secret Seal
Ranulf-atte-Newgate	Principal Clerk in the Chancery of the Green Wax, Corbett's henchman
Chanson	Corbett's Clerk of the Stables
Malfeson	French royal clerk, a member of the Chambre Noire
Rahmel	Royal clerk in the service of Queen Isabella

The Templars

Jacques de Molay	Grand Master of the Templar order
Sir Giles Fitzalan	High-ranking officer in the Templar order
Raoul Clombier	Templar executed for an attempt on the life of Enguerrand de Marigny
Hugh de Payens	Founder of the Templar order
Hildegarde	Franciscan nun and close friend and ally of Cartaphilus
Cartaphilus, the 'Great Wanderer'	Close adviser to Hugh de Payens

The Black Robes

Brother Norbert	Confessor in Westminster Abbey
Brother Ricard	Benedictine monk from Westminster, chaplain at the Twilight tavern

The Twilight Tavern

Henry Malling	Minehost and proprietor
John Appleby	Steward and co-host
Stigand	Chief porter and doorkeeper
Matilda	Morning maid
Rachel and Rebekah	Henry Malling's two daughters
Spikenard	Ratcatcher
Lotham	Spit boy
Cuthbert	Chief cook

The Rifflers

William Sarasin	Riffler chieftain
Gruffeld	London riffler
Walter Mappe	Former riffler chieftain, an assassin

Seafarers

Sir Miles Kynaston	King's Admiral
Louis Luytens	Captain/master of the Flemish war cog *The Basilisk*
Brasov	Frisian pirate, captain/master of *The Hirondelle*

The Court of France

Philip IV	King of France
Joanna of Navarre	Wife of Philip IV
Louis, Philip, Charles	Sons of King Philip and Queen Joanna
Marguerite, Jeanne, Blanche	Wives of the above three princes
Gautier and Philippe D'Aunay	Knights and members of Marguerite's household
Enguerrand de Marigny	Adviser to Philip IV
Guillaume de Nogaret	Adviser to Philip IV
Amaury de Craon	Envoy of Philip IV

Others

Lady Maeve	Corbett's wife
Edward and Eleanor	Corbett's children
Megotta	Moon-girl, mummer, Corbett's spy
Ap Ythel	Corbett's friend, captain of his escort, the Tower archers
Malachi	Ensign, officer in command of a cohort of Tower archers
Robert Swinton	Justiciar
Elias Poulter	Wine merchant
Ursula	Washerwoman in the queen's household
Madcap	Local lunatic
Thirston	Leech
Magpie	Hangman of Queenhithe ward

Jacques Henri	Priest in Paris, confessor to those condemned to death
Clement V	Pope, residing in exile at Avignon
Brother Philippe	Augustinian monk and doctor, a member of the community at St Bartholomew's in Smithfield
Richard Puddlicott	Failed merchant, leader of the coven who broke into the Royal Treasury at Westminster in 1303
Adam Warfeld	Wicked Benedictine Prior who conspired with Puddlicott
Robert the Bruce	King of Scotland

HISTORICAL NOTE

January 1313, the new year has swept in the cruellest weather. The cold so intense even the Thames has frozen. Nevertheless, the blood still runs hot along the narrow runnels of fourteenth-century London. The lords of hell, London's dark and treacherous underworld, fight to control all the sinister business of the city. Their retainers, the rifflers, defy the freezing cold to plot and plan further mischief and mayhem. One dark lord in particular, the riffler Sarasin, leads the pack. He rides high and mighty before he can be brought down then brought to book.

Denizens of London's underworld such as Sarasin work hand in hand with the great lords of the soil, hungry for even more power and wealth. None more so than King Philip IV of France. He has crushed the mighty Templar order, seizing their wealth and consigning the Templars to dungeons the length and breadth of his kingdom. Philip has also urged his son-in-law,

King Edward of England, to follow suit. Both kings have sown a truly bitter harvest. Nevertheless, the time of an even crueller reaping has arrived ...

The quotations I cite before each section originate from a contemporary chronicle *Vita Edwardi Secundi* – The Life of Edward II.

PROLOGUE

France might be dangerous for him.

From all my terrors, Lord, set me free.

Père Jacques Henri, former soldier and now a retired priest, with a comfortable benefice in the shadow of Notre-Dame cathedral, mumbled his prayer and crossed himself. He then turned once more to stare up at the abomination on the lofty execution platform beneath the gallows of Montfaucon, the great and gruesome gibbet ground close to the Porte Saint-Denis. One of the stipulations behind Père Jacques being granted the benefice was that he would hear the confessions of the condemned as they waited to welcome hollow-eyed Death in the dungeons of the Palais de Justice. Today had been no different, except there was only one execution, that of Raoul Clombier, former serjeant in the now proscribed order of the Templars. Clombier, Henri concluded, was as mad as a spring hare. A poor unfortunate who had tried to kill Philip IV's leading minister, Enguerrand de Marigny, as he processed through the Gingerbread Fair close to the

Petit Châtelet. He had certainly paid the price for his unsuccessful murderous attempt, ranting and raving in the slimy-walled death pit where those condemned to die waited for sentence to be carried out. Père Henri had visited him but could make no sense of him.

Everyone knew the story of the Templars, the great military order with its myriad of houses, priories and fertile estates in both France and beyond. Philip IV of France, however, was not impressed by its supposed dedication to recovering the Holy Land and all those sacred places visited by Christ. Oh no! Philip had attacked and ruthlessly dissolved the military order. He had then encouraged other princes in Europe to follow suit, and they certainly had. Some with enthusiasm, others more reluctantly. He was also fully committed to persuading Pope Clement V to support him. Philip had seized all the properties belonging to the Templars. He had thrown their leading officers, men such as their Grand Master, Jacques de Molay, into prison, where his torturers could obtain any confession they wanted.

Père Henri stared up at the darkening sky. He pulled his cloak closer about him, settling his hood to protect his head and face against the icy drizzle now beginning to fall, and glanced around. He had to stay here and pray for the recently departed, mouthing the verses from the psalms till the bells tolled for vespers. He took a few steps closer to the execution platform, pushing his way through the crowds now breaking up, everyone eager to be away from this place of stinking, horrid death. A beggar approached with his clacking dish. Père Henri knocked this away and lifted his right hand to display the Ave beads wrapped around his stubby fingers, a sign that he was praying. A Dominican priest, garbed in the black and white robes of his order, shouted at him to be more compassionate. Henri just ignored him.

He reckoned that vespers was imminent. He had one more task to complete before he could scurry back to his comfortable candlelit chamber in the schools of Notre-Dame. He opened his small leather satchel and took out his asperges rod, a sprinkler containing holy water. Muttering a prayer that his belly would not betray him, he climbed the greasy steps. The bearded, rough-voiced men-at-arms stepped aside so the priest could stand on the top step and stare at the abomination that had once been Serjeant Clombier. The former Templar had suffered the full rigour of the law, being flayed alive, his genitals severed, his head struck off. The grisly remains had then been dragged to one side of the gallows where, skinless, what remained of his corpse was strung up by its elbows and arm joints.

Henri hastily lifted the asperges rod and sprinkled the remains. He rushed a prayer for mercy, then, as the bells of nearby churches began to toll for vespers, he fled the execution platform, ignoring the mocking laughter of the men-at-arms. As soon as he was through the palisade that cordoned off the execution ground, he paused to vomit. Once his belly had settled, he straightened up, staring into the gathering dark, wiping his mouth on the back of his hand. He caught his breath as two shadows emerged out of the murk to stand either side of him.

'Père Henri?' one of them whispered, thrusting a small wine skin at the priest. 'Drink!' he urged. 'Drink! *Pax et bonum*, Father, we mean you no harm.'

'Who are you?' Père Henri stuttered.

'Messengers. Please drink, and here is something for your time.'

He felt a small clinking purse being pressed gently into his hand. He grasped this more tightly before lifting the wine skin to take a most generous gulp. He coughed, took another mouthful and handed it back, striving to keep his nerve.

'What is it?' he murmured. 'I can see you mean me no harm, do you, sirs?' He tried to relax, to ignore the calling of the rooks and ravens circling in to feast on the blood-drenched scaffold.

'What do we want, Père Henri? The answer is simple. Nothing, really. Yes,' the shadowy visitor whispered, 'we want nothing. Serjeant Clombier now hangs dead. All we want is for you to tell those who are the cause and source of all this carnage . . .'

'Tell them what?'

'That the Poor Soldiers of Christ are not yet finished. Vengeance comes. Vengeance on a king who destroyed our order. Threefold vengeance on the father, the daughter and the grandson: Philip, Isabella and Edward. Three names, three Capetians, three objects of God's anger. Vengeance is coming on them all! They will taste the same fire, the same horror of the flames as our brothers in the Templar order.'

'No, no!' Père Henri shook his head. 'Edward is but a baby, hardly a few months old.'

'Vengeance is mine, said the Lord, even to the third or fourth generation. Tell them, priest. Tell those who caused such destruction about the storm that is brewing.'

'And your names?'

'No names, priest! No names! Now, close your eyes and slowly recite the Pater Noster, the Our Father. Do so with your head down, eyes closed!'

Père Henri obeyed. He bowed his head and closed his eyes. One of the shadows seized his right arm and thrust something cold into his free hand. Then silence. He finished his Pater Noster, took a deep breath and opened his eyes. He glanced around. 'Nothing,' he murmured. He opened his hand and stared at the waxen seal and the image printed so distinctly upon it: two knights sharing the same horse.

'Templars!' He exclaimed. 'God have mercy on them all.'

On that same day, at around the same hour, between nones and vespers, Brother Norbert, a Benedictine monk at Westminster Abbey, was sitting on the mercy seat in one of the chantry chapels deep in the darkness of that ancient church. He was there to assoil, shrive and give ghostly comfort to any sinner seeking it. Norbert was, by his own admission, a veteran priest, a shrewd observer of human foibles. He was an experienced confessor, though constantly surprised by the sins of others. Today, however, was different; there was no one to surprise him, at least so far.

The abbey lay silent. Nothing but the scrabble of questing mice and the clatter of some iron-studded door being slammed shut. This was the time of the twilight terrors: the hour of the bat as well as that of the ghost, those wandering spirits still seeking solace after death. God knows Norbert had a surfeit of such tales. The good brothers constantly maintained in their daily gossip that the abbey was a haunted hall crammed with the spirits of the dead who refused to move on. Given its long history, Norbert mused, it was little wonder that such tales became commonplace. Moreover, the imminent arrival of Sir Hugh Corbett, Keeper of the King's Secret Seal, together with his henchman, Ranulf-atte-Newgate, Clerk in the Chancery of the Green Wax, had certainly disturbed the harmony of the abbey, causing a real flutter among the good brothers, and with sound reason. Brother Norbert grinned and clutched even tighter the small crucifix he held.

'Oh yes,' he whispered to himself. 'Corbett returns, and so will the ghosts.'

Ten years ago, the abbey had been swept up in the richest of scandals. A cohort of the Black Robes, the Benedictines, had certainly proved they were black of both heart and soul. Under the leadership of the wicked prior, Adam Warfeld, these monks had conspired with a bankrupt merchant named Puddlicott, along with a band of London rifflers, to rob the Crown Jewels, which were kept secure, or so people thought, in the cavernous, well-fortified crypt beneath the abbey. Prior Warfeld had organised parties in the dark hours around midnight. Food and wine, only the very best, had been imported into the abbey together with a bevy of beautiful courtesans, who certainly kept the Black Robes, or at least some of them, very busy. So much so that when dawn broke and the bells tolled for divine office, these monks could hardly climb the stairs or stand in their stalls to chant the psalms. In the meantime, Puddlicott and his merry band had forced their way into the crypt, crossed the deep divide and descended into the treasure chamber. They had robbed it clean, taking so much that they left a trail of plundered loot from the abbey doors to their barges waiting at a nearby quayside.

At first the robbers had their way, becoming the toast of all who dwelt in the dark, those minions from the manor of Hades, London's shadow-crowned underworld. Oh yes, they had swaggered and congratulated each other until Sir Hugh Corbett arrived in their midst. The royal clerk, on the direct order of the old king, had swept like an avenging angel into the city. He would brook no opposition and ignored all privileges. No one was safe. Puddlicott took sanctuary in a London church, only to be dragged out by Corbett's mercenaries. Lawyers and priests protested that the rights of sanctuary were being violated. Corbett refused to listen and had the robber chieftain tried before a special commission in the Tower. Puddlicott was condemned to death and hanged at Westminster Gate. Corbett, again at the old king's instruction, had his corpse peeled and the skin nailed to the door leading into the abbey refectory so that the good brothers, before they dined and wined, could clearly see what happened to those, cleric or not, who violated the king's peace. The skin hung there still, becoming drier and more shrivelled but a constant reminder of royal power. The abbey had petitioned for its removal, but Corbett proved implacable, refusing to exercise any clemency, even though the Black Robes maintained that Puddlicott's ghost now stalked the abbey and would know little peace until the skin was taken down and buried.

Perhaps, Brother Norbert reflected, chewing the corner of his lip, the abbot could petition again. After all, Corbett was apparently to be lodged in the royal palace and work in the main chancery office, both of these only a brief stroll from the abbey. Surely the abbot could use this visit to mend bridges with the royal clerk? The monk swallowed hard. Corbett made them all nervous. The brothers gossiped about why he was taking up residence. Father Prior had intimated that he was coming to Westminster to harry and hunt William Sarasin, a former member of Puddlicott's coven, a criminal guilty of a veritable litany of horrid crimes.

He startled as a door in one of the transepts opened and shut with a crash. Footsteps echoed. The door to the chantry chapel opened. Brother Norbert ensured that the screen was in place. He listened intently as his visitor made himself comfortable at the prie-dieu on the other side. He was sure the would-be penitent was a man, fairly rich, as he could smell the perfumed oil his visitor must have rubbed into his hands and face.

'Good evening, my son,' he intoned. 'You have come to be shriven?'

'No, I have not.' The voice was harsh, peremptory. It startled the Benedictine. 'I have not come to be shriven but to warn.'

'About what?' Brother Norbert gasped, dabbing at the sweat that had broken out on his forehead. 'My son,' he pleaded, 'this is sacred ground and a sacred space. Be prudent.'

'Sacred ground, sacred space?' The voice became jeering. 'No space here or elsewhere can atone for those spaces once occupied by my brethren, the Poor Soldiers of Christ.'

'You mean the Templars?'

'Who else?'

'But they are to be dissolved by the Holy Father, Pope Clement V, in Avignon. He has issued—'

'He has issued nothing of the truth. Clement is no more than Philip of France's puppet, as is our own king. Nevertheless, vengeance is coming, threefold vengeance on father, daughter and grandchild, retribution sweeping across three generations. Fire will consume them as it has so many of our brothers. Oh yes, the avenging angel will be a tongue of living flame. Philip and his ilk will experience the same terror and pain as our good brothers.'

'What is this? Who are you?' Norbert could only stammer.

'Listen, Black Robe. Tell those who will be hurt by this warning what I have said. Now I shall leave you. You will stay until I have gone. Good day, Brother Norbert.'

PART ONE

He was Master of the Seas.

PART ONE

He is a Man of the Sea.

The Twilight was a most magnificent hostelry, overlooking the prosperous and busy quaysides of Queenhithe, a place where ships, galleys, cogs and other craft came in to disgorge their goods and take on different cargos, produce that poured in from the country estates of England. It was a majestic three-storey mansion with a finely decorated main entrance guarded by a porter. This individual was always quick to inform travellers not to use the grand entrance but instead to enter through one of the many side doors either side of the great hostelry bounded by its soaring crenellated curtain wall. A small village in itself, the Twilight housed stables, outhouses, storerooms and smithies, as well as a farmyard containing poultry, piggeries, hen coops and chicken runs, a rabbit warren, and a duck and carp pond.

Many of the tavern's lower chambers were considered to be the most comfortable in London. Sir Hugh

Corbett and his henchmen certainly agreed with such a judgement. The royal clerks had taken over the tavern to execute royal justice: to investigate certain crimes against the Crown, in particular the wilful murder of Louis Rahmel. Rahmel had been a squire, a body serv- ant of Isabella, Queen of England. His murder had actually taken place in the tavern's spacious, beautifully decorated taproom. Sir Hugh, together with Ranulf- atte-Newgate, had been authorised by the Crown to conduct an inquiry into the murder as well as other felonies associated with the squire's violent death. He had accepted the charge with alacrity, even more so when he learnt that the accused was none other than William Sarasin.

Ten years ago, Corbett had pursued Puddlicott's gang, who had been accused of the theft of the Crown Jewels from the crypt at Westminster Abbey. He had tracked down and dispatched to the gallows Puddlicott and his leading henchmen. Sarasin, however, had escaped. Until now! Corbett could have insisted that the case be heard before King's Bench in Westminster Hall, but he had decided to implement a more ancient custom: to try the offence where the crime had been perpetrated. The Twilight would become an extension of King's Bench, and the Royal Exchequer solemnly promised to reim- burse Master Henry Malling, owner of the tavern.

The taproom was swiftly transformed into a true court of King's Bench. The chamber's dais, leading into a spacious window embrasure, became the heart of the court. As at Westminster, the judgement bench was a long trestle table covered with a thick green baize cloth. Three justices would sit behind this bench, Corbett and Ranulf being joined by a local justiciar and landowner, a benevolent former royal clerk, Robert Swinton. Symbols of royal authority proclaiming the full power of the English Crown were carefully laid out across the table: a sword of justice, a book of the Gospels and a small whip, along with the royal warrants, licences and letters authorising the court, Sir Hugh Corbett in particular, to act in the pursuit of God's justice as well as that of the king. In this, the two were always the same. The jury empanelled by Swinton sat on benches to the right of the table, witnesses to the left. The floor had been swept clean, and fresh rushes sprinkled with fragrant herbs had been carefully strewn. A merry hearth fire leapt like a dancer, giving off heat, sparks and perfumed smoke. The air turned sweet as the scented logs snapped and cracked under the flames. The taproom was well lit. A veritable host of candles shed pools of shifting light, while a thick red-ringed hour candle on its heavy bronze stand carefully marked the passage of time.

On that particular morning, Sir Hugh Corbett was not so concerned about time, for this was the last day of the trial. Its outcome had never been in doubt, but due process had to be rigorously followed. He had risen early that morning. A barber had shaved his olive-skinned face, now lined and furrowed, and had then trimmed his hair, once raven-black, now streaked with lines of silver. Corbett had finished dressing, murmuring a prayer against the cold as he slipped on fresh linen followed by socks, shirt and leggings. These were as thickly padded as his jerkin, which boasted the royal arms on both the right and left shoulder. He had pulled on his soft Spanish leather riding boots and carefully put on his bracelet and three rings: one a gift from his wife Lady Maeve, the second the Keeper's unique signet ring. Finally, the wedding ring his mother had worn so many years ago. She had tugged it off with her near-dead fingers, smiling faintly as she thrust it into the palm of her beloved's son's hand.

Corbett paused before the hearth to murmur a requiem for his parents. He then donned his cloak, strapped on his war belt and left his chamber for the taproom, where everything was ready. He scrutinised the layout of the judgement bench but could find nothing amiss. Ranulf had done an excellent job. The spiky-haired clerk knew all Corbett's foibles, and 'Old Master Longface', as Ranulf secretly called him, would not accept sloppiness, particularly in matters judicial. Corbett sat and waited for the bell for terce and, when it sounded, he gave the order for the court to be convened.

Chanson, Corbett's Clerk of the Stables, had been dragged away from his beloved horses to serve as an official usher. He now began to summon the witnesses, clerks and, most importantly, the twelve jurymen. Once they were seated, Corbett stared around. Two people were missing. The prisoner waiting chained in the cellars below, and the enigmatic Malfeson. As if in answer to Corbett's hushed mention of his name, Chanson opened the door and ushered the French clerk to a chair to

Corbett's left at the far end of the judgement table. Tripping like a dancer, yet silent as a shadow, Malfeson stopped in front of Corbett, bowed and took his seat, asking that his chancery desk be brought closer. Ranulf arranged this, ensuring the desk contained inkpots and other necessities.

Corbett seized the opportunity to scrutinise Malfeson. The French clerk had only recently arrived from Paris, dispatched by King Philip to serve Queen Isabella. Fluent in English, Latin and Norman French, he had presented the case against Sarasin. In Corbett's view, his presentation had been superb, teasing out from Sarasin shreds of evidence to build a solid case against him. From the very beginning, Queen Isabella had insisted that Malfeson act for her and her household. The Crown lawyers declared they could see no reason to refuse such a request, while King Edward also agreed, being determined not to alienate Isabella's father. The trial had begun late, as they had waited for Malfeson's arrival. Corbett, however, hoped that today would still be the last before judgement, for he was determined to impose summary sentence. As for Malfeson, who he truly was and what he was really doing in Westminster, Corbett quietly promised himself that he would discover more. He suspected that Malfeson was not just an ordinary chancery clerk but a high-ranking member of the Chambre Noire, Philip IV's secret chancery. Why had he come? Corbett closed his eyes. What other mischief was brewing?

'Sir Hugh,' Ranulf whispered, 'all is ready.'

'Yes, all ready for the dark,' Corbett retorted.

'Now . . .' He raised himself in his chair, pointing at Captain Ap Ythel, who commanded the retinue of twelve Tower archers who always accompanied the royal clerk. 'Captain Ap Ythel, bring up the prisoner.'

A short while later, Ap Ythel and three of his archers pushed and shoved Sarasin into the taproom and made him sit in the chair directly opposite Corbett just below the dais. The prisoner was heavily manacled and chained. Ap Ythel, however, was also determined that Sarasin could not even move on the chair, and lashed him more securely with thick, heavy rope. Once the archers had all taken their places behind the accused, an eerie silence descended. Corbett stared at Sarasin, who glared back at the clerk who had brought him down, eyes like those of an angry stallion, his mouth twisted in a never-ending litany of curses. Ten years ago, Corbett had shattered Puddlicott's conspiracy, recovered most of the treasure and dispatched a goodly number of Sarasin's confederates to the heavenly court. Sarasin had been forced to flee abroad, but had then returned armed with a royal pardon earned by long, arduous service in the royal array. Once he had this, he had reverted to his old ways, soon making himself a powerful riffler captain who could stir up the city mob and command the allegiance of the ruthless London gangs.

'Sir Hugh?' Malfeson got to his feet, scraping back his chair, and went to stand behind the prisoner, who twisted and turned like some savage beast struggling to break free from a net. 'I am finished in presenting my case and that of my royal mistress before this court.

In brief, the creature Sarasin, the prisoner you have before you, is guilty of the wilful murder of a French royal clerk here in this very taproom. Louis Rahmel was going about his local business—'

'Which was what?' Corbett intervened. 'Remind the court.'

'Sir Hugh, we do not know why he came here just after the Angelus bell on that fateful day.'

'Well, do *you*?' Corbett pointed at the prisoner. 'Do you know why Rahmel came here?'

'Piss off, Corbett.' Sarasin collected phlegm in his mouth and spat it out. Corbett nodded at Ap Ythel, who went round the chair and roundly smacked the prisoner's face.

'For my part, Sir Hugh,' Malfeson spoke up, 'the evidence indicates that a dispute arose between the accused and Rahmel, which ended in the prisoner drawing his dagger and piercing Rahmel to the heart.'

'Self-defence,' Sarasin bawled.

'Against whom?'

Sarasin just shook his head.

'This is all a nonsense,' Malfeson continued. 'We have the testimony of Rachel and Rebekah Malling.' He pointed across to the two young women who, white faced and nervous, sat on the witness bench. 'Not to forget their father Henry Malling, who also witnessed the murderous attack. Remember, Sir Hugh, Rahmel was unarmed. Sarasin, on the other hand, was steeped in his drink. He was malmsey enough to commit murder, which he certainly did, on that innocent clerk.'

Corbett nodded, keeping his own counsel. He could not decide if Rahmel was as innocent as Malfeson portrayed. After all, what was a French royal clerk doing in a tavern on Queenhithe?

'Sir Hugh,' Malfeson continued, seeming to guess what Corbett was thinking, 'Rahmel was a royal clerk. He could go wherever he wanted, and he did. On this occasion, unarmed. He had every right to visit a splendid tavern such as this to chat to the fair-faced daughters of the taverner. All the evidence shows that on that particular day, Sarasin picked a quarrel with Rahmel, drew his dagger and killed him.'

'Do we know anything of what passed between the two?' Ranulf asked.

'None, sir,' Malfeson replied.

'Will you help us?' Swinton asked, pointing at the prisoner.

'Piss off.'

'So what is your defence in all this?' Swinton demanded.

'Self-defence,' Sarasin snarled again. 'Rahmel was armed. He drew his dagger and I drew mine in self-defence.'

'That's a lie,' Malfeson retorted. 'We have witnesses who testify against you.' He lifted his hands in supplication. 'Sir Hugh, with all due respect, how long must this mummery go on?'

Corbett glanced at Ranulf, who simply shrugged, and then at Swinton, who did likewise.

'Sir Hugh,' Ranulf whispered urgently, 'we have gone

through all this time and again. Sarasin is a felon of gross disrepute. We do not know, and I don't think we ever will, why Rahmel came here on that particular day or what provoked his dispute with Sarasin.'

'Nevertheless,' Swinton interposed, 'on one thing we are certain. Sarasin killed a defenceless man in cold blood without good cause.'

Corbett nodded in agreement and rose to his feet. Everyone followed suit. He looked to Ranulf.

'Members of the jury,' Ranulf intoned, 'we await your verdict. Who will deliver it?'

'That will be me, your Honour.' A small, rotund man stepped away from the benches, his faced laced with sweat, his breath coming in short gasps.

'Your name?'

'Elias Poulter, sir, wine merchant.'

'Very well, Master Poulter, you and your companions will retire to prepare and confirm your verdict.' Ranulf pointed across to a door leading into the great buttery. 'Captain Ap Ythel will guard you there.'

'He'll be no real defence,' Sarasin bellowed, struggling against his bonds. 'I am the Immortal. Whatever you decide, I shall return.'

'Not from hell,' Ranulf retorted. 'Satan will hold you fast.'

Corbett retook his seat and stared hard at the accused, who now sat with his shoulders hunched, head down. He was intrigued by Sarasin's outburst, but there again, men about to die often made such vain threats and promises. He was about to question the prisoner more closely when the buttery door flew open and Poulter, the foreman, full of his own self-importance, led his fellow jurors back to their seats.

'No surprise,' Corbett whispered to his two colleagues. Ranulf murmured his agreement, then raised his voice and called for silence.

'Members of the jury,' Corbett declared, 'have you reached a verdict?'

'We have, your Honour.'

'And is that verdict the judgement of you all? Of each and every one of you?'

'It is, your Honour.'

'So, Master Poulter, foreman of the jury, look upon the accused. On the first charge of the wilful murder of the clerk Louis Rahmel. Guilty or not guilty?'

'Guilty.'

'On the second charge of being a violator of the king's peace in this city and across the shires beyond. Guilty or not guilty?'

'Guilty.'

'And your recommendation? Is mercy to be shown?'

'None.'

'So what is your sentence?'

'To be hanged by the neck until dead.'

A deathly silence fell on the taproom. Corbett wondered if the ghosts were beginning to gather. The demons eager to seize Sarasin's soul. He rose to his feet and tried to pass sentence, but Sarasin was now in full voice, threatening them all with dreadful visitations from beyond the grave. Sick and tired of this masque,

Corbett eventually ordered Ap Ythel to gag the prisoner. Sarasin continued to protest behind the gag. If he hadn't been tied, he would have cast about and tried to attack as many as he could. Consequently Corbett decided that sentence was to be carried out immediately. He declared this to be so, and that the gibbet would be the tavern signpost.

'It's lofty and sturdy, Sir Hugh,' agreed Ranulf. 'Just place a ladder against it and the rest can be done swiftly enough.'

'And if it's to be done,' Corbett replied, 'then it's best done quickly. Sarasin is a killer. If he has the opportunity, he will kill just for the sheer sake of it. So quick now,' he urged. 'Fetch the ward hangman. Captain Ap Ythel, see if the prisoner requires a priest, but for the time being, take him back down to his cell until all is ready for his last walk on God's earth.'

Sarasin, bound and gagged, could do little as he was dragged away. The clerks, spectators and witnesses joined the jurors in the great buttery. Only Malfeson remained.

'A satisfactory conclusion, Sir Hugh.'

'Most satisfactory, sir.'

'I shall report the same to her Grace. She will be pleased.'

'As will the king,' Corbett declared. 'Not to mention the Lord Mayor of London and his Guildhall coterie. Sarasin was a riffler chief, the most violent of them all: his fearsome reputation attracted the true nightmares of London's underworld.'

'I would certainly swear to that.' Ranulf, who'd re-entered the taproom and was now sitting in a window seat, got to his feet and walked towards Corbett and Malfeson on the dais. 'Oh yes,' he continued, 'the angels of the light will certainly rejoice at Sarasin's departure from this vale of tears, while the spirits of the dark will welcome him into eternal night.'

'Quite poetic,' Malfeson mused.

'And you are most skilled,' Corbett retorted. 'You presented a powerful, convincing indictment.'

'Thanks to you, Sir Hugh. I received great help and assistance from your clerks in both the Chancery and King's Bench and was able to draw up a veritable litany of crimes that could be placed at Sarasin's door. And that did intrigue me . . .'

'Why?'

'Well, Sir Hugh, why didn't the Crown, given Sarasin's lies and depredations, not deal with him years ago?'

'Simple enough, monsieur. The Crown could not summon witnesses against him. Oh, we certainly tried, but you can guess what happened.' Corbett waved a hand. 'Witnesses changed their minds, became ill, too sick to testify. Or they simply disappeared. On Rahmel's death, however, there was no wavering. Master Henry Malling, owner of this spacious tavern, together with his two daughters, Rachel and Rebekah, swore, as you yourself witnessed, that Rahmel was unarmed. He was wilfully slain by Sarasin: their testimony alone was enough to dispatch the wolfshead a hundred times over to the scaffold.'

'I suspect both ladies were sweet on our charming young French clerk,' Ranulf declared, 'with his courtly words and handsome manner.'

'I agree.' Corbett nodded. 'And they undoubtedly persuaded their father, who apparently dotes on them, to sing the same hymn they did.'

'But what about Sarasin's henchmen and the other rifflers? Wouldn't they have come to his aid?'

'Monsieur,' Corbett gestured around, 'that is why we detained him here to follow due process of law. He was kept well away from Newgate, Westminster and the city wards. More to the point, some of the other riffler lords would be only too pleased to see the back of an arch-rival.'

'And there are other considerations,' Ranulf added. He paused to fill three beakers of morning ale, two of which he duly served to his companions before sipping from his own tankard. 'Everything was kept secure at the Twilight. Woe betide any of Sarasin's coven who tried to enter here to perpetrate mischief: to interfere with the work of royal justices is a capital crime. Oh yes, Sarasin was well and truly trapped.'

'And you, sir,' Corbett pointed at Malfeson, 'you are a lawyer?'

'Of sorts.'

'And you crossed to England in the retinue of Marguerite of Burgundy. So let me cut to the chase. Are you a member of the French secret chancery, the Chambre Noire?'

'I am, Sir Hugh, the loyal subject and sworn servant,

body and soul, in peace and war, of his most excellent Majesty King Philip of France and his beloved daughter Isabella, Queen of England. Louis Rahmel was the same. Much beloved by my mistress, hence my presence here over the last few days. To ensure justice was done and Rahmel's murder avenged.'

'And now what—' Before Corbett could finish his question, there was a knock on the door and Sir Robert Swinton entered, leading an eerie-looking individual garbed in black and white from head to toe, whom he introduced as Magpie, hangman of the ward. A lean and lanky man, long of arm and leg, sharp featured and hollow eyed, Magpie seemed uneasy as he stood bowing and scraping before them.

Corbett rose to his feet and clasped the hangman's outstretched hand, which was slippery with sweat. 'All is well?' he queried.

'All good, Sir Hugh. I am just very nervous. William Sarasin must be a soul bound for hell.'

'He certainly is,' Corbett replied, retaking his seat. 'And you are to send him there, the sooner the better.' He turned to Sir Robert. 'Monsieur Malfeson and Master Ranulf will accompany you.'

'Sir Hugh . . .?'

'No, Ranulf, I need to have my own witness.'

'Yes, Sir Hugh.'

'Let it be done swiftly. Time passes, the hour candle burns, the night beckons. God be with you.'

The four men left to go down to the cellar where Sarasin lay manacled and chained. Corbett heard Ranulf rapping out orders to Ap Ythel and the hail of obscenities Sarasin, now free of the gag, hurled at his captors. Doors opened and slammed shut. The scrape of steel mingled with the clatter of chains and manacles. At last the chaos and clamour from below subsided, to be replaced by shouts and yells from the front of the tavern.

Corbett could imagine what was happening. Two ladders would be placed against the signpost. The hangman would go up one, while Sarasin would be pushed up the other by Ap Ythel's archers. The prisoner would be bound hand and foot but still able to move as he mouthed a tirade of obscenities. The noose would go round his throat, the knot tightened. Once ready, the Magpie would scuttle down his ladder, then pull the other one away to leave Sarasin turning and twisting as the rope tightened and he strangled to death. Corbett had insisted Ranulf be an official witness because that was part of a justiciar's task – he represented the king and must ensure that his judgements were enacted – but he knew the source of his henchman's reluctance to watch the hanging.

Ranulf-atte-Newgate was the by-blow, the illegitimate son, of a priest who'd fled both his vows and his parish. As a young man, he had joined the ranks of London's rifflers, running as wild and as savage as the worst of them. Eventually he was caught, tried and sentenced to hang. Corbett, who was inspecting the prisoners being pushed into the death carts, had, for God knows what reason, plucked him out for a pardon, then appointed the young riffler to be his henchman.

Ranulf had escaped the gallows, but their shadow still hung over him. He would never forget that long, cold wait in the death pit as the Crown organised his hanging at Tyburn or Smithfield.

'It's over, Sir Hugh.'

Corbett glanced up. Ranulf stood in the doorway.

'Sarasin has gone to judgement.'

'God have mercy on him and on us,' Corbett replied. 'Come, my friend, let us toast the end of this business. Let's hope and pray it remains as closed as it seems. Now, what should we do?'

In the end, Corbett decided to stay the night at the Twilight. He gave instruction to Chanson that the horses be saddled and the sumpter ponies be ready by first light. He intended to make swift return to Westminster, but he also wanted to stay and thank those who had played such a prominent part in what he described as 'The destruction of one of London's most notorious outlaws. A man of blood, guilty of many sins and crimes. A real threat to both Crown and Church.' He paid for a sumptuous meal to be served in the privacy of the comfortably furnished great buttery. Malling the taverner proclaimed the menu: soup of ground capon thickened with almond milk and seasonal fruits; roast lamb, venison and baby pork, the dessert being a frumenty, a porridge made with a mixture of eggs, milk and more fruit.

As the tavern settled after the execution, Magpie, along with Malling the taverner, had pleaded with Corbett for Sarasin's unsightly corpse to be taken down and conveyed to the great mortuary near St Mary atte Bow. Once there, it would be sheathed in a cheap shroud and tossed into one of the many lime pits. Corbett had been quick to agree. Justice had been served; the king's peace proclaimed. Moreover, he knew full well that the corpse of a hanged man was a great attraction to the wizards and warlocks who prowled both banks of the Thames. They would love to cut Sarasin's corpse and morsel the flesh to use in their macabre midnight rites and rituals.

He had watched as the Magpie had cut the corpse down, shouting that it was still warm but as dead as a roast duck, then left with it on a cart. As soon as the hangman returned, Corbett ordered the celebrations to begin. He toasted the Mallings, the jurors, Sir Robert Swinton, Elias Poulter and the Magpie. All those who had aided and supported the cause of the king and his council. He had tried to persuade Malfeson to stay and join them. However, the French clerk, courteous as ever, pleaded that he had urgent business with the queen. So perhaps some other time . . .?

'Perhaps some other time,' Corbett murmured as he sat in his own chamber on the gallery overlooking the main door to the Twilight. He had left the entertainment because he wanted to awake refreshed and well rested. Now he sat in the window seat staring at the moonlit path leading down to the main gate in the curtain wall, only a short distance from the tavern sign. This now creaked in the night breeze, shifting slightly as if it too had been afflicted by the gruesome burden fastened to it a few hours earlier. He turned away. Sarasin was gone. Corbett had finished his task, yet he felt a sense of discomfort. Something was not quite right. Did the ghost of the riffler still hover close, provoking this disquiet? Dismissing his anxieties as a result of tiredness, Corbett changed for bed. He then recited three Aves for the Lady Maeve and their two children, Edward and Eleanor. Once finished, he crossed himself and lay down. As he rested his head against the bolsters, his mind slipped away, revisiting what had happened earlier that day.

Corbett and his henchmen returned to Westminster late the following morning. The Keeper of the Secret Seal immediately became embroiled in all the work that had accumulated during his absence. He returned in particular to the preparations for the king's planned journey to France to meet his redoubtable father-in-law and confront whatever that wily prince was plotting. Nevertheless, despite his absorption with this, the feeling of unease he'd experienced at the Twilight did not dissipate. Indeed, it grew even sharper. He began to wonder if Sarasin's execution would prove to be the end of the matter. In addition, the involvement of the French royal clerk Malfeson intrigued him.

'Something,' he confided to Ranulf, 'is wrong in the French camp. But what?' Edward and Isabella were happy enough. The upstart royal favourite Gaveston had been executed. The great barons of England were now satisfied that they'd had their way and slunk back to their estates. Edward was able to move freely about his kingdom. Above all, Queen Isabella had given birth to a lusty boy whose entry into the world of politic had greatly pleased both Edward and Philip. So why did all this unease persist? 'I sense a change in the body politic of Philip's court. Something is happening, but what? Philip should be pleased, contented. His daughter is now a mother, the apple of her father's eye. Feted and courted by both France and England, she has recently been joined by her sister-in-law Marguerite, Countess of Burgundy, the wife of Louis Hutin, Philip of France's eldest son and heir.'

'We also have our old friend Monseigneur Amaury de Craon.'

'Oh yes, Ranulf. The red fox of Paris. Sly, totally devoted to the House of Capet. And that's another mystery. De Craon is an accomplished envoy. A skilled spy. In his eyes Philip of France is God. He is the French king's devoted slave. In fact, I admire him for that: his loyalty can never be questioned, nor can his cunning. So why has Monsieur Malfeson, undoubtedly like de Craon, a high-ranking officer of the Chambre Noire, been sent to England? Attached very closely to the queen and her council? Surely de Craon could do what Malfeson is involved in? Has there been a shift in power? Ah well,' Corbett murmured. 'Time will tell.'

He returned to his myriad of tasks, though he still remained distracted about events at the Twilight. On the morning of the fourth day after Sarasin's hanging, his fears were proved correct. A stable boy, dispatched by Malling, presented himself at the porter's lodge of the main chancery house and demanded to speak to the Lord Hugh Corbett on an urgent and most important matter. Corbett and Ranulf were hastily summoned and the lad blurted out how Sir Robert Swinton and Elias Poulter had stayed on at the Twilight. Sir Robert had business in the city, while Poulter's expenses were being met by the Royal Exchequer so he had decided to stay a little longer.

'And?' Ranulf demanded. 'What is so urgent?'

'Sir Hugh,' gasped the lad, 'Sir Robert and Poulter had their own chambers: this morning we found both rooms locked and bolted from within, yet we cannot arouse either of the men. They are definitely within but do not answer.' The messenger closed his eyes, lips moving soundlessly as he tried to recall the rest of the message. 'My master realises Sir Robert is a knight of the shire, a justiciar. He believes he does not have the authority to force entry into such a lord's chamber—'

'But I do,' Corbett interrupted. He snapped his fingers at his two henchmen. 'Swiftly, Chanson! Get the horses ready! Ranulf, let's grab cloak and sword and make ready to leave.'

They arrived at the Twilight within the hour. They found the tavern strangely quiet. The groom who took their horses whispered that many of the guests had fled, not wanting to be drawn into any investigation. The rest had simply locked themselves in their chambers to await the outcome of whatever was happening. Corbett sent for the taverner and was shocked at the shambling, shuffling figure who emerged from the gloom of the poorly lit taproom. Malling's appearance was truly alarming; he was a mere shadow of his former self, his face all haggard, his hair and beard unkempt, his clothing stained and smelly. He clasped hands with Corbett, then wearily sat down in a chair. Corbett told Chanson to look after the horses while he and Ranulf made themselves comfortable. Malling offered wine or ale, but Corbett refused, glancing quickly at the entrance to the kitchen. He realised that the stoves and ovens had not been fired, and the same was true of the braziers arranged around the taproom.

'What is the matter?' he demanded, leaning across the table. 'What has happened? Where are your daughters? Master Malling, what has happened here? Where is everybody?'

'Sir Hugh,' Malling replied wearily, 'I shall tell you later. What concerns me now is Sir Robert and Master Elias.'

'True, true,' Corbett agreed. He turned to Ranulf. 'Organise a small group of servants, no more than four. They are to find and bring a good stout log. So, Master Malling, let's go up to the chambers.'

The taverner, muttering and mumbling under his breath, took the two clerks up the staircase to Swinton's chamber at the far end of the main gallery. Corbett tried the door, but it held fast.

'Locked,' he murmured.

'Yes, Sir Hugh,' Malling agreed. 'With two bolts, one at the top and the other at the bottom.'

'We will have to force entry,' Corbett declared.

'I agree. There is no other way in. The windows are shuttered and would be difficult to force from outside. In any case, I doubt a fully grown man could fit through them, as they are very narrow.'

'And what of this?' Corbett tapped the eyelet, or squint hole. This was a small rectangle with iron bars that would form a grille when the hatch was pulled open. 'Is it significant?'

'Sir Robert Swinton used it.'

'Why on earth would he do that in a tavern he used almost as his second home?'

'He had become very nervous, suspicious. I noticed his change of mood yesterday. Very secretive, he was. He would pull back the hatch to scrutinise any visitor.'

Corbett paused in his questioning as Ranulf returned, accompanied by four servitors, burly men who easily managed the huge fire log they brought with them. Corbett and Malling stood back as Ranulf supervised the pounding of the heavy door until it buckled, cracking and snapping as the hinges burst loose, followed by the lock and the two bolt clasps. At last it broke free, turning slightly before falling sheer and hard as a drawbridge.

The chamber beyond was dark, the only slivers of light being the shafts piercing the window shutters. Corbett asked Ranulf to fetch two cresset torches. The fluttering flames of the sconces bathed the floor in pools of darting light that made Swinton's corpse even more hideous. It lay in a pool of drying blood, head turned slightly sideways. Corbett gently shifted it so he could see the ravaged face of the victim. Swinton had been killed outright by a crossbow bolt. The barb had smashed into his forehead, bursting apart skin, flesh, brain and bone. The dead man's eyes had virtually disappeared, his nose and mouth a gruesome mess of flesh and congealed blood.

Corbett, holding a torch, moved around the chamber. Ranulf organised more candles, trying to ignore Malling, who stood in the doorway moaning to himself as he rocked backwards and forwards. Corbett crossed to comfort him.

'Go to your chamber, Master Malling,' he urged. 'Take a goblet of wine and stay there until I come for you.'

Malling was about to object when a voice shouted his name. A man was forcing himself through those gathering in the gallery outside the murder chamber. Corbett immediately recognised John Appleby, Malling's household steward, a pleasant-faced and courteous man who had helped his master after the trial was finished. He asked him to take care of Malling. The steward promised he would, and gently coaxed the taverner into the chamber next to where Swinton had been murdered.

'Sir Hugh?' Ranulf murmured. 'We should open Poulter's room.'

'Wait, wait, Ranulf. Let us first inspect this chamber closely, lest there be interference in whatever evidence is available. Come.'

Ranulf followed Sir Hugh back into Swinton's chamber. Corbett took a counterpane off the small four-poster bed and hastily covered the corpse. He and Ranulf then searched the room, scrutinising everything carefully, but they could not detect anything amiss.

'Nothing,' Corbett whispered. 'Except that gruesome corpse and an overturned stool. No tainted wine or food. Nothing!'

He walked over to where Swinton had left his panniers. Picking these up, he handed them to Ranulf.

'Search them,' he urged. 'And then search this chamber one more time for anything out of the ordinary.' He paused. 'I shall wait outside for Appleby. Once he returns, we will force Poulter's chamber. Only God knows what we will find.'

Corbett walked back out onto the gallery, ordering the servants to return to their duties. He stood there for a while listening to Ranulf go through Swinton's saddlebags. The clerk shouted that they contained nothing significant, then returned to a careful scrutiny of the chamber and its contents. He had barely finished when Appleby came out of Malling's chamber.

'My friend has drunk a great deal of wine,' the steward declared. 'And now he is sleeping it off.'

'Fine,' Corbett exclaimed. 'Now let's go and see if Master Elias still breathes God's air. Master Appleby, get those four sturdy men with their ram to break into the chamber. It's the only way.'

Corbett and Ranulf waited until Appleby returned with his cohort.

Poulter's chamber stood on the gallery above them, and its door soon gave way, almost springing off its thick leather hinges. Corbett ordered everyone to stay outside as he took a cresset torch from Appleby and went into the room. Poulter's corpse was sprawled across the floor with the chamber key lying close by, and he swiftly examined it, despite the poor light. In his view, the man had been dead for some time: his flesh had that cold, hard, waxen feel. His face was livid, sightless eyes popping, mouth half open; saliva had dribbled down onto his chest and fat, distended belly. Corbett picked up the chamber key and pushed it smoothly into the lock. It turned easily. He beckoned Ranulf and Appleby to join him in his scrutiny of both corpse and room. The window shutters were heavy and covered in cobwebs, proof enough that it had been some time since they'd been opened. Nothing else seemed to be amiss. He sniffed at the wine jug but could detect no tainted odour. Nevertheless, he gave both the jug and the pewter goblet to Ranulf, along with dried scraps of food on a platter.

'Take these down into one of the outhouses. The rats will soon devour what is left, and we'll know for sure if the food and drink were poisoned. As for the rest, I can detect nothing amiss, just a room with a man lying dead on the floor. But why? How was he killed and, more importantly, who was responsible?'

'Sir Hugh, Sir Hugh!' Chanson's voice rang loud and clear.

'What is it?' Ranulf called back.

'Sir Hugh, you have a visitor.'

Intrigued, Corbett asked Ranulf and Appleby to

continue with the survey of both corpse and room, as well as ensuring that the rats feasted on the wine dregs and the morsels left on the platter. He then went down to the taproom, exclaiming in surprise as Malfeson emerged from the shadows. The French clerk told his escort to wait elsewhere while he beckoned Corbett into a far window seat.

'My friend,' Corbett began, making himself comfortable, 'you are going to ask me why I am here?'

'Well,' Malfeson spread his hands, 'I am curious.'

'Why?'

'I came looking for you at Westminster. I was informed by the porter guarding the main chancery door that you and your henchmen had left in great haste for this tavern. So,' he shrugged, 'I decided to follow.' He paused as Appleby strode into the taproom to declare he had found nothing of note in Poulter's chamber.

'Very well.' Corbett nodded. 'Master Appleby, I would be grateful if you would arrange for both corpses to be moved to the mortuary in St Bartholomew's Hospital overlooking Smithfield.' He opened his wallet and took out a wax replica of the secret seal. 'Show this,' he declared, 'and ask to speak to Brother Philippe. He is an Augustinian friar, a priest. He is also one of the most skilled physicians I have ever encountered. Ask him to arrange both corpses for a requiem mass, followed by burial as their kin decide. However,' he held up a hand, 'although it is obvious how Sir Robert Swinton was murdered, the death of Elias Poulter is the real mystery. I could detect no open wound nor the effect of some violent blow. Philippe will surely cast more light on the enigma. Nevertheless,' Corbett pointed at Appleby, 'stay with us for a while. Monsieur Malfeson, you know what has happened here?'

'Yes, I had words with the servants on my arrival. Two murders, Sir Hugh?'

'Yes, my friend, two murders. You know both men. Swinton, who acted as a fellow justiciar, and Poulter, foreman of the jury. Both slain during the hours of darkness. Yes, Master Appleby?'

'So it would seem, Sir Hugh. They both retired early last night.'

'How were they?' Corbett demanded. 'What happened?'

'What happened?' Appleby echoed, licking his lips. He paused as Ranulf entered the taproom and, at Corbett's bidding, drew up a chair.

'I went back to scrutinise Elias's corpse,' the clerk explained. 'Removing both his jerkin and leggings.' He shook his head. 'Nothing at all, Sir Hugh, as you yourself concluded. However, looking at the colour of the dead man's face, perhaps poison was used. But there again, I fed the dregs and food mixed into a mash to the rats teeming in the barn and, as far as I can see, none were affected. I have asked the stable boy to keep watch and report to me if he notices anything untoward. I don't think he will.' Ranulf glanced at Appleby. 'What happened here?'

'I have asked the same question,' Corbett declared. 'So for the moment, let us establish the facts. Oh, by the way,' he added, 'Master Appleby, tell Brother Philippe that all costs and expenses for removing the two corpses and their burial will be met by the Exchequer. He is to submit all bills as well as one for his own work and trouble.'

'Strange,' the steward mused, 'you talk of expenses, Sir Hugh. Both victims stayed here because of expenses.'

'True,' Corbett agreed. 'They were paid for a fixed period of time. The trial was very swift, so they had money left over and the Exchequer has to accept that.'

'Indeed,' Appleby agreed. 'Sir Robert stayed on here at the expense of the Crown. He declared he had business in the city. Poulter was the same. He claimed that he would enjoy the peace and quiet after the rigours of the trial.' He shrugged. 'You cannot blame them, Sir Hugh.'

'I agree,' Corbett said. 'But what truly happened here? Sarasin was hanged on Monday last. The following morning, we returned to Westminster. We left everyone here hale, hearty and healthy. What changed all that so drastically?' He tapped the table. 'Malling is like a man sorely wounded. Why the transformation? How did it happen? And when?'

'It happened about midweek.'

'Who else came here?' Ranulf demanded.

Appleby screwed his face up, concentrating on the question, then smiled. 'Ah yes, the royal battle-boat *The War-dog* left Queenhithe on Wednesday manned by Tower archers.'

'What was that doing here?' Malfeson demanded.

Corbett sighed. 'His Grace the king has his treasures

deposited in the Tower under close lock and key. Now he is planning a royal visit to Paris and we are doing our best to facilitate this. Weapons as well as luxuries go with him, including a treasure chest, be it good coin or jewels. He and the queen need this to manifest themselves in all their glory at the receptions Philip will stage in their honour. Such impedimenta, baggage, coffers and chests, are taken along the riverbank to Queenhithe, where they are collected by an armed escort and placed in *The War-dog* for transport across the river. They are then moved to a royal residence in Canterbury or, better still, the fortified arca in Dover Castle, from where they can be easily carried to a royal cog waiting in the harbour.'

'You seem to know a great deal about it, Sir Hugh.'

'Oh monsieur, such matters cross my gaze in the secret chancery. The sailing of *The War-dog* is in the main kept confidential. So, Master Appleby, on Wednesday last . . .?'

'Sir Hugh, whatever the treasure was, it arrived here by cart from the Tower. The archers, seven in all, relaxed and drank in the buttery. Once finished, they loaded their cargo and left.'

'They didn't meet here in the taproom?'

'Oh no, Sir Hugh, they commandeered the buttery. Master Malling himself served them food and drink. I really didn't pay much attention. The officer in charge made it very clear that they be left alone.' Appleby shrugged. 'And so we did. *The War-dog* left under the cover of darkness, manned by the archers as well as a skilled river navigator. They offered us no trouble. They did nothing to disturb the peace and harmony of the Twilight.'

'And Master Malling?'

'For a short while he seemed happy enough, but then he abruptly changed.' Appleby shook his head. 'I don't know why, but . . .' He tapped his chest. 'Well, I too have fought in the royal array. I have seen men shattered by what they've witnessed. Master Malling was like that. Sometimes he mouthed gibberish.'

'Such as?'

'He ranted about the Immortal drawing closer and closer but, before you ask, I do not know what he meant. Anyway, I must see—'

He startled as the door to the taproom crashed open and Malling strode in, a manic look on his face as he held up a battleaxe in one hand, a jagged stabbing dirk in the other.

'You bastard!' he bawled at Malfeson. 'You are responsible, all of you. You should all die. My poor daughters, my tavern.' He lowered his weapons as if exhausted, then abruptly lunged forward in a desperate attempt to strike Malfeson, but the French clerk was swifter. Drawing his own dagger, he quickly moved to the left, blocking Malling's blade before delivering a cut that sliced open the taverner's throat. Malling staggered, choking on the blood that squirted from his mouth and nose to mingle with that cascading down his chest. He gave one final strangled gasp, then collapsed to the floor.

'The Lord have mercy on him,' Corbett murmured,

getting to his feet. 'God only knows what turned his wits so grievously.'

'You saw it, Sir Hugh.' Malfeson coolly used a rag from a nearby table to cleanse his dagger. 'I had no choice but to kill him. He was intent on my death and, I suggest, that of everyone else gathered in this taproom.'

'It was self-defence, I agree.' Corbett nodded. 'Monsieur Malfeson, be assured you will receive a full and complete pardon for Malling's death. As you said, we all witnessed it, and you had no choice. So let's have the corpse removed and this place cleaned.'

A pale-faced Appleby, helped by some cowed servants, removed the blood-soaked body. Malfeson and Ranulf poured deep-bowled goblets of Bordeaux, and the three men drank as they waited for the steward to return. When he did, Corbett explained that he wanted him to take them on an inspection of the tavern, and Appleby seemed to brighten up at the prospect of showing off, as he put it, the Twilight's comforts and attractions. He first took them out into the freezing fresh air and showed them the garden, now held fast by a severe hoar frost that had whitened the herb and vegetable plots. The water on the carp pond was frozen hard, the rest of the garden buildings almost hidden under a coverlet of snow. He pointed out the dovecote, the benches and tables, the small summer house and the occasional arbour, all ringed and protected by the soaring curtain wall.

Corbett half listened to the steward's chatter, becoming more concerned about the lowering grey clouds, which threatened heavy snow. The heralds of this were already floating down, thick, rich flakes, to lace ledge, windowsill and shelf. At Corbett's insistence, the party returned to the main building. The steward led them along highly polished galleries and up a gleaming oak staircase to the various chambers. Finally he showed them the pride of the tavern, a luxuriously appointed solar that led into a small chapel properly furnished for sacramental and liturgical use. The walls were painted a gleaming white, which emphasised the dark wooden crucifixes and triptychs hung around this holy place. There were also benches and prayer stools as well as a cushioned prie-dieu placed before the dais on which the altar stood.

'Very good, very comforting,' Corbett murmured, echoing the praise of his companions.

'Most singular,' Malfeson declared.

'It certainly is,' Corbett replied, 'but why have a chapel in a tavern?'

'Because God's work must not be confined,' a powerful voice intoned, and a shadowy figure entered through the narrow door to the right of the altar.

The newcomer, a Benedictine monk by his black robe, tapped his walking cane against the paving stones, then shuffled forward to greet Corbett and his companions.

'You are most welcome.' He sat down on a wall bench and sighed with relief. 'Welcome, welcome, welcome,' he exclaimed, 'to the Chapel of St Christopher, the patron saint of travellers.' He gestured at Corbett. 'Please sit, Sir Hugh . . . It is Sir Hugh, isn't it?'

'Yes, Father, it is.'

'Sit down, sit down. I am Brother Ricard, chaplain here.'

Corbett's companions hurriedly pulled up benches to sit opposite the monk. Corbett studied Brother Ricard. Despite his infirmity, the monk seemed vigorous enough. A man of medium age, he was completely shaven, both head and face, while his large, expressive eyes reflected an amused if not cynical attitude to everyone and everything around him. He had rubbed some perfumed nard on his sallow-skinned face. Corbett also noticed the Benedictine's long, clean fingers, his neatly pared nails. He had a prayer bracelet around his left wrist and a heavy bronze ring, that of a fully professed Benedictine monk, on the middle finger of his right hand. The royal clerk sensed that this was a man completely in control of his appetites and humours. A monk who would find it easy to converse with whomever he met.

'You study me, Sir Hugh.' Brother Ricard abruptly tapped his walking stick against the paving stone. 'You certainly are a hawk. You watch and you wait.'

'For what, Brother Ricard?'

The Benedictine threw his head back and laughed, the sound echoing loudly across the chapel. 'Why, Sir Hugh, for whatever passes beneath your hawk-like gaze. Now, you are here because of the dire events that have occurred in this tavern.' He gestured towards the steward. 'You told me what had happened when I met you in the death house to anoint all three corpses. Poor souls, God assoil them.'

'So, Father—'

'Let me anticipate what you are going to ask, Sir Hugh. You are wondering how a tavern such as this has a chantry chapel and a chaplain?' The Benedictine pointed to a triptych on the far wall depicting a burly individual carrying the infant Christ on his shoulder across a river. 'St Christopher shows us the way. Travellers need special graces. Now the Twilight, as you know, is a splendid hostelry, as stately and dignified as any manor house. Master Appleby caters for the body and I minister to the souls of all travellers, be it along the river or up and down the various trackways. I celebrate mass, I shrive souls and I try to give ghostly counsel; that's why I'm here.' He leant on his cane. 'Oh, I remember you, Sir Hugh. Your visit to our abbey in pursuit of that disgraceful miscreant Richard Puddlicott? You were the cat who certainly landed firmly among the pigeons.' Ricard laughed softly to himself. 'All gone now,' he continued, 'Puddlicott and his coven dangling by their necks on gibbets and gallows around the abbey.'

'I don't remember you.'

'Of course you don't, Sir Hugh. I was here, as I have been for the last few years. The Bishop of London eventually reached a compact with my lord abbot and Master Malling that a chapel be set up dedicated and consecrated in honour of St Christopher. I am a monk of many years.' He half smiled. 'Once I was a mailed royal clerk. I saw military service in Gascony before I discovered I had a vocation and became a follower of St Benedict. Anyway, I am now part of this tavern. I have, as Master Appleby will tell you, a very pleasant room above stairs as well as licence to dine here.'

'You are treated as a special guest,' Appleby declared. 'As you richly deserve to be.'

Corbett nodded as he listened. He would remain quiet as the memories flooded back of those dramatic days when he confronted and hunted to the death Puddlicott and his black-robed coven.

'Sir Hugh?'

He glanced up. Brother Ricard grinned wolfishly at him, his lips parted to display strong white teeth.

'You have questions for me, Sir Hugh?'

Corbett smiled back. 'Sharp as sharp can be, Father. You know I have questions.'

'Then ask them.'

'Do you know anything about the dreadful deaths here?'

The Black Robe shook his head. 'I became aware that an eerie strangeness, a brooding silence, seemed to descend on this tavern and those three men in particular. I did visit them all. They admitted me to their chambers but seemed most unwilling to talk. I offered them the sacrament. Malling was too agitated, but Sir Robert asked to be shrived. One of the few things he said was that he was still proud of playing his part in Sarasin's downfall. Nevertheless, he added, Sarasin's execution seemed to have cast a deep black cloud over the tavern.'

'And did Malling ever provide a reason or share an explanation for his abrupt change of mood?'

The Benedictine pulled a face and shook his head.

'Did he talk to you about the Immortal, whoever or whatever that might be?'

'Ah, yes.' The Benedictine held up a bony finger. 'Good man, Sir Hugh. You have jogged my memory. Malling certainly did mention the Immortal, but I thought it was just a part of his ranting. God knows what the poor man meant. I don't know . . .'

A knock at the door made the Benedictine pause. Appleby went to open it, and Lotham, the spit boy, almost fell into the room, followed by Cuthbert, the chief cook, who looked similarly agitated.

'What is it?' Appleby demanded.

'Master,' Cuthbert gasped, 'we all know about the deaths.'

'Murders,' Ranulf interposed.

'Whatever.' Cuthbert sank down onto a wall bench. He patted the seat and called the spit boy to join him. He then brought out from beneath his food-stained apron a small but thickly wrapped linen parcel. 'Let me explain,' he began. 'I sent Lotham here to Master Malling's chamber to collect a silver bucket, my pride and joy. Master Malling had borrowed this last midweek just as he started becoming strange. I wanted to ensure that it was returned safely to my care. I mean—'

'I am sure you are very honest and conscientious,' Corbett broke in, 'but why are you here?'

'I went into the master's bedchamber,' Lotham blurted out, his high-pitched voice quavering.

'What then, lad?' Corbett asked gently.

'I found the bucket. The master had hidden it behind

an aumbry. I took it down to the cook, and only then,' he hurried on, 'did I notice the linen parcel inside it.'

'I opened it,' Cuthbert declared.

'Let us see for ourselves.' Corbett unwrapped the thick linen covering and, as he did, several red blotches became more noticeable. Ignoring the exclamations of the others, he eventually laid the folds of linen back to expose two forefingers, their nails painted, on each, above the clean cut, a blue-stoned silver ring.

'Hosts of heaven,' Appleby whispered. 'Those rings belong to Rachel and Rebekah, Malling's daughters. They have not been here. Malling said they'd left to visit relatives in Faversham, in Kent.'

Corbett lifted the parcel to study the severed fingers. Corruption had already set in, and he caught the whiff of decay.

'Severed some time ago,' he declared. 'I would say at least a few days.'

'But they left for—'

'No, Master Appleby, I doubt very much whether they journeyed to Faversham. I suspect that they left this tavern to do some shopping or something of the like. Two young ladies, arm in arm, easy victims to the rifflers prowling close by. I believe they were abducted and most grievously abused. The severed fingers are a clear, stark warning.' Corbett paused. 'A dire warning to Malling. Little wonder his wits were turned.'

'But he did little to hurt anyone,' Brother Ricard pleaded. 'He was just a generous-hearted taverner . . .'

'Whose hostelry,' Ranulf declared, 'was used for a

commission of oyer and terminer that ended in the execution of one of London's most notorious rifflers. More importantly,' he continued, 'Malling's daughters provided evidence that dispatched Sarasin to the gallows.'

'I agree.' Corbett nodded gravely. 'This is the work of a demon, hounding and harassing, pounding and paining to his heart's content.' He wrapped the severed fingers back in the linen, then handed the parcel to Appleby. 'Of your goodness, sir,' he said, 'keep these here for a while, for only God knows what will happen next.' He pointed at the steward. 'Both ladies resided here?'

'Of course.'

'Well, Master Appleby, take my good friend Ranulf to see their chamber. Let us see what is there.'

Ranulf and Appleby left the chapel. Malfeson, who had remained silent throughout, went to talk to Father Ricard about his work at the tavern. Corbett, lost in thought, crossed to the narrow slit window. He pulled back the small horn-filled window door and looked out. The snow was falling thick and fast. The darkness was deepening, creating a silence broken now and again by noises from the tavern.

'Sir Hugh, I appreciate . . .'

He turned to face Malfeson.

'What do you appreciate, monsieur?'

'What has happened here is a truly murderous masque. It may well be rooted in the dangers we too are facing.'

'Such as?'

'Sir Hugh, the sooner we return to Westminster, the sooner we will all find out. Or at least begin to.'

'I agree.' Corbett broke off as Ranulf and Appleby re-entered the chapel.

'Nothing!' Appleby exclaimed. 'Nothing to show they packed panniers or were leaving for a visit. It's as if,' he shrugged, 'they slipped out of here to shop at the stalls and would be back very soon.'

'Yet they never will be.' Corbett sighed. 'God have mercy on those two ladies. Brother Ricard, please remember Rachel and Rebekah at prayer. Ranulf, tell Chanson to prepare the horses. We will soon leave for Westminster.'

PART TWO

What does it serve to resist the King?

Brother Ricard got to his feet, sketched a blessing and hobbled out. A short while later, Corbett and his party left the Twilight, their horses carefully picking their way along the river path leading down to Westminster. The snowfall had been incessant, creating a world of whiteness as it covered everything like a shroud. Buildings lay silent. Houses and shops stood firmly fastened and shuttered against the harsh weather. Here and there other travellers stumbled their way along the river path; lanternlight bobbed, sconce torches blazed, their leaping flames kissing the white darkness. They passed the gibbets and stocks. Corpses hung by their necks; the snow created what looked like coffin cloths to wrap around them. The occasional beggar tried his luck, cowering in enclaves and recesses along the riverbank. Corbett and Ranulf spun them coins and urged their horses forward, cautiously following Chanson, whose Scottish garron delicately picked its way along the treacherous trackway. At last they reached Westminster, a monument of soaring carved stone, now blanketed white.

Corbett and Ranulf left their horses in the royal courtyard and made their way deep into the palace buildings. When they reached the visiting chambers, they swiftly prepared themselves and gratefully accepted the chamberlain's offer of goblets of heavily spiced posset. They drank quickly but had hardly finished when Malfeson arrived accompanied by a royal official, who led them to the elegantly furnished Jerusalem Chamber. This most splendid of rooms was carpeted with turkey rugs, its walls lavishly decorated with richly hued tapestries displaying scenes from the history of the Holy City.

Corbett, Ranulf and Malfeson took their seats at the end of the oval council table. This was covered with a cloth of gold, a splendid silver nef placed in the centre. Ranulf opened his chancery satchel, which Corbett had asked him to bring, and took out rolls of parchment and other accessories. He was still busy with this when the chamberlain returned to announce the imminent arrival of their Graces. Edward and Isabella followed almost immediately. Corbett and his companions sank to their knees, then stood up and waited as the king loosened his blue-gold cloak. He almost threw it at the waiting chamberlain before turning to help his wife to the throne-like chair at the end of the table. He then took his seat to her right.

Once settled, he gestured to Corbett and his

companions to sit. Corbett used the preparations for the meeting to study the royal couple. Edward looked tired and harassed. He had still not recovered from the loss of his 'beloved brother' Gaveston, his Gascon favourite. Gaveston had risen high and glorious like some fiery comet searing the heavens. Despite being officially claimed as 'the king's own brother', however, he had fallen, and what a fall it had been! He had been seized by the great earls, led by Thomas of Lancaster, the king's cousin. The favourite had been given a mock trial, then summarily executed, savagely decapitated in some lonely copse close to Warwick Castle. Edward's grief at his death was so acute he had even refused to have his embalmed corpse buried, so it continued to lie in state at the royal manor of King's Langley. Nevertheless, Gaveston's death did achieve something. Civil war between the king and his earls had been narrowly averted, the two factions uniting against the growing threat of Robert the Bruce and his Scottish rebels.

Edward was truly restless, Corbett could detect that. The king was dressed in a quilted silken doublet fashioned in the colours of the Plantagenets. A beautiful gold chain circled the royal neck. The medallion on it shimmered in the light, as did the jewelled rings on Edward's fingers and the silver circlet around his head. Nevertheless, 'the baubles of kingship', as Corbett called them, could not hide the king's disquiet. Edward's usually smooth face was now wrinkled. Dark shadows had formed beneath his deep-set eyes, while his blond hair, moustache and beard were not so cleverly clipped and coiffed as was usual.

Queen Isabella, however, looked truly radiant in a costly gown of dark blue sarcenet decorated with shiny gold suns and glittering silver stars, her luxuriously blond hair hidden beneath a gauze veil held in place by a jewelled circlet. Isabella's perfectly formed face always fascinated Corbett. He truly believed it was like that of an angel, with her deep-set blue eyes that could crinkle in amusement or turn ice-hard in her now notorious hot temper. Corbett watched her and came to the conclusion that, despite all her splendour, this was a day when one should be extremely wary of the queen. Just for a few heartbeats her smile would fade, her face becoming hard, her lips compressed, eyes averted as she played with the tassel around her waist or the bracelet on her wrist. Corbett, however, tried to relax as the servants busied themselves pushing scented braziers closer to the table. Honey cakes were served on silver platters together with goblets of Alsace and cups of steaming hot mulled wine.

Edward sat drumming his fingers on the table, now and again drinking noisily, draining a goblet in one great gulp. The queen turned slightly to glare at him. He just shrugged and tapped the rim of his goblet as a sign for the wine butler to pour a refill. Corbett realised they were waiting for someone or something. He was about to whisper to Malfeson about what it might be when there was a knock on the door and Marguerite, Countess of Burgundy, escorted by two young knights, swept into the Jerusalem Chamber. Corbett recognised her immediately and rose to his feet, tugging at Ranulf's jerkin as a sign to follow suit. All three clerks bowed. Marguerite fluttered a hand in languorous acknowledgement, then took the chair to the left of the queen. Once she was comfortable, she smiled at Corbett.

'So long, Sir Hugh. You have not aged at all.'

'And neither have you, your Grace,' Corbett replied. 'Indeed, you look even younger.'

Marguerite laughed. 'You flatter me, Sir Hugh.'

'Your Grace, I would only speak the truth to you, daughter-in-law of the illustrious Philip of France, sister-in-law to our own beloved queen and last, but certainly not least, wife of Louis, heir apparent to the crown of France.'

The dark-haired, sensuous Marguerite simpered behind her fingers before introducing the two young knights – her bodyguard, as she laughingly described them – Philippe and Gautier d'Aunay. She then dismissed her escort with a snap of her fingers before snatching a goblet from the wine butler. She held this up in toast to both king and queen, who responded in kind. For a while there was silence, broken only by the last peals of the compline bell.

'Greetings to you all, and welcome to you, Sir Hugh and the faithful Ranulf.' Edward leant forward in his chair, looking down the table. 'And of course I welcome the ever-loyal Malfeson.' He paused as his wife lightly brushed his hand.

'And I,' Isabella declared, 'extend my welcome to you

and your companions, Sir Hugh, as does my loving sister Marguerite.' She kept her voice steady. 'I am glad,' she continued, 'to draw strength from my husband, from my family, from my court.'

She paused at a knock on the door and a chamberlain ushered in Monsieur Amaury de Craon, Philip's envoy to the English court. De Craon bowed and scraped, mouthing his apologies for being late. Edward waved him to a chair beside the countess, who smiled and patted his hand as if he was her pet monkey. Corbett watched the envoy settle himself. In his eyes, de Craon, with his russet hair and neatly clipped moustache and beard, looked what he really was: a fox to the very marrow, the most treacherous of creatures. As Corbett had confided time and again to Ranulf: 'De Craon would not know the truth if it bit him on the nose.'

'You are most welcome. I am so glad that you have eventually arrived,' the queen snapped, glaring haughtily at the latecomer.

De Craon, surprised by the tart rebuke, sank lower in his chair. Corbett hid his smile. The French delegate would have to learn how to deal with a much more imperious mistress than before. Married at the age of thirteen to Edward, the years had been kind to this truly beautiful woman. Isabella had given birth to a lusty baby boy now closeted with his nurses, and had more than fulfilled the main condition of her marriage: to become a more powerful figure in the byzantine politics of England, France and elsewhere. She was truly a force to be reckoned with, no longer some innocent young girl but a woman of outstanding ability with the power to match.

'Let us begin,' the queen continued, 'and let us move swiftly.'

'I agree with that,' Edward declared in a ringing voice.

'Monsieur Malfeson?' The queen's own voice now turned soft and gentle, showing the sudden change of mood that disconcerted so many.

'Your Grace, I will be as swift as a hawk on the wing.' Malfeson bowed his head. 'Let me first introduce into our conversation a French priest, Père Henri Jacques, an old servant of the Church who was given a benefice in the city of Paris. In return for this, Père Henri acted as the chaplain, the sin-shriver, to those sentenced to hang on the gallows at Montfaucon. Anyway, about three weeks ago, he was mysteriously approached by two hooded and masked strangers close to the great scaffold. The old priest was discomforted. The day was freezing and he wanted to be away. However, the strangers insisted that he listen to them because they brought a warning, a clear threat, to Isabella, Queen of England. They declared how her father's destruction of the Templar order was about to provoke punishment. Many Templars had suffered grievously, been tortured by fire. The same would happen to the Capetian dynasty across three generations, father, daughter and grandson. In other words, Philip, his daughter Isabella and her newly born son, Edward, Prince of Wales, would suffer an ordeal by fire.' Malfeson paused at the growing clamour his words had provoked, with the king loudly cursing as he rapped the table. Then Malfeson asked, 'King Philip and his court also view this as a very real and deadly threat, yes?'

De Craon and the Countess of Burgundy, talking hurriedly between themselves, nodded in agreement. Malfeson said nothing in reply. He just sat stony faced, staring into the distance.

Once again Corbett wondered about the true nature of this clerk who moved so softly, so swiftly like a shadow across the wall. He broke from his reverie as Ranulf nudged him. The queen, although she must have heard all of this before, was clearly furious. She now gave vent to a torrent of expletives at the threat posed not only to her but to her beloved father and her treasured baby boy. Corbett decided to assert himself.

'Your Graces,' he called out, tapping the table noisily, 'I need to know why I am here and what I am supposed to do. What I hear now is truly dreadful. However, I need to know all the facts. If your Graces would be so kind as to let Monsieur Malfeson tell his tale.'

'And tell it he will,' the queen retorted. 'Malfeson?'

'Père Henri,' the French clerk continued, 'realised the sinister threat being posed. Alarmed, he immediately visited the Chambre Noire. Of course, as Monsieur de Craon will attest, both he and myself sensed the deeply malicious menace of what Père Henri reported and the danger it posed. Highly treasonable, a blow against the very heart of France.'

'I agree with that,' Marguerite of Burgundy called out. 'When I heard about this threat, I journeyed to

England not only to pay a family visit to their Graces but to provide any help or assistance they might need. I came as soon as I could, only to discover that another threat had been delivered about the same hour and on the same day as Père Henri received his.'

'What?'

'Countess Marguerite is correct, Sir Hugh,' Malfeson declared. 'The second warning was delivered here at Westminster.'

'Where in particular?'

'To an old priest, a venerable Benedictine, Brother Norbert, who was accustomed to sit on the mercy seat in one of the chantry chapels at Westminster Abbey. Sir Hugh, you know how it is. Anyone who wishes to be shrived can come and kneel on the prie-dieu before the curtains that divide them from the confessor on the other side. Brother Norbert was approached by a sinister visitor who delivered the same warning. A threat of vengeance to Philip and his daughter as well as her beloved son. He heard this very clearly. Vengeance by fire in retaliation for the destruction of the Templars.'

'And then?'

'Nothing more, Sir Hugh,' Isabella retorted. 'Nothing at all. No indication of who this criminal is.'

'A traitor,' Edward hissed, 'who must be caught and torn apart at Smithfield.'

'So,' Corbett hurried on, 'you have the same sinister threat delivered in two places, very distant from each other but at the same hour, on the same day.'

'Impossible!' Ranulf exclaimed.

'No, Ranulf,' Corbett replied, 'not if the Templar order was involved. The Templars owned houses and estates across Europe. True, all these estates have been seized, but members of this fallen order still shelter in both Paris and London.' His words were greeted with murmurs of agreement. 'Consequently,' he continued, 'it would be easy to facilitate occasions such as the delivery of this threat. However, more importantly, I ask who is truly responsible and why have they delivered their threat now?'

'Precisely,' Malfeson agreed. 'Let me make it very clear, Sir Hugh. Philip of France views this threat to himself as most serious, and even more so those levelled against his daughter and grandson.'

'One question.' Corbett stared at the king. 'Her Grace the Countess of Burgundy has been informed . . .'

'As indeed has all the royal family,' Isabella declared. 'Philip has asked us to be most vigilant.'

'Of course, I understand that,' Corbett replied. 'But, your Graces, I am the Keeper of the King's Secret Seal. Why wasn't I told immediately?'

'I was waiting to speak to you, Sir Hugh,' the king's tone turned apologetic, 'but the monks of Westminster apparently move very slowly. Brother Norbert informed his abbot, who in his own good time then deigned to inform me. I believe,' he added drily, 'the good monks of Westminster first regarded all this as some feckless jest, a mummer's tale. Indeed,' he struck his chest in mock sorrow, 'I confess so did I. However, now that we have the same threats being published at the same time in both France and England, we must take it very seriously.' He waved a ringed hand. 'There's more. Monsieur Malfeson?'

'Shortly after I arrived, Sir Hugh, I began to scrutinise all members of the queen's household, be they English or French. I met Louis Rahmel, a clerk in her Grace's chamber. A most likeable fellow.'

'I appointed Rahmel.' Isabella spoke up. 'I truly liked him. He began his service as a page, but soon excelled himself, be it in clerkly matters or the battlefield. He became a mailed clerk, a young man dedicated to protecting me. He was courtly and kind. Most presentable.' Her voice quavered. 'I trusted him.'

'I decided,' Malfeson continued, 'to bring this delightful squire under closer scrutiny after I discovered he frequented the Twilight tavern, as did a number of undesirables. Eventually I made my decision. I invited Rahmel to a tavern along Cheapside and questioned him closely about his friends and his wanderings. He might well have been very charming, but he was a weak man, given over totally to the pleasures of the flesh.'

'Most men are!' Isabella declared tartly.

'Be that as it may,' Malfeson continued hurriedly, 'Rahmel had formed a friendship with Sarasin, who introduced our lecherous clerk to a house of pleasure in Cripplegate, an establishment that offered comely maidens and handsome young boys for men such as Rahmel to consort with as they so wished.'

'In heaven's name,' Corbett breathed.

'Sir Hugh, matters turned most serious – and before

you ask, I will explain why this was not revealed during Sarasin's trial.'

'Oh, I can answer that myself,' Corbett replied. 'First, there was no need. I had enough cause, reason and evidence to hang Sarasin. Second, I suspect they are matters of concern for the royal families of both England and France?'

'Precisely, Sir Hugh. So there was no need to proclaim them to all of Europe. These matters would then be taken up in the Commons, the Church, not to mention every alehouse and tavern the length and breadth of this realm. What good would that do?'

'I agree,' Corbett retorted. 'However, matters involving the Crown are covered by the treason laws, with the most horrific punishment of being hung, drawn, quartered and castrated on the public gallows.' He shook his head. 'As for Rahmel, he was a fool.'

'Indeed, Sir Hugh. However, he did not realise the real danger he was courting until it was too late. Sarasin began to question him about her Grace the queen, especially her movements. What escorts she might have and so on. Rahmel eventually realised he was plotting the most rank of treasons: the abduction of her Grace along with her infant son. Deeply agitated, he eventually confessed everything to me, including Sarasin's threats of exposure and the possibility of the most horrid death on the public gallows. His panic intensified. What could he do? He would be marked down for death both in this kingdom and beyond the Narrow Seas. Now, as yet he had done nothing wrong except been grossly foolish. I became his confessor. He said it was like being shrived at the mercy pew. He asked me what he should do. I told him to see what more he could learn but then break with the riffler. Once he had, I would take him to her Grace and beg for her pardon.' Malfeson paused as Corbett raised his hands. 'Sir Hugh?'

'Why?' Corbett demanded. 'Why kidnap and abduct our queen? For ransom? Or for some other deeply nefarious reason?'

'Sir Hugh, I don't truly know, and neither did Rahmel. I did question him constantly on this, but he could tell me no more. He just had a feeling that the abduction was being organised by conspirators who lived deep in the shadows, be it here or abroad. He had the distinct view that Sarasin was working for someone else. But,' Malfeson shook his head, 'who that might be remained a complete mystery. He also had the impression that Sarasin was going to be lavishly rewarded for his treachery.'

'So what happened next?' Corbett demanded.

'Well, Rahmel twisted and turned, but Sarasin had him trapped hard and fast. I do not know what occurred during Rahmel's last hours. As I said, he did frequent the Twilight, being made most welcome by Rachel and Rebekah, Malling's comely daughters. On the day of his death, Sarasin followed him there. An argument broke out, probably caused by Sarasin's threats and Rahmel's change of attitude over supplying details about the queen. Violence erupted. Rahmel was a mailed clerk, but he was no match for Sarasin, who drew his dagger and cut him down.'

'So blatantly, in full view of all,' the queen protested. 'I cannot understand that.'

'Your Grace, I have already explained this to Malfeson. Sarasin was an outlaw, a prince among rifflers. He swaggered and he threatened, he wounded and he killed without a second thought. He would do this to anyone who protested or bore witness about his felonies. Woe betide anyone who took the oath against him. They knew they would suffer grievously.' Corbett shrugged. 'However, killing Rahmel when he did was a grievous mistake. Rahmel, as was his wont, had made himself the close, even intimate friend of Minehost Malling's daughters, Rachel and Rebekah. From what I gather, they were both deeply smitten by him. When he was killed in their father's tavern, they were only too willing to bear witness against his assassin. They even persuaded their father to do likewise. All three came down to King's Bench in Westminster to deliver sworn statements.

'The justiciars were delighted to receive their depositions. The Judas men and the thief takers were alerted and, for a few silver pieces, they sniffed out where Sarasin lurked. Of course, the felon had left the Twilight cocksure that he was safe. So he swaggered about, easy prey for the Tower archers to seize him. He was arrested, indicted and tried within days. I ordered his execution to be immediate, and so it was. He was not given the opportunity or time either to flee or to organise any of his coven to come to his aid. For all I know, his comrades in Hades, London's gloomy, dangerous underworld, might have been only too pleased to see a rival chieftain so ruthlessly removed.'

'Yet it is not finished.'

'No, Monsieur Malfeson, you are correct. It is certainly not finished.'

'What then?' Isabella asked, playing with a tendril of hair that had broken free of her coronet.

'Yes,' de Craon drawled, 'why have you not finished this malicious mischief?'

Corbett stared coolly across at this French clerk, a master in the Chambre Noire. A man who, he realised, hated him with a vigour past all understanding.

'Hugh?' The queen's voice now turned plaintive.

Corbett held up a hand for silence. 'Your Graces, and you, my friend . . .' he tried to keep the sarcasm out of his voice as he glared at de Craon, 'for the moment I am merely collecting information.' He then gave a pithy report on recent events at the Twilight, which provoked gasps of surprise and shock from his listeners, the queen in particular. He also noticed how agitated the rest were, except for the king, who just sat slouched, his heavy-lidded eyes almost closed.

Once he had finished, Corbett shook his head at the litany of questions from his audience. 'I cannot say,' he declared. 'I cannot reply. I have very little at this moment in time to offer you. Monsieur Malfeson, I do have one question for you, however.' He waited for silence. 'In your meeting with Rahmel, did he ever mention any associates, accomplices, friends or allies?'

'I suppose he had his coven of sinful souls, as did

Sarasin, who once informed Rahmel that he preferred the Twilight because it housed someone who watched his back.' Malfeson pulled a face. 'But I learnt nothing more about this. Perhaps in time . . .' His voice trailed away.

'Sir Hugh,' Countess Marguerite spoke up, 'I have one observation to make among many, but my main concern is that those who brought about Sarasin's conviction and execution are now being ruthlessly punished. Vengeance for his death seems almost immediate and inevitable.' She dabbed at her lips. 'The list is already long enough. Swinton, Malling, Rachel and Rebekah, Poulter, the foreman of the jury.'

'My good sister has it right,' agreed the queen. 'Vengeance seems to have set up camp in the Twilight. It now wreaks cruel and deadly retribution to those involved in Sarasin's death.'

'This begs more questions.' The king now asserted himself, sitting up in his throne-like chair, tapping the table with his empty goblet. 'First, who could be the mysterious avenging demon inflicting such bloody chaos? Second, did Sarasin really die on that gibbet? Did he somehow survive being strangled?'

'I doubt it.' Ranulf shook his head. 'Your Grace, I have seen many men hang. I watched Sarasin die. However . . .' he undid the collar of his shirt, tapping his throat, 'the garotte is a common tool for assassins, professional or otherwise.'

'Meaning?'

'Meaning, your Grace, that in the dank, dark dungeons of Whitefriars, where the midnight people cluster, there is a band of outlaws who call themselves the Guild of Assassins.'

'Never!' Edward retorted. 'My sheriffs—'

'Your sheriffs,' Ranulf answered, 'with all due respect, my lord king, know very little about the underworld of Whitefriars and elsewhere.' He glanced quickly to Corbett, who nodded as a sign to continue. 'These assassins, members of their guild, go hunting in pairs. One will surprise the victim and hold his hands fast as his accomplice wraps the garotte rope around the unfortunate's throat. He then begins to tighten it while his partner searches the victim and steals anything of value.'

'And the point of all this?' de Craon sneered. He then paused, head down, as the king pounded the table.

'Master Ranulf, you have not yet finished informing us about this guild.'

'Your Grace, my argument is that not a few of your London citizens, merchant or clerk, wear a special collar to protect their throats so the garotte cannot be tightened.' Ranulf spread his hands. 'Now I ask myself, was one of these used at Sarasin's hanging?'

'Do you think so?'

'No, your Grace,' Corbett declared. 'Indeed, Ranulf watched that malefactor die.'

'Yet it is possible?' Countess Marguerite questioned.

'Your Graces,' Ranulf straightened in his chair and cleared his throat, 'I am merely informing you of any possibilities that might explain the murderous mayhem in and around the Twilight tavern.'

73

'You mention Queenhithe,' the king abruptly exclaimed. 'Sir Hugh, I think we need you there more than any other place. I will grant you a full commission of oyer and terminer. You'll be armed with all the powers of King's Bench. There are other challenges you must face.'

Corbett kept his face impassive. He had dearly hoped to return to Leighton to spend Candlemas with his lady wife and two children.

'Sir Hugh,' the queen smiled dazzlingly, 'I can read your thoughts, but please, for my sake and that of the king, see this business through.'

'You and Master Ranulf were instrumental in the capture, indictment and execution of Sarasin,' warned Malfeson. 'If a war of vengeance is being waged, and it certainly seems so, you are both marked down for death.'

'A constant shadow, monsieur,' Corbett retorted. 'A deep, dark shadow that hangs over my life and that of my friend here.' He pushed back his chair. 'I must—'

'Sir Hugh,' Marguerite called out, leaning against the table, head slightly back. She peered imperiously at this clerk as if trying to assess Corbett's true value.

'My lady?'

'You mention Sarasin's execution. However, during his trial, I hear that little reference was made to his friendship with Rahmel.'

'My lady, we kept it simple and distinct. Sarasin killed a royal clerk, an unarmed man, in cold blood. That was enough to hang him. He certainly wouldn't have mentioned his relationship with Rahmel, as that could lead to a charge of treason. No, when I organised my indictment, I concentrated solely on Louis Rahmel's unlawful death.'

'Thank you, thank you.' Marguerite fluttered her fingers.

'Sir Hugh,' the king declared, 'I will issue you with the commission because there is more mischief at Queenhithe. When I heard of it, I groaned. What I tell you is already being gossiped about and, like any fire, the gossip will be fanned into flames and become common knowledge.'

'Your Grace?'

'Yes,' Edward murmured, 'I am your Grace, and now I hope for God's grace.'

'Inform him,' the queen snapped.

The king took a deep breath. 'Last Wednesday, a cohort of Tower archers, six in number, under their ensign, Malachi, collected treasure from the Tower consisting of jewellery, silver and gold ornaments, bracelets, rings and neck chains. Most of this belongs to my lady wife. Malachi and his cohort, as was customary, fetched the treasure chest and adjourned to the Twilight. Here they hired a gubernator, or navigator, to take them across the river to some designated inlet where the chest would be handed over to royal officials. These in turn would ensure it would be transported to some secure place, in this case a royal manor house, where it would remain until my lady wife and myself journey down to cross the Narrow Seas.' He waved a hand. 'Sir

Hugh, you must know of such arrangements, treasure taken with little ceremony or show. The transport of such precious cargo must be kept as secret and silent as possible.'

Corbett nodded in agreement. The transport of anything precious was best covered by a pall of secrecy. Indeed, he was part of that secrecy, being involved in the current preparations for the royal couple to cross to France. The arrangements were complicated and needed careful management, especially against pilfering or any type of theft. Such felonies were almost endemic in the royal household, a facet of court life he had to constantly deal with.

'So,' he declared, 'the treasure leaves the Tower by cart, yes? Down to Queenhithe, close to the Twilight tavern, where it is met by Malachi and his band of merry men. They also collect a navigator.' He paused. 'Who would appoint him?'

'Malachi would. The task is offered to any seasoned gubernator who presents himself to the officer in charge, which duly happened.'

'And then what?' Ranulf asked, fascinated by what he was hearing.

'When they were ready, Malachi, the navigator and the six archers would board the battle-boat *The War-dog* and cast off from Queenhithe.'

'Your Grace?'

'Yes, Ranulf?'

'I have heard whispers that something went wrong – just chatter, gossip.'

'It certainly did go wrong,' the king snapped. 'I am talking about the disappearance of an entire battle-boat, its crew and its cargo. The navigator was important. He would know everything there is to know about the Thames, its inlets, coves and currents. Now my admiral advises me that *The War-dog* should have reached midstream before turning to starboard, heading towards Southwark side. Except,' he clapped his hands abruptly, 'all gone! Vanished like mist before the sun.'

'Hard to believe,' Corbett exclaimed.

'Perhaps Malachi and his escort were suborned,' Ranulf suggested.

'No, no, that would be impossible.' Corbett shook his head. 'Those Tower archers are hand picked. King's men, body and soul, in peace and in war. Moreover,' he made himself more comfortable in his chair, 'if they *were* suborned, if they are thieves, where is the battle-boat? How and where did they berth it and then move a heavy treasure chest across open countryside?' He tapped Ranulf on the arm. 'Think, my friend, the boat has to move from its original course. It has to choose a place to hide. The men stumble ashore. They must have accomplices waiting there with a cart and some horses. Moreover, if Malachi and his men were responsible for the theft, they will not remain at liberty for very long: someone will see them.'

'I agree,' the king declared. 'However, the disappearance of the battle-boat, its crew and precious cargo is cloaked in mystery. So, Sir Hugh, move your banner from Westminster to Queenhithe. Investigate the disappearance of *The War-dog* as well as the other malicious mysteries confronting us. The Chancery will commission you with the usual letters and licences, warrants and proclamations.' He fell silent, eyes closed. 'Strange,' he murmured, opening his eyes. 'Strange and stranger still.'

'Sire?'

Edward turned in his chair and smiled at the queen. 'The treasure on board *The War-dog* contained precious stones – *your* precious stones, my dear. It also held the assassin's dagger.' He pointed at Corbett. 'You remember that, Hugh?'

'Of course, your Grace.'

'Then refresh our memories and inform the company what that dagger means.'

'Years ago . . .' Corbett cleared his throat. He was becoming impatient: the day was drawing on and, from what he could see, the snow was still falling. Moreover, despite the crackling braziers, the chamber had grown colder.

'Sir Hugh, we are waiting,' Countess Marguerite called out.

'Years ago,' Corbett repeated, 'the king's father of blessed memory went on crusade in Outremer. Edward the Prince, as he was then called, had earned the reputation of being a formidable warrior. Now, in the mountains close to Aleppo lurked an Islamic sect led by one who styled himself the Old Man of the Mountain. In truth, they were assassins: their leader fed them on hashish, then would dispatch them in pairs to kill anyone he had marked down for execution. He turned on our prince camped near Acre. Edward was emerging as a real threat, so the assassins wanted him dead. At first the Old Man's emissaries were successful. They managed to slip into the prince's personal pavilion. According to the accepted story, Edward killed both assassins. However, before he did, one of his attackers wounded him with a dagger smeared with poison. He would certainly have died in agony but for his beloved wife Eleanor. Your devoted mother actually sucked the poison from his wound and spat it out, thus saving his life. Your father, in solemn thanksgiving, dedicated the dagger as a talisman, a memorial of his deliverance thanks to the incredible courage of his warrior-queen wife.'

Corbett paused and glanced at Isabella, who was listening, eyes closed, while her husband sat with his hands covering his face. Corbett knew the king was crying, as he always did whenever his beloved mother was mentioned. Edward had truly feared his redoubtable father, but he had adored his mother and considered her a saint in the heavenly court.

'Such items, Hugh,' the queen spoke up, 'were in that coffer. You must find those responsible and recover that chest. Once done, we promise, you will have a well-deserved rest from all of this at Leighton Manor.'

Corbett murmured his agreement. The king made to leave, but the royal clerk raised his hand.

'Your Grace, a moment . . .'

'What is it, Hugh?'

'You mentioned how the threat against the queen proclaimed that she would suffer by fire as many Templars allegedly have. So has there been any hint of this happening? I appreciate our beloved queen is always carefully guarded and protected. Nevertheless, some assassins have the fanaticism to see their plots through. They are quite prepared to face death as long as they achieve what they have planned. So I repeat. Have there been any incidents where the queen has been threatened with fire?'

'Well, one time,' Isabella spoke up, 'there was what you might call an incident here at Westminster. I was with my sister Marguerite.' She looked at the countess, who signalled her agreement. 'A candle,' the queen continued, 'suddenly tipped over.'

'Sweet sister, it was more than that,' the countess declared. 'It was an eight-branched spigot. God knows what caused it to fall. Anyway, some manuscripts and items of clothing caught fire.'

'But the flames were soon doused,' Isabella added. 'My devoted sister seized a curtain that had been rolled up on the floor. It had been taken down from the windows and was heavily laden with dust. Marguerite quickly smothered the flames with it.'

'For which,' the king interjected, 'she has our most grateful thanks.'

'But it was an accident, or at least I think it was,' Isabella went on. 'A chilling coincidence with no proof or evidence that it was malicious.'

'And now I really must go,' the king declared, rising

to swing his cloak about him. He kissed his wife affec-
tionately on the brow, nodded at the rest of the company
and left, calling for his bodyguard. Isabella, however,
remained seated, indicating that Corbett and Ranulf
should also.

For a while there was a great deal of bustle as servants
served fresh wine while other royal retainers filled the
brazier with more charcoal. Eventually matters calmed
down. The Countess Marguerite and de Craon took
their leave, the French envoy acknowledging Corbett
with a sketchy bow and a sneering smirk. Corbett just
sat staring across the room until he had gone. Malfeson
stayed, seemingly lost in thought. Ranulf excused
himself, murmuring that he had to visit the jakes closet
on the gallery outside. Isabella murmured that they
would wait until he returned. The queen continued
tapping the table, lips moving soundlessly as if she was
trying to memorise something.

Corbett rose and crossed to a lancet window filled
with painted glass. He peered through, glimpsed the
snow still steadily falling and decided he would not
leave Westminster until the morning. Ranulf returned.
The queen asked Corbett to secure the door and make
sure it was locked fast. Once he had done so, she asked
all three clerks to draw closer, her voice hardly above
a whisper.

'Sir Hugh, I need to speak to you and Master Ranulf.
You must know,' she pointed at the French clerk, 'that
Malfeson is no ordinary clerk. He is a high-ranking
seigneur in the Chambre Noire and has been armed

with a special mandate.' She sipped from her goblet. 'I will not take long,' she continued. 'I need to be swift and sure, to the point. First let me tell you that I have Malfeson's agreement to share this with you.'

'A special mandate?' Corbett declared. 'What secret is this?'

'My task is quite simple,' Malfeson replied. 'I am to concentrate on the other lords of the Chambre Noire. I am to watch them as a hungry cat would a mousehole.'

'*Quis custodiet ipsos custodes*?' Corbett replied. 'Who will guard the guards themselves?'

'Precisely, Sir Hugh, and, believe me, I have a great deal to watch. I have, as an important part of my mandate, to ensure that these great seigneurs do not wander from the path laid out for them.'

'And what is that path?' Corbett asked. 'Though I do have a suspicion about what it might be.'

'Nothing more, nothing less,' Malfeson replied, 'than the will of the King of France. Different individuals have different perceptions. They must, however, ignore all these in the struggle for the common good.'

'Which is the will of King Philip?'

'Very perceptive, Sir Hugh.'

Corbett half smiled. Malfeson's reply held a gentle sarcasm.

'Can you tell me any more?' He spread his hands. 'I suspect you cannot.'

'I'm afraid that's true, Sir Hugh. I cannot.'

'So why are you telling me this?'

'First,' Isabella interjected, 'so that you can trust

Malfeson in everything he does on my behalf. I am the Queen of England.' Her voice was almost a hiss. 'Sometimes I believe I am surrounded by serpents, vicious snakes waiting to strike. I trust Malfeson completely, as I do you, Sir Hugh, because he protects me, and because my father has told me to trust him.'

'And why has King Philip done that?'

'Because Malfeson is my half-brother. My father's illegitimate son, born of a lady at the court. His birth and his provenance were kept secret and have, in the main, remained so. England and France,' Isabella continued, 'circle each other like swordsmen looking for an opening, a weakness, an opportunity to impose themselves; that, Sir Hugh, is the game of kings. However, other games, just as deadly and dangerous, also take place. Malfeson makes sure that both myself and my interests are zealously protected. These threats of violence against me, the question of who is responsible and why they are doing this, fall within his remit. In a word, Hugh, Ranulf, he is your closest, handfast ally. Once this game has finished, he'll return to what he does best: watching and plotting.'

Corbett stared across at Malfeson, who held his gaze then smiled, proffering his hand for the royal clerk to grasp. Malfeson tightened his grip then let it go.

'Trust me, Sir Hugh,' he murmured, 'in this business involving the queen, I am a sure and certain ally. I cannot tell you more, not now. We must wait to see how the game unfurls. I will say—'

The three men sprang to their feet as a brazier just

behind the queen's chair erupted, its blazing coals seeming to turn to liquid fire as the flames cascaded onto the floor. Corbett immediately seized the queen and pulled her towards him. Another brazier erupted, followed by a third close to the buttery table. He snatched up his heavy cloak, shouting at the others not to open the doors or use water to douse the flames, but instead to use any dust-laden cloth they could find. Without hesitation, Ranulf and Malfeson grabbed heavy winter cloaks hanging on wall pegs and threw these over the flames and the thin rivulets of fire curling like snakes across the turkey rugs. Outside, others had gathered, alarmed by the shouts and crashing as well as the tendrils of smoke seeping out through shutters and beneath doors.

'Do not open anything!' Corbett yelled. 'There is a strong draught that will only fan the flames.'

They continued to beat at the fire, smothering the flames while keeping well away from the rest of the braziers. At last, confident that the blaze was under control, Corbett unlocked the door and stood aside as the king and members of the royal household swept into the chamber. Edward, shouting questions no one could answer, immediately embraced his wife. They were joined by Countess Marguerite, who gently coaxed a distressed Isabella to leave the chamber. Chamberlains and household knights swiftly formed a circle of steel around all three. Shutters were then pulled back and lancet windows opened to allow the acrid smoke to curl out.

Once the royal entourage had left, Corbett, Ranulf and Malfeson, faces and clothing smeared with dirt, examined the contents of the three braziers, now little more than smouldering ash.

'Nothing really,' Corbett murmured. He carefully bent down and sniffed at the hot dust.

'The cause, Sir Hugh?' Ranulf asked.

'Oil, perhaps,' Corbett suggested. 'Or black powder, the type used on culverins and bombards.'

'But how did it happen?' Malfeson demanded.

'Monsieur, I do not know. But with God's help I will find out.'

Corbett and his companions continued their examination of the braziers, gingerly using their daggers to sift the greying remnants. However, they could find nothing significant to explain the abrupt eruption of flame and fire. The chamberlains' men came into the room and started busily clearing the mess, begging the three clerks to leave. Corbett, however, asserted his authority. He summoned the chief chamberlain and his acolytes, then, with Ranulf beside him, sword and dagger unsheathed, walked among the household men studying each of them. He could detect nothing except fear and apprehension at what had happened. All these retainers were garbed in tunics and jerkins boasting the royal arms. They had a certain way about them, yet Corbett hoped he could find at least one individual whose presence in the room could be deemed suspect. But though he stared closely at all of them, he could sense nothing untoward. He returned to stand beside Ranulf, who sheathed his weapons and raised his hand for silence.

'Gentlemen,' Corbett exclaimed, 'I ask you, on your loyalty to the king, did any of you on this day, before or after their Graces arrived, notice anything untoward, be it a stranger in your midst or a person acting suspiciously either here or outside?'

'Sir Hugh,' the chief chamberlain replied, 'I have asked the same questions and received the same reply. We are king's men to the very marrow. We can tell you nothing.'

'Are you sure?' Malfeson demanded. The French clerk's agitation was obvious, his smooth face now tense, eyes wary as he walked through the ranks of the assembled retainers. 'Are you absolutely sure?' he repeated, only to be answered with firm denials.

'In which case, gentlemen,' Corbett declared, 'we will leave you to your work.'

Malfeson followed Corbett and Ranulf as they left the chamber. 'You are to return to the Twilight?' he asked. 'You will lodge there?'

'That,' Corbett replied, 'is the king's wish.'

'In which case, I shall be with you.'

'And I welcome that.' Corbett clasped Malfeson's hand. 'I will not leave till tomorrow morning. The snow falls heavy and lies thick. I am tired. The queen is resting and so must I. However, believe me, Malfeson, the evil we confront never sleeps. Tomorrow the struggle continues, be it here or at the Twilight.'

PART THREE

He awaits the blaze of hellfire.

Megotta the Moon-girl, 'Daughter of the Sun', leading mummer lady in the acting troupe known as the Apostles, under their flamboyant leader Lord Janus, wondered what was happening in her life. She had received Corbett's summons as she sheltered with the rest of her troupe in the makeshift bothies strewn across the fields of St Mary Overy on Southwark side, close to London Bridge. Corbett had sent her a memorandum summarising what had happened at the Twilight tavern with the murders of Poulter and Swinton. He had then described Malling's turn of madness, which had led to his slaying by Malfeson, a high-ranking French mailed clerk in the service of Queen Isabella. He had also expressed his deep concern about the disappearance of Malling's two daughters and the hideous injury inflicted on both young women. He had concluded his missive by asking Megotta to hasten 'as swift as a swallow' to the Twilight and keep everyone and everything under close scrutiny.

Megotta had hurried across London Bridge, arriving at the tavern just before the snow began to fall. She now sat ensconced in a window enclave nursing a pot of ale as she stared across the cavernous taproom and the crowd milling there. The harsh, bitter weather had, despite the macabre happenings at the tavern, encouraged those who congregated there to stay and revel in the warmth and sweet-smelling comfort of Queenhithe's leading hostelry. The taproom was well lit, and Appleby, the tavern steward, had ensured that the fire, roaring like a demon in the great hollow hearth, was regularly fed with logs by the spit boys. These urchins of the alleyways also turned the spits to roast the huge chunks of spiced meat that permeated the air with mouth-watering smells. In the meantime, the cooks in the kitchens were busy cutting up the produce, piling the cooked meat and scanty vegetables onto wooden platters for the horde of hungry customers.

'The world and his wife,' Megotta whispered to herself, 'are certainly here tonight.'

She loosened the clasps of her gown to counter the deepening heat of the taproom. She had hurried from London Bridge, glad to be away from the icy wind, which tore at both the bridge and the houses and shops either side of it. On reaching the Twilight, she had quickly changed her clothing, donning the shift, flounced skirt and low-cut chemise of a street-walker. The mummers' girl was protected by Corbett, who had instructed Appleby in no uncertain terms that she was a member of his household. Appleby was not to reveal this to anybody, and was to provide this remarkable young lady, as Corbett described her, with every assistance. She must be allowed to come and go as she wished.

Megotta had slipped into the tavern dressed as a modest, shy-faced young woman, her face flawless, teeth as white as the snow falling outside. In a short while she had transformed herself into one of her favourite roles: the witch-queen of the Old Testament, Jezebel, the consort of that king of sinners Ahab, a prince who constantly put God to the test. The transformation was complete. No one would have guessed the truth of the mummer girl.

For a while she played the part as she moved from table to table trying to capture the essence of the place as well as learn more from the constant chatter and gossip. Confident in her disguise, she stared around, studying the motley throng. She was correct in her assumption. The world, his wife and all their children appeared to have wandered into the tavern. Jongleurs and minstrels with their trained monkeys. Balladeers offering to sing or chant a poem. A street herald with news from the city. A teller of tales from Byzantium who claimed to have crossed seas coloured a deep, rich blue where gold and silver triremes loosened their majestic billowing sails. Relic sellers elbowed their way through the crowd offering the most surprising artefacts: a needle once used by the Virgin, a bone from the leg of St Alphege and a feather from the dove dispatched by Noah to discover whether the Great Flood had receded.

Of course, the inhabitants of the dark, dire landscape of London's underworld had also swarmed into the tavern: the pickpockets, naps and foists; the sewer squires; the heralds of the alleyways; the bum boys along with a flock of ladies of the night. The street-walkers soon noticed Megotta, but kept their distance. After all, she was young and strong and carried at least two daggers sheathed on the battered war belt around her waist. She looked and moved as if she was skilled in weaponry and, if she was confronted, the consequent dagger play would certainly end in a death.

As she strolled between the tables, slapping away questing hands, Megotta learnt a great deal more about what had actually happened in this magnificent tavern. She had then decided to give it a rest, sitting in the enclave near the window. She leant back, eyes half closed, as she wondered about the mysteries many of the customers were discussing. She was keeping a particularly sharp eye on a group seated around a table on the far side of the taproom. She was certain that the scruffily attired men were rifflers. Despite their tawdry, dirty clothes, they seemed well armed, with war belts and baldrics within easy reach should violence erupt. More significantly, they all had a small whistle on a cord slung around their necks: the symbol that according to their own code meant they should not clash with a brother from another riffler group or tribe. Megotta had passed this table several times, even letting a couple of them snatch at her bodice. She regarded this as part of the price to pay for getting closer and lingering to listen before moving on. She had overheard remarks about the execution of Sarasin and the emergence of someone called the Immortal.

'Scraps of loose threads,' she murmured, 'but still all a-tangle.' She sipped from her tankard as she sprawled in the high-backed chair, legs apart, her raven-black hair hidden beneath the most tawdry blood-red wig. She moved, scratching herself, then gulped at the ale while keeping a constant watch on the rifflers. The noise of the tavern had begun to subside.

'Are you well, my dear?' Megotta spun round and stared up at the kindly face of a Black Robe. He was lean and sinewy, yet he had to rest on his silver-topped walking cane. 'I am Ricard,' he declared, offering his hand so she could shake it.

'And I am Imelda.' Megotta had decided on that name as soon as she'd entered the tavern. She pointed at a stool close by. 'Sit down, Father.'

The Benedictine crossed himself as he sat down gratefully. 'You are not from around here, Imelda?'

'No,' she replied in a voice that held echoes of the western shires. 'I have travelled from Corfe in Dorset. I came to London to make my fortune. Anyway, Father, I could ask the same of you. What is a Black Robe doing here at such an hour?'

'If Christ came to London, he would certainly visit a place like this,' the monk replied. 'He would settle down comfortably in the company of sinners.'

'Such as myself, Father?'

'Even worse,' he quipped. 'Naughty Benedictines, Black Robes, who keep one eye on God and the other on the sins of the flesh.'

Megotta laughed in a fine display of blackened teeth.

'I am harvesting souls,' Ricard went on. 'This busy tavern stands at a very important crossroads. The river is close by, where great cogs are moored. Such ships could take you to the farthest horizon, while the lanes and trackways around here spread out like a spider's webs for travellers who wish to cross the shires.' He paused as Megotta offered him a sip from her tankard, which he gratefully accepted. 'My lord abbot of Westminster,' he continued, 'recognised that a place like the Twilight needs its own chaplain to cater for travellers and the horde of customers who flock here. My chapel lies close by, a simple whitewashed chamber but still a sacred place within a sacred space. You should visit it.'

'I may well do so, Father. But what has happened here? I sense a deep tension.' Megotta scratched her cheek. 'I hear stories about a gruesome hanging and other hideous deaths.'

'Such stories are true.' The Benedictine's face now turned solemn, his light blue eyes staring sadly at Megotta. 'At this moment in time,' his voice fell to a whisper, 'this place is the hunting run of demons. Killers prowl deep in the shadows. So, my lady, keep close watch over yourself. If you stay here and need advice or help, come speak to me.'

He stood up, resting on his cane as he blessed Megotta,

then hobbled away. The moon-girl returned to her own scrutiny, watching as the coven of rifflers conversed, their heads close together as they whispered among themselves. She was sure that they were preparing to leave. She also believed they would not be returning to their nests but were intent on some murderous mischief. She watched carefully as their leader, a balding hulk with a slit nose and cropped ears, glanced towards the great hour candle on its large metal spigot. The candle burnt fiercely, its flame melting the wax as it moved down to the next red circle.

Megotta was determined to follow them wherever they went, so she slipped like a flitting shadow from the enclave up to her garret on the top floor, where she changed, swiftly donning men's clothing, including a deep capuchon pulled close around her head with a woollen visor to cover the bottom half of her face. She then returned to the noisy taproom and waited. The flame on the hour candle had now reached its ninth red circle. The rifflers rose, strapping on war belts and fastening cloaks. Megotta grasped the clubbed walking stick she had collected from her chamber and followed them out onto the long pathway leading down to the tavern gate. Once there, they turned right, heading towards Salt Wharf and Timberhithe. The snowstorm had begun to subside, but the snow now lay thick and crisp across the rutted lane and laced every ledge, sill and cornice.

Megotta continued to follow the rifflers. It was not so hard because they carried between them two huge lanternhorns, their light bobbing on the snow as good as any beacon. Here and there they passed pools of blood created by the night creatures, the feral dogs and cats that hunted the legion of rats and other vermin infesting the riverside. The night had turned bitterly cold. A razor-sharp breeze swept in from the river, which ran dark and sullen as if it too resented the freezing weather. They passed the stocks and pillories where prisoners still languished, neck and wrists held fast by the iron clasps. Bonfires burnt the day's refuse left by the markets, the flames drawing in the cohorts of the damned, the beggars, night-walkers and dark-dwellers.

Megotta could do little to help these unfortunates, while the club and dagger she carried gave clear warning to any would-be assassin that she be left alone. Whores and doxies, clustered in doorways or at the mouths of alleyways, called out stridently to the rifflers. They, however, just continued on, loudly cursing the rutted, ice-frozen trackway. Candles glowed eerily from covered lancets or through the gaps between closely barred shutters. The birds of the night, driven away from the river by the intense cold, turned and screeched in their desperate hunt for food. Megotta tried to ignore all these distractions, determined to keep a sharp eye on the rifflers, though sometimes she struggled to maintain her footing.

After some time, they reached Broken Wharf, now nothing more than a great slab of stone and rock jutting out over the river, decorated here and there by dilapidated ruins. These stark black shapes loomed up against the light of the night. Megotta paused. Other rifflers were already assembled there, standing around bonfires, their leaping flames piercing the darkness. The ones she had followed were greeted with good-natured catcalls and jeering. She crouched and watched from behind her vantage point, the ruined wall of a derelict warehouse. 'All the comforts!' she whispered to herself as some of the rifflers broached a cask of ale while others thrust pieces of meat onto makeshift grills laid over stoves. The air stank of beer, sweat and crispy meat.

She carefully watched the rifflers move about. Now and again one of them would go to the mouth of an alleyway that debouched onto the wharf. 'You are waiting for someone or something,' she whispered, 'but what?' She prayed that whoever or whatever it was would arrive soon. The falling snow had faded, but the freezing cold was like a blanket wrapped about her.

At last her prayer was answered. A hunting horn brayed and a macabre procession made its way out of the alleyway. Four torchbearers came first, two either side of the horn carrier, who once again blew a strident blast full of imminent threat. These were followed by a cohort of armed men who ringed an impressive figure garbed in a purple robe and hood. He walked slowly with all the pomp of a bishop attired in full pontificals. Behind him staggered three prisoners, their wrists tightly lashed and nooses around their necks. Megotta breathed in deeply, trying to calm herself. She did not recognise the man, but she guessed the two women were Rachel and Rebekah, the taverner's daughters who had supposedly gone to Faversham. Corbett was correct, they had been abducted and held prisoner. Both women were in a pitiful state. They tried to walk as closely together as they could. Each had her right hand heavily bandaged. Again Corbett was correct. The severed fingers had been cut from the two women.

The procession stopped in the middle of the wharf, between two bonfires that cast a lurid light on this macabre visitation. The purple-garbed figure raised his hands, as if in prayer, and his escort, followed by the rest, knelt in homage. 'We are here,' he trumpeted in a ringing voice, 'to carry out justice, my justice, the justice of the Immortal. How say you all?' He turned to receive the raucous roars of approval from his comitatus, their Aves ringing out through the darkness. He seemed fully at ease. Megotta reckoned that Broken Wharf, and all the stinking runnels leading onto it, would be closely guarded by this riffler lord.

Eventually the acclamations subsided. The purple-clad Immortal rapped out an order, and the three prisoners were dragged to stand along the ruined quayside. The nooses, tight around their necks, were lashed to an iron clasp embedded deep in the concrete. Megotta's mouth went dry, and her stomach lurched. She sensed what was about to happen. Once, when the Broken Wharf was a busy quayside, executions had been carried out here. Persons sentenced to hang would be either drowned or strangled. The three captives also realised this. The man, who Megotta now believed to be Magpie the hangman, screamed in protest while the two women crouched down together, moaning in terror. The purple-garbed leader shouted out another order, and the rifflers forced all three prisoners into silence. Once again the dreadful apparition raised his hands.

'Behold!' His rich, carrying voice echoed sombrely across the ruined quayside. 'Behold the condemned who dared raise their hand against the Immortal who cannot die.'

'All hail to the Immortal!' The shouts of the rifflers turned into a chant, then faded away.

'Listen to this,' the riffler leader continued. 'I am the Immortal. I never die. I have returned. I who have walked the corridors of hell and met the janitors who hold the keys to the gates of the underworld! Oh yes. We must now have retribution on those who have lifted their hands against me. First, the Magpie, the self-styled hangman. Guilty or not guilty?'

'Guilty!' roared the horde of rifflers.

'Then punishment.' The self-styled Immortal, accompanied by his bodyguard, walked quickly forward and shoved the Magpie, who toppled screaming into the fast-flowing river, where his screams continued then abruptly ended. 'Now,' the Immortal continued, 'those two wenches of wickedness who dared offer testimony against me. Guilty or not guilty?'

'Guilty,' came the shouted reply.

The Immortal strode towards the women and, helped by a henchman, pushed his shrieking victims into the icy water to either strangle or drown. Megotta watched as the riffler leader and his retainers then began to celebrate.

'I could do nothing,' she whispered to herself. 'I could do nothing. God send them a speedy death and have mercy on their souls.'

Corbett echoed Megotta's prayer as he stood over the three river-drenched corpses, cruel parodies of what they had once been. The backs of their heads were grievously wounded, the river having battered them against the stone ledge of Broken Wharf. Their faces and bellies were ravaged, eyeballs popping, loose mouths gaping as if they were still trying to gag what they had been forced to swallow. The clothing of all three victims was tattered and rent.

He sighed and crossed himself as he walked to the window, pulling back the battered shutters so he could breathe in fresh air. Resting against the wooden frame, he stared out across the swiftly melting snow. He had risen early that day to find the snowstorm had subsided, then dawn had broken with a glorious cloud-free sky that had ushered in a swift thaw. He had attended the first mass of the day in the chantry chapel of Edward the Confessor in Westminster Abbey. Once it was finished, he'd ordered his retinue to make a swift return to the Twilight. They'd arrived back at the tavern as the church bells rang out for prime. A cold, hard journey, the ground underfoot turning into a slippery icy mush. Nevertheless, they had travelled safe and sound to be greeted and welcomed by a heavy-eyed Appleby.

Corbett, Ranulf and Malfeson were given chambers on the first gallery. Chanson, as expected, chose to sleep in the stables with his beloved horses.

'Don't try to sing them to sleep,' Ranulf teased. 'And keep your weapons neatly sheathed.'

Chanson simply pulled a face, recognising that he was notorious for being the poorest singer on God's earth while, if he became involved in any dagger play, he would do more damage to himself than to any assailant. Captain Ap Ythel and his Tower archers also chose to lodge in the stables and outhouses. Like all veteran soldiers, they soon made themselves comfortable and warm so they could eat, drink and carouse to their hearts' content.

Corbett had hardly settled into his own chamber when Megotta, still in disguise, slipped like a ghost into the room. Pale faced and agitated, she had informed him about what she had witnessed the night before. Corbett sat down on the bed beside her and embraced her. Ranulf offered some wine, but she just shook her head. Corbett then decided to act as if the news of the three murders had been brought to the Twilight by one of the harbourmasters. 'No one,' he had declared, 'must suspect you of being involved in this. So quick as you can, go to the Tabard further along Queenhithe. Maintain your disguise and lodge there until I send for you.'

Megotta agreed and left, and Corbett ordered Ap Ythel to take his cohort down to Broken Wharf. He was to bring back the three corpses in a cart taken from the courtyard below. The captain of archers had moved with his usual swiftness. Broken Wharf was not far, and he returned quickly with the cadavers laid out on the cart. Once they were lodged in the tavern death house, Corbett, accompanied by Ranulf and Malfeson, carried out his inspection of the dead. He had hardly finished when there was a knock on the door and Father Ricard hobbled in, his cane rapping the stone floor.

'In God's name,' the Black Robe breathed, 'what is all this, Sir Hugh?' He gestured at the cadavers. 'Look at these corpses. Poor souls. Such a dreadful death. Let me bless them.'

Corbett agreed, and he, Ranulf and Malfeson sank to one knee as the Benedictine solemnly blessed the dead in the hope of their souls moving into the light of God's grace. Once finished, the monk sat down on a battered stool and peered up at Corbett.

'You have just returned from Westminster?'

'Yes, Father.' Corbett gestured at the French clerk. 'You know Monsieur Malfeson?'

'Oh yes, I do, Sir Hugh. I recognise all three of you,' Ricard smiled, 'as God's workers.' He sketched a cross in the air. 'Blessings on you all and the work you do.'

'Which is?'

The Benedictine laughed. 'That, Sir Hugh, is for you to tell me. The game of kings does not concern a Black Robe. Nevertheless, if I can help you in any way, please let me know.' He was about to get to his feet but sat back as Corbett raised a hand. 'Sir Hugh?'

'Father, you minister here?'

'I try to, yes.'

'Have you seen or heard anything that has a bearing on the recent dire occurrences?'

'Sir Hugh, as I have said, I know nothing about these deaths at Broken Wharf. I just minister here. Ask Appleby or any of the servitors. I move among the customers. Some bless me, a few curse me and the rest are basically indifferent. I keep myself to myself. I have little to do with those who brutally kill, either here or elsewhere.' He gestured at the corpses. 'Rachel and Rebekah were two delightful young women. Poulter was a busybody but good at heart, Swinton a dedicated royal official, while poor Malling was the best of taverners until he lost his wits. As for my other customers, they are all God's creatures.'

'One further matter, Father. I appreciate the sacrament of repentance. I know that canon law protects what a soul confesses on the mercy stool – that it must never be repeated or disclosed to anyone else.'

'True.' The Benedictine peered up at Corbett. 'I know what you are asking. Is there anything I have heard that may be of interest to you that is not, and I repeat not, covered by the sacred seal of confession?' Corbett nodded. 'Well, Sir Hugh, the answer is no. But believe me, you have my utmost support, and if I can help in any way, I will. Now, gentlemen, I have a mass to celebrate before what must be the smallest of congregations.' He sketched a blessing and left.

Corbett walked back to stare down at the three corpses. He asked Ranulf to seek out Appleby for thick cloths to serve as shrouds. He must also ensure that the corpses be taken down to the death house at St Mary atte Bowe. 'But first,' he declared, 'let us with all due care and reverence thoroughly search the remains of these unfortunates.'

Assisted by Malfeson, he began to strip the mangled corpses. All three were bruised, battered and cut. The two clerks whispered the prayers and invocations for the dead as they worked. Once they had finished, Corbett scrutinised the naked bodies as well as their clothing. He picked up a smock belonging to one of the women and held it up to the light. He turned and was about to put it down when he felt something hard in the waistband. Apparently this had become unstitched to create a small pocket that held a tiny roll of the coarsest parchment. Using his dagger, Corbett was able to pluck the damp parchment out. He then took it across to the window and, in the bright morning light, unrolled it. He scrutinised it carefully, but all he could make out were two unfinished words: 'calcul' and 'cucul'. The ill-formed letters had been etched in thick black ink.

'What is this?' he murmured, handing the parchment to Malfeson. 'Can you make any sense of it?'

The French clerk studied the script. 'Could it be a receipt?' he wondered. 'Or maybe an account from the tavern. This word could be the first six letters of "calculus", while "cucul" could be the first part of the Latin word for hood or cowl.'

'In which case,' Corbett replied, 'why keep it? Why hide it away? Unless it's an accident, mere chance. Ah well.' He rolled the parchment up and slipped it into his belt wallet.

Ranulf returned with the corpse sheets, and he and Malfeson helped Corbett shroud the three cadavers. Once finished, they returned to Corbett's chamber in the main building, where they washed their hands and faces at the two-branched lavarium, Corbett loudly savouring the Spanish soap and the thick woollen drying cloth. He and his companions then adjourned to the buttery for strips of venison roasted in red wine, and light morning ales. They had hardly finished their meal when Appleby knocked on the door to announce that Corbett had a visitor: a Brother Philippe from the hospital of St Bartholomew.

The tall, sharp-featured Augustinian, garbed in the grey robes of his order, strode in. He and Corbett exchanged the kiss of peace, and the usual introductions followed. Brother Philippe had met Ranulf on a number of occasions, but when Corbett declared who Malfeson was, the monk just stood, head slightly to one side, and studied the French clerk.

'Father, what is the matter?'

'You say your name is Malfeson?'

'It certainly is, Father. Why?'

'Let me see, let me see. I feel sure we have a mutual acquaintance.' Patting the sweat from his face, the Augustinian gratefully sank into the chair next to Corbett.

'Brother Philippe, why are you here? Let me hasten to add that you are most welcome.'

'Sir Hugh, I had to see you. We Grey Robes are not daunted by a little snow. My journey was easy enough, stimulating and relaxing.' Philippe placed a restraining hand on Corbett's arm as the clerk made to rise. 'You are very courteous, Hugh, but I don't need any refreshment. Let us move to the business in hand. I carefully scrutinised those two corpses you dispatched to me. The first one had lost most of his face, being killed by a crossbow bolt delivered very close.' He leant across and tapped Corbett's brow. 'Indeed, the assassin could not have got any closer. Now, as for the second . . .'

'Poison?'

'No, Hugh, not poison. Well, nothing like deadly nightshade, but something just as powerful.'

'Which is?'

'Fear! Indeed, a real and lasting attack of the terrors. To put it bluntly, that poor man died because his heart gave out. Something or someone literally terrified the life out of him, so that he collapsed and died.'

'Good Lord,' Corbett whispered. 'And what could be the cause of that?'

'Hugh, I have given you my conclusions, nothing more, nothing less.' The Augustinian rose as if he was about to leave, but then sat down again while pointing a finger at Malfeson. 'Monsieur, as you know, I am a physician. I study medicine, I study physic. I have examined corpses on the battlefield, on the scaffold, in hovels and in the stateliest mansions. I have a fascination not so much with death but with its cause. Anyway, quite recently I had a visitor from Outremer, a man who called himself Cartaphilus. Do you recognise that name? He certainly mentioned you, among others.'

Malfeson remained stony faced, yet Corbett was sure that the name Brother Philippe had mentioned was known to the French clerk, despite his shake of the head.

'Brother Philippe,' Corbett declared, 'Monsieur Malfeson is a high-ranking royal clerk at the court of Philip of France. He's an official envoy to England.'

'I know all this, because Cartaphilus told me.'

Corbett sighed and sat back in his chair.

'Hugh, let me tell you what happened. I was busy in my kitchen, as I call it, concocting certain powders and potions. A lay brother came to announce that I had a visitor, who had been lodged in the waiting room of our guest house. I washed my hands and went across to meet him. He was very well dressed and carefully presented. He looked like a rather wealthy merchant. He was dark, sallow faced, a man used to working under the sun. He in fact admitted that he had journeyed long and far across Outremer as well as the kingdoms along the Great River. He said he was collecting herbs, potions, remedies, like all of us doctors and physicians who love to enquire and probe. He asked after you, Sir Hugh. I told him you were well. He then enquired if I had met you, Monsieur Malfeson. I said no. Cartaphilus, as he called himself, just smiled at this and said that he and his comrade wanted a meeting with both of you, though that might have to wait.'

'A strange conversation,' Corbett mused.

'I agree. I think he simply wanted me to know that

he was in England, that he had knowledge of you and Malfeson. I imagine he wants to meet you to resolve certain matters, to discharge items of business, but that is only a feeling I have. I possess no evidence to confirm it. So, Hugh, I have told you what I know. I have offered my conclusions. Now,' Brother Philippe got to his feet, 'I must go. There is an apothecary close by who sells a certain tincture I need.' He made his farewells and left.

For a while Corbett and his two companions sat in silence.

'Cartaphilus. What is the significance of that name, monsieur? Why should a visitor from Outremer be so interested in you?'

'Sir Hugh, I cannot answer that. Perhaps one day when I find out more I might be able to reply. However, at this moment in time, the name means little to me.'

'Right.' Corbett pulled himself up in his chair. 'Ranulf, seek out Megotta at the Tabard. I asked her to wait there. Do not act as if she is your friend. Do not tease her. Tell her to dress in disguise then wander the taverns and alehouses along Queenhithe. And Ranulf,' Corbett jabbed a finger at this most loyal of henchmen, 'please remember, as must you, Malfeson, all three of us were instrumental in bringing Sarasin to justice. Consequently, we are marked men, walking possibly into the greatest danger. So go well armed, not only with weaponry but with sharp wit and keen sense. Now, Malfeson, let us explore this tavern, and the murder chambers in particular.'

Ranulf made to leave. Before he did, however, Corbett

whispered, 'Take a survivor, if you can.' Ranulf exclaimed in surprise, but then shrugged and departed. Once he had gone, Corbett and Malfeson began their inspection. They first visited Swinton's chamber. As they walked along the gallery, Corbett had to admit that although Appleby was downcast at the dreadful happenings at the Twilight, the steward had done his best to rectify matters. All had been swept clean, while the door to Swinton's chamber had been refurbished and rehung.

Once inside the room, Corbett closed the door and turned on the French clerk, grasping him by the shoulder. 'Monsieur,' he whispered, 'do not be alarmed, but I need you to act as quickly as you can. Grab your cloak and war belt and follow Ranulf when he leaves.' He paused. 'He is more recognisable than you, but still, put on your cloak and pull your hood forward as far as you can with a visor across your face. Keep to the wall and watch! Hurry now and see if Ranulf is being followed and, more importantly, that he does not encounter any malice.'

'But Sir Hugh . . .' the Frenchman stuttered.

'Please,' Corbett urged. 'Swift as a sunbeam, and do not leave by the main entrance, but through some postern door. Ranulf will not hurry, that's his way. Don't catch up with him, but keep him in sight. And believe me, monsieur,' he tapped the Frenchman on his shoulder and grinned, 'I never thought I would reveal as much to a clerk from the Chambre Noire.'

'And I, Sir Hugh, never thought that one day I would be protecting a clerk of the Secret Seal with my life.'

'Matters turn, monsieur, while surprise awaits around every corner.'

Malfeson smiled his agreement and hurried out. Corbett listened to him go, then, ensuring the door was firmly shut, he glanced around the murder chamber. All had been put back in order. Furniture had been polished and fresh turkey rugs lay strewn across the floor. The four-poster bed was neatly made and the air was sweet with the smell of some astringent used to clean the chamber. However, none of the braziers had been lit, so it was uncomfortably cold, an added incentive for him to finish his search and leave. He moved briskly, crossing to the door and pulling back the small iron grille. He peered into the squint hole and ran a finger through the space between the iron bars, then sighed in satisfaction. Leaving the chamber, he climbed the stairs to where Poulter had lodged on the second gallery. The door to this room was rehung and locked, so he had to wait for a servant to bring the key before he could enter. Once again, he noticed how everything had been cleaned and tidied. Very cold, but still comfortable.

'Now,' he whispered to the darkness, 'I'll go back to my own chamber and reflect on what I have seen, what I have heard and what I have felt. I shall then work to find that loose thread, which, if I tug and pull, will reveal a great deal more.'

Ranulf-atte-Newgate swaggered along the broad quay-side of Queenhithe. He knew the Tabard from his youthful days when he had run wild with the rest; a true roaring boy. Ranulf loved the city. He revelled in all its rich, thrusting clatter and clamour. Snow may have fallen, the frost may have hardened, but the morning sun had persuaded many of the citizens to leave their houses and flock to the numerous markets along Queenhithe. The strumpets and the whores, the tinkers and the traders, the tumblers and the toast men surged along the pathways, shouting and pushing to their hearts' content. The prisons had been emptied and the malefactors, heads and faces cruelly shaven, had been shoved out to stand on the pillories and stocks. Once displayed, passing citizens could curse them and throw whatever was at hand, be it dried dogshit or a dead rat. Moveable gallows had also been brought in to hang those who had tried to use the weather as a pretext to break into the deserted houses and shops. Caught *infangentheof* – red handed – the housebreakers were to be left to twirl and dance in the air. Ranulf averted his gaze. The noise around the scaffold was incessant: shouts, catcalls and curses that competed with the chanting of the troubadours as well as the strident music of the fiddle and the bagpipes. Priests, shrouded in clouds of incense, took the viaticum to the sick and the dying. Funeral parties sang their dirges, desperate to get the coffins they carried buried in the hard earth as swiftly as possible. Pack ponies, hooves scraping, brought in produce, as did the carts, their iron wheels shattering both stone and ice.

Now and again Ranulf would pause to watch something that caught his attention, be it a painter sketching some scene on a piece of canvas held tight between two rods, or a quack informing his audience about the powerful potions he could sell them. He was also certain that he was being followed. Indeed, that was to be expected. What intrigued him was why Old Master Longface would send him out by himself. And that whisper before he left about taking a survivor if he could? He was certain Corbett not only wanted a message delivered but also to discover something else. Only time would tell what that was.

He turned into a narrow runnel leading to the Tabard, brushing aside a mountebank who hurried up behind him claiming he owned a magic pig. Walking on down the runnel with the pig owner still proclaiming the attributes of his precious animal, he became suddenly aware that something was wrong. He could feel it: a prickling of sweat on the nape of his neck, an awareness of how silent the approach to the tavern had become. He walked on. The pig man had followed him, still shouting; then abruptly, the litany of praise for his beast ceased. Ranulf immediately drew his weapons and turned, just as the pig man closed. He lunged at the clerk, who sidestepped, his sword scything the air to slice open his attacker's face from eye to chin. The pig man sank screaming to his knees, then gasped as Ranulf advanced, blade glittering, to inflict the death blow across his throat.

Ranulf immediately kicked his assailant away and retreated to the wall to protect his back as four more attackers emerged from the murk of the alleyway. He glimpsed the small whistles slung on cords around their throats. Rifflers! They were garbed in motley rags, faces all visored, tattered hoods pulled forward, but they were armed with gleaming sharp blades. Two of the assailants lunged. One of them slipped and crashed cursing onto the rutted trackway. Ranulf danced forward, turning sideways to deliver a deep thrust to the second man's protuberant belly. The swordplay continued. Ranulf moved swiftly with all the assurance of a skilled swordsman and a born street fighter. The attackers drew back, gasping for breath, edging closer to each other. They were about to lunge again when a voice shouted, 'For the glory of St Denis,' and Malfeson came hurrying down the alleyway. He did not swerve or stop but crashed into the rifflers, knocking them aside and exposing them to the death blows from both himself and Ranulf. Sword and dagger blades glinted in the light. Blood spurted like wine from a ripped skin, then it was over. Three corpses, almost swimming in their own life blood.

Ranulf pointed to the one injured survivor, moaning and cursing as he nursed a grievous wound to his ankle. 'Earlier, before I left, Corbett told me to bring back a survivor. I wasn't too sure what he meant. Now I do.' He whistled under his breath. 'Old Master Longface plotted this. Cunning old fox, this is what he intended.' He crouched beside the injured man. 'My master wants you. God knows why. If I had my way, I would slit your throat and have done with you.'

Ranulf and Malfeson cleaned their blades on the dead men's clothing. They then quickly searched the corpses but found nothing but a few coins. Malfeson took these with him to the mouth of the alleyway. Ranulf returned to crouch beside the surviving assailant, who was still writhing in pain. He tapped his dagger beneath the man's chin, driving the point in until it pricked blood.

'The mercy cut,' he whispered. 'When it comes, I'll make it quick.'

'But not yet!' Malfeson called. 'Not yet!' The French clerk had collected a wheelbarrow from somewhere. He placed this close by the corpses, then rubbed his arms against the cold. 'Master Ranulf, do what business you have to in the Tabard while I look after this miscreant. I have promised the dark-dwellers they can have our assailants' weapons and clothing, but only after we have left. Until then they must leave us in peace.'

Ranulf nodded his agreement. He got to his feet, gave the injured man a kick and made his way towards the tavern. However, he had hardly gone far when Megotta, still disguised as a whore, flounced out through the doorway. She acted as if full of curiosity at what was happening in the alleyway, blowing Ranulf a kiss then staring at the injured assailant, who was being shifted by the denizens of the dark. Ranulf pretended to drive her off. However, even as he did so, he whispered Corbett's brief message. She replied with a litany of rich abuse and flounced back into the tavern.

Ranulf returned to the injured prisoner, who had been secured in the huge wheelbarrow. This was now to be pushed by four ragged dark-dwellers with the assistance of another two running either side. 'We have

Sir Hugh's prisoner,' he whispered to Malfeson, 'as well as an escort back to the Twilight. These dark-dwellers have no love or care for rifflers, who will now think twice before springing some ambuscade against us.' He turned to his escort, who were milling about, chattering among themselves in the patois of the city. 'Gentlemen,' he declared, 'once we have reached the Twilight, the prisoner is mine, but as we have already promised, the clothing, weapons, chattels and all other accoutrements of the fallen are yours.' He paused and grinned. 'To protect your property, collect it now, as a token of our honour and trust in such loyal subjects of the king.'

Ranulf and Malfeson watched in astonishment as the dead were swiftly stripped of anything of value, which disappeared into large sacks that seemed to materialise from nowhere. Once filled, the sacks were taken across to a shadowy enclave, leaving the corpses nothing more than white slabs of frozen dead flesh, soaking in their own blood.

'The scavengers will remove the corpses,' Ranulf declared. 'We are finished here.'

They returned to the Twilight without incident to be greeted by Corbett and Appleby. The dark-dwellers disappeared. Corbett ordered the prisoner to be taken to an outhouse in the tavern garden, while Appleby arranged for a local leech to be summoned to treat his wounds. Because of the sudden deep thaw, the tavern was even busier than usual, so Corbett adjourned to his own chamber, inviting Malfeson and Ranulf to join him. Once they were relaxing in the warmth and sipping goblets of hot posset, Corbett raised his cup in toast to his companions.

'My friends,' he declared, 'I do truly thank you. Ranulf, believe me, I did not see you as a sacrificial lamb. I just needed to discover as much as I could about these rifflers. If I had gone to the tavern myself without Ap Ythel and his burly boys, that would have created suspicion. The Keeper of the King's Secret Seal visiting a tavern without any protection?' He shook his head. 'Oh no, that would have achieved nothing. The same could be said about you, Ranulf, except they know I use you as a messenger. They may have thought we had made a mistake or that the business was so urgent I dispatched you without an escort. I gambled that the prospect of attacking Ranulf-atte-Newgate, who played such an important role in the capture and execution of Sarasin, could not be resisted. And so it was.' He smiled. 'I also have every confidence in your sword skills, while Monsieur Malfeson is equally efficient, and so the dice was thrown, and we won this small game of hazard.'

He rose and walked over to the hour candle. 'When the flame reaches the eleventh circle, come back here. We will be going to the garden to meet our prisoner. I intend to interrogate him, so Appleby must be with us, ready to fetch anything I may need.'

'You will torture him, Sir Hugh?'

'If necessary, Ranulf. I have no pity. Think of poor Magpie and those innocent young women.' Corbett waved a hand. 'If torture is needed, then yes. Now, my friends, I need some time to myself.'

When Ranulf and Malfeson had left, Corbett sat at his chancery desk writing down in cipher the various strands twisting and turning around the malicious mayhem he must confront. He was finishing a paragraph when he heard hurried footsteps followed by a sharp knocking on the door.

'Sir Hugh, Sir Hugh,' Malfeson called, 'you are needed downstairs. Appleby has . . .' He paused as Corbett unlocked the door and flung it open.

'Stay there,' Corbett ordered. He pulled on his boots, collected his cloak and war belt and followed the breathless Malfeson down the stairs and along a passageway leading to the garden door. Ranulf stood there, sword drawn. On a wall bench nearby sat a fearful, pale-faced Appleby. Next to him, Matilda the morning maid and Stigand the doorkeeper.

'Ranulf?'

'Sir Hugh, monsieur, follow me.' Ranulf turned to the three sitting on the bench. 'Stay here, guard the door. No one is allowed into the garden without my say-so.' He then beckoned his two companions to follow him out.

The air was bracingly cold, but the canopy of thick snow that had laced every surface was rapidly turning into a constant dripping from trees, bushes and ledges. The ground underfoot was slippery as they made their way through a small orchard onto a stretch of desolate wasteland. The only building was a whitewashed shed with its door flung open. As they approached, two ravens, beaks smeared red, hopped out of the shed, wings flapping, croaking and cawing at being disturbed from their gruesome banquet, a truly ghastly sight. Blood had seeped out of the riffler's decapitated torso, while his severed head had been placed on a narrow ledge facing the door. Corbett took one look and, hand covering mouth and nose, turned away from the gruesome scene. Malfeson did the same, cursing in French as he tried not to gag at the foul, fetid stench.

Corbett went back and stood in the entrance, moving carefully to avoid the brimming blood. He examined the clasp on the inside of the door, with a similar one on the outside, then gazed around. The outhouse contained little furniture, nothing more than a battered wooden table, a stool, a narrow cot bed and a brazier. Turning away, he walked around the outside of the building. He could detect nothing suspicious. The full horror lay inside that box of stone. Deciding he had seen enough, he gestured at his two comrades and they returned to the tavern. Appleby ushered them into the small buttery. He, Matilda and Stigand sat on one side of the table, Corbett, Ranulf and Malfeson on the other.

'Very well,' Corbett began, 'does anyone require any refreshment?'

'Not now.' Ranulf spoke up. 'My belly is still protesting at what my eyes have just seen.'

'So let us proceed quickly. What happened here? I am not carrying out judgement on any of you. I fully admit, though, that I should have left a guard close to that outhouse.'

'But it was freezing cold,' Ranulf replied, 'and you, Master Appleby, assured us that there was only one entrance to the garden.'

'And I guarded that,' Stigand declared. 'Believe me, no one went by me without my knowledge. Your archers, Sir Hugh, put the prisoner in that outhouse. He could scarcely walk. He moaned and groaned as he was taken outside. I followed the archers there. After they pushed the prisoner into the outhouse, I checked that the outer bolt was firmly pulled across, then I went back to my post. I can't tell whether he bolted the door from the inside.'

'Stigand is very trustworthy,' Appleby said, trying to control the quaver in his voice.

'So tell me,' Corbett demanded, 'who did actually go through into the garden with your permission?'

'Well, there was the leech,' Appleby replied.

'Who is he?'

'A local man, Sir Hugh, Master Thirston. Venerable and learned in good physic.' The steward shrugged. 'He arrived and I took him across to the outhouse. I waited outside. Once he had examined and treated the prisoner, he came out. I made sure the outside bolt was firmly embedded in its clasp, and we both heard the prisoner securing the inner one. We then walked back to the tavern. I asked Master Thirston about the prisoner. He replied that he had tightly bound the man's ankles and given him a potion to ease the pain. I have dispatched a messenger to bring the leech back here.'

'Good, good,' Corbett replied. 'So, Master Appleby

and Thirston go out into the garden. They deal with the prisoner, then return to the taproom. Our captive is held secure. No one else went into the garden, eh, Master Stigand?'

'No one, Sir Hugh, except Matilda, the morning maid.'

Corbett smiled at the neat little woman sitting opposite. 'Tell me what you did,' he said gently, 'in your own words.'

'I am very conscientious, sir,' she replied, in a voice barely above a whisper.

'I am sure you are. Continue, please.'

'I carried out refuse for the fire pit. I didn't hurry as it was so slippery underfoot. Master Appleby is most strict. No rubbish to be left strewn across the garden. Anyway, I did hear something and I saw a strange sight . . .'

Corbett leant forward and pushed across the table a coin he had taken from his belt wallet.

'I didn't tell anybody,' Matilda continued. 'I didn't think I should tell anyone until I was asked by somebody in authority.' She shifted her gaze from Corbett to stare intently down at the coin. Corbett pushed it closer to her.

'That's for your trouble, my dear. So speak up, be brave and inform me about what you saw.'

'When I had emptied my basket of rubbish in the fire pit, I stood there for a while listening to the sounds from the garden. I love to hear the birdsong, especially the robin, which can be constant, and—'

'Very good, very good,' Corbett interrupted. 'And then?'

'I heard a voice, a man's voice, deep and carrying. He said he was the Immortal. Sir, I just turned and stared. The man was tall, garbed in a purple jerkin and cloak, then he was gone, moving like the hunters I have seen in Epping Forest – that's where I was born, sir.'

'A beautiful place.' Corbett nodded. 'Is there anything else you have to tell me?'

'No, no, Sir Hugh, as I've said, I was staring at the fire pit and I heard that sound behind me. I turned to see the strange figure standing between two bushes. He said what he did, then vanished as softly as a shadow.'

'Thank you, very well said.' Corbett pushed the coin into Matilda's hand, then gave another to Stigand. 'So,' he declared, 'there is no other entrance into that garden except the door leading into it, and that was guarded by you, Master Stigand?'

'Closely guarded, sir.'

'I am sure it was. What about the curtain wall?'

'Sir Hugh,' Appleby retorted, 'go study that wall: it is high and sheer, with no footholds. You would need a scaling ladder to get in and out. Now, are we finished here? I am sure Master Thirston must have arrived. I did send our swiftest pot boy.'

'Yes, yes, Master Appleby. For the time being we are finished. Go and search out Master Thirston.' Corbett got to his feet. 'Master Stigand, Matilda, thank you very much.'

Both made their farewells and followed Appleby out of the buttery.

Corbett sighed and sat down. Ranulf went to speak, but Corbett lifted a finger to his lips.

'The walls have ears!' he quipped. 'Let's leave any discussions until we are elsewhere.'

He'd hardly finished speaking when Appleby knocked and ushered Thirston the leech into the buttery. An old man, hook nosed and watery eyed, he was garbed in a powder-stained robe. He looked quite overcome by the attention he was receiving. Corbett introduced himself and his companions. He then put their visitor at his ease, giving him a coin followed by a pot of morning ale. He let the leech slake his thirst, then asked about the prisoner.

'I can tell you little,' Thirston replied, 'except for one thing that might interest you. Your prisoner was lost in his pain. I realised he was a riffler and asked if Sarasin had been his leader. He replied that Sarasin had returned and now proclaimed himself to be the Immortal.'

'Impossible!' Corbett breathed.

'That's what I said, sir, but it's the truth.'

'Tell me,' Corbett asked, 'when you left to rejoin Master Appleby, you bolted the door from the outside?'

'Yes, Sir Hugh, as the prisoner did from within.'

'You are sure?'

'I heard the bolt being pushed across.' The leech shuffled his feet. 'Why didn't you leave a guard, Sir Hugh?'

'Because the prisoner was crippled and unable to flee. He was locked in an outhouse with Master Stigand guarding the one door that led into the garden.'

'You believe his own coven killed him?'

'I suspect that. They knew I would interrogate him. They had to silence his tongue once and for all.'

'I am grateful to you for telling me that, Sir Hugh. I can say no more.'

Corbett thanked Thirston and the leech left, wishing them well.

'It's time we rested,' Corbett declared. 'I need to reflect, to think, to let my mind ponder on what I have seen and heard. Ranulf, you should do the same. Do not leave the tavern, and remain vigilant. If you have to go out, speak to Ap Ythel. He will provide an escort.'

Corbett slept long and deep until he was roused by knocking on the door of his chamber. Rubbing his eyes and shivering at the cold, he found Ranulf outside.

'Sir Hugh,' Ranulf declared, 'my apologies for disturbing you, but we have visitors from the court. Come, see.'

Corbett, now fully awake, swiftly pulled on his boots. He made himself ready and followed Ranulf down to the great buttery, where the Countess Marguerite's two household knights were sipping wine.

'Monseigneur Philippe, Monseigneur Gautier.' Corbett tried to make himself sound friendly. 'You are most welcome.'

He and Ranulf exchanged the usual pleasantries with the d'Aunay brothers, insisting that they enjoy a platter of savouries from the tavern's kitchen. Ranulf, sensing that Corbett might still not be recovered from his abrupt awakening, chatted to their visitors, diverting them, while Corbett studied both men closely. Court fops, he concluded, who revelled in luxurious clothes, soft beds and delicious food. Dangerous men, though, full of their own importance, jealous of their honour and quick to quarrel. Beneath their pure wool cloaks, they were garbed in costly jerkins with puffed, lace-edged sleeves. They each wore a thin Milanese war belt with weapons sheathed in the Italian style. They had taken their belts off and hung them on wall pegs, and a pair of costly looking gloves sat on the table between them. Definitely the work of some Parisian craftsman with their gorgeous purple cloth and, on the back of each glove, a golden fleur-de-lis. Corbett commented on their exquisite beauty. The two brothers seemed slightly embarrassed by his interest in them; they each snatched one of the gloves and tucked it away in the folds of their cloaks.

'Sir Hugh.' Gautier, the elder of the two, spoke up, both his tone and manner ingratiating.

'Yes, my friend?'

'Countess Marguerite asked us to visit you here. Let me assure you that both the countess and her Grace the queen send their compliments. Nevertheless, they do wonder what progress has been made.'

'None as yet.'

Both knights looked startled at such a blunt response. Corbett, however, simply repeated his reply as he watched these two court fops with their manicured nails, clean-shaven faces and crimped dark hair. He recalled his first impression of the pair. They might talk and act like ladies of the court, but they were probably ferocious dagger boys. He breathed in deeply. He must watch his tongue and not give either of them cause for provocation.

'So,' Gautier drawled, 'you wish us to take that message back to your queen? Are you sure?'

'Monseigneur, you may add that once I have made progress – and rest assured I shall – I will return to Westminster to account to her Grace the queen and the Countess Marguerite. Now, gentlemen, is there anything else?'

'The countess wanted you to see these.' Gautier drew a small leather pouch out of his purse and handed this to Corbett, who undid the string around the neck and shook out three hard waxen seals. All bore the insignia of the Templars: two knights sharing the same bare-backed horse, which proclaimed the poverty of the Knights of Christ.

'Even though they stopped being poor,' Corbett murmured.

'Sir Hugh?'

'Where and when were these found?'

'When the Jerusalem Chamber was being cleared and cleaned after the fire.'

'So,' Corbett mused, 'was the blaze the work of the Templars? Now this is an item I would like to discuss with their Graces.'

'There is one other matter,' Gautier declared. 'Naturally both the queen and the countess still feel extremely vulnerable. They could move to the Tower, but the queen especially . . .'

'Yes, yes, I know exactly what you are about to say.' Corbett chewed the corner of his lip. 'Her Grace does not like the Tower.' He smiled wryly. 'Few do! Once within its walls, you enter a maze of gullies, lanes and runnels. It's a village in itself, with markets, stalls and a whole flock of traders surging in and out. Of course, there is also its grim reputation as the House of the Red Slayer.' He shrugged. 'Or so people call it. I can well understand why her Grace is most reluctant to move there.'

'And so where?' Gautier asked. 'Where would you recommend? The countess believes they should move into the abbey.'

'I would agree,' Corbett replied. 'The abbey's lodgings are positively luxurious, and they stand in their own quarter, which can be securely guarded. Oh yes,' he added, 'I must, and I shall, visit her Grace. But not at the moment, gentlemen.' He rose to his feet. 'Now, if there is no further business . . .?'

There wasn't, and the d'Aunays left. Once they had gone, Corbett, Ranulf and Malfeson adjourned to their chambers to rest before assembling once again in the buttery for a very late supper. They ate in silence and afterwards talked in desultory fashion about the morrow. They were finishing the last of the sweet wine along with a small platter of marchpane when Appleby knocked and entered. He sat on a stool, mopping his sweaty face.

'A busy day,' Malfeson murmured. 'But I am sure you've had busier?'

'But not as hideous.' Appleby shook his head. 'Thank God for Stigand. He is an old soldier. He even fought in Outremer, where he served as a medicus.'

'And?' Corbett asked, trying hard not to sound testy.

'Stigand cleaned the prisoner's corpse,' Appleby continued blithely. 'He filled both the torso and the head with sawdust, then sealed it.'

'I understand that,' Corbett retorted. 'The Exchequer will pay for any expenses.'

'Sir Hugh, I thank you. Your bill is growing longer by the day. Anyway ...' Appleby opened his wallet, chatting away. Ranulf seemed half asleep, but Malfeson was staring hard at the taverner as if seeing him for the first time. 'Ah yes, here it is,' Appleby declared, emptying the wallet onto the table. He pushed aside a few coins and picked up a tau cross fashioned out of dark wood, about two inches long and the same across.

'The tau symbol.' Ranulf became more alert. 'That's what it is, isn't it?'

'Indeed,' Corbett replied. 'A cross in the form of the letter T, the first letter of the Greek word for God, *theos*. It's the sign St Francis of Assisi chose to confirm his letters. The use of the tau symbol became very common-place in Outremer, a practice that then spread across Europe. It was favoured especially by the Templars.' He grasped the cross. 'People carry it or wear it on a cord around their necks.'

'Why,' Appleby queried, 'should a riffler, the most violent of men, carry such a thing? Stigand found the cross on the dead prisoner.'

'As protection, spiritual protection. Remember, Master Appleby, it's difficult being an atheist when you are facing violent death. Heaven knows why this riffler carried it, but I will keep it.' Corbett slipped the tau into his own belt wallet. 'Now, gentlemen, if there's nothing more, I will bid you goodnight. As for tomorrow morning, I think we will meet with Admiral Kynaston. We must see if we can discover anything about the disappearance of the battle-boat *The War-dog*.'

PART FOUR

The criminal is always fearful.

Corbett was all dressed and ready the following morning as the church bells tolled for terce. Admiral Kynaston arrived. The rugged, stern-faced master of the king's ships was brought up to Corbett's chamber, where greetings were exchanged. Once done, platters of food were served so they could all break their fast following the early-morning mass. After the servants had left, Corbett instructed Chanson to guard the door while he and the admiral discussed the disappearance of the battle-boat.

'A total mystery.' Kynaston sighed. 'Sir Hugh, I swear, I have never encountered anything so strange.'

'Miles, Miles,' Corbett soothed, 'let us start at the beginning.'

'Hugh, you probably know the way such matters are organised.'

'Miles, as Keeper of the Secret Seal, I am more than aware of the movement of precious items from the treasure hall in the Tower. What I am keen to know is what happened on that fateful evening. I mean, a treasure chest and the battle-boat carrying it completely disappeared from God's earth, along with its escort of seasoned archers!'

'Well,' Kynaston replied, 'the treasure chest was taken from the Tower in a cart under the command of Master Malachi, one of Ap Ythel's henchmen, together with six Tower bowmen well known for their honesty and loyalty. They would take the chest along the riverside to the Twilight with as little ceremony and show as possible. Once they reached the tavern, they would unload their precious cargo and carry it into the buttery. They would then eat and drink while Master Malachi hired a navigator to ensure safe passage across the river.'

'To where?'

'To Southwark side, then downriver to the royal manor of Kennington. Each journey has its own plan depending on the destination: it might be to Southwark then further north to wherever.'

'And who would know about the destination?'

'The barons of the Exchequer and Malachi; the latter would keep it highly confidential.'

'And the navigator?'

'Always hired at the last possible moment. Easy enough. The Twilight is a famous riverside tavern patronised by those who work along the Thames. A navigator is always used because of the river's ever-changing moods. Such an expert would know about any challenges the crossing might face at the dead of night during deep winter. He would ensure safe, swift passage. Hiring him at the last moment means he, or indeed anyone else, would not have the time to plot any mischief.' Kynaston sipped at his morning ale. 'Anyway,' he continued, 'how could a simple river man, unarmed except perhaps for a dagger, pose any danger to seven burly veterans of battles the length and breadth of this kingdom?'

'And if anyone,' Ranulf interjected, 'tried to pose as a navigator, he would be quickly discovered.'

'He certainly would. The Thames has little mercy on those who do not know her.'

'Continue,' Corbett urged.

'Well, Sir Hugh, Malachi and his cohort finished their eating and drinking. They collected the navigator from the taproom. Only then would Malachi share information about their destination. Once the navigator was instructed, the archers would carry their precious cargo down to the quayside, where the battle-boat, taken from the royal quayside at Westminster, would be waiting.' Kynaston cleared his throat. 'Malachi and his archers would then load their cargo and prepare to leave. The battle-boat needed six rowers, three either side. Malachi would sit in the stern while the navigator positioned himself in the prow along with two lanterns and a horn so as to warn off approaching craft.' He pulled a face. 'Not that the Thames was busy that evening. Nothing amiss was reported.'

'So *The War-dog* left the quayside?'

'Apparently it quit its moorings, turning to go midstream, then just disappeared!'

'Totally?'

'Totally, Hugh. As if it had been plucked off the river and cast into the deepest darkness.' Kynaston shook his head. 'The river never conceals a mishap for ever. If a craft capsizes, there's always some detritus, but not from *The War-dog*. Eight men were on that vessel. All strong and capable. Nevertheless, we haven't discovered a shred of evidence that tells us what happened to them or their boat. Nothing! Nothing at all.'

'Impossible!' Ranulf whispered. 'I was born and reared in London. We have a saying, "The Thames always gives up its dead".'

'True,' Kynaston agreed.

'And there were no witnesses?'

'Now that, Hugh, is where matters turn a little strange. No one saw or heard anything amiss except for one poor soul whom I will come to in a while. There were no proper witnesses, though my spies – and they are legion – have swept both banks of the Thames. They have questioned the river people most closely, but to no avail whatsoever.'

'I cannot understand it.' Malfeson, who had sat silent as a statue, spoke up. 'The Seine in Paris regularly takes boats and their crew as if some beast lurks beneath the surface. Nevertheless, I have never heard of such a disappearance as the good admiral has described.'

'Let us look at one possible solution,' Corbett suggested. 'Did Malachi and his crew decide to forfeit their loyalty to the Crown and flee with the king's treasure chest?'

'No, no.' Kynaston shook his head. 'They could've kept rowing down to the estuary. For what? Some waiting cog? But if that had happened, they would have been seen. If they had come ashore on either bank, again someone would have noticed. They'd have had to hire a cart and horses and have these ready: that would be very difficult to hide from the river people. And of course,' he added, 'Malachi and his men were most trustworthy. Moreover, think, Hugh, of all they would have to do if they turned malevolent and criminal. They would have to find a deserted inlet, get rid of the battle-boat, load the treasure onto the cart and then slowly plod their journey undetected to God knows where. They would be taking a most dangerous risk; the theft of the king's treasure would be defined as treason, with all its hideous sanctions.'

'I agree. But what about the navigator?' Corbett demanded.

'We don't know who he was. Malling may well have known, but he is far beyond telling us. I understand,' Kynaston pointed at Malfeson, 'that you killed him?'

'In self-defence,' Corbett retorted, 'for which a pardon has already been granted.' He paused and swiftly crossed himself. 'God save us all,' he murmured. 'Oh, Miles, who was waiting for *The War-dog* on Southwark side?'

The admiral grinned and tapped his chest. 'It was I, Sir Hugh, in a designated place not far from the manor of Kennington. We were to take the chest, stow it away and await further instruction from Westminster.' He pulled a face. 'It was all part of the king and queen's expected crossing to France, either this year or when-ever.' He sighed. 'Of course, nothing came. We waited and waited. The weather was bitterly cold, so eventually we retreated to the manor, and the rest you know. We thought *The War-dog* might have berthed at a nearby quayside, but that never happened. So there you have it. Treasure taken from the Tower was the first step. Transferred to *The War-dog* is the second; the third step, a navigator is hired. Fourth step, Malachi and his company refresh themselves in the Twilight. Fifth step, *The War-dog* casts its moorings and makes its way midstream. Sixth step, it disappears into the mist never to be seen again.'

'Those Tower archers,' Corbett declared, 'were a cohort of trusted royal retainers, but the navigator was just a tradesman selling his skill. Nevertheless, surely someone must have made enquiries about his disappear-ance. Someone worried about a father, a lover, a son . . .'

'Well, if they did, Hugh, they did not approach me or mine.' Kynaston sipped from his tankard. 'I know about the Black Robe who resides here at the Twilight. Have you questioned him?'

'No, but I agree he is a possible source of fresh information. One I should visit when we have finished here.' Corbett rose, turned and stretched himself to ease a slight cramp. 'One thing, Miles. You mentioned how someone might have seen something untoward.'

'Ah yes, Hugh, but brace yourself.' Kynaston half smiled. 'There's a wild man who haunts Queenhithe. He's called Madcap and, believe me, he is well named.'

He got to his feet. 'It's time you met him. He is truly fey, but the glint of silver helps calm his humours. I'll fetch him up myself.'

The admiral left, returning a short while later with Madcap leaping beside him. Even though Kynaston put a restraining hand on his shoulder, Madcap twisted and turned, his tongue stuck out.

'You truly are well named,' Corbett whispered.

'And who are you?' Madcap bowed. He would have knelt down before Corbett, but Kynaston, now helped by Ranulf, forced him to stand. He did so while performing a jig as if in the room by himself.

Corbett studied him closely. Madcap had sandals on his bare feet and wore a tattered black robe, probably a gift from the monks. Over this he had pulled a jerkin fashioned out of fishnet, a hood of the same material half covering his bald head. He had a stubby face with the upturned nose of a dog and the bulging, frenetic eyes of a March hare. He stopped his jig as soon as Corbett slipped a silver coin from his belt purse and twisted it before his eyes. The wild man licked his lips and would have seized the coin, but Corbett drew it back.

'So what does monsieur want with poor Madcap?' His voice had turned to a whine.

'What did you see the night that the battle-boat *The War-dog* left the quayside close to the Twilight only to disappear?' Corbett asked.

'Aye, aye, it did, it did.' Madcap performed another brief wild jig.

'Tell me what happened,' Corbett insisted, his hand

falling to the handle of his dagger. Madcap grinned and tapped the side of his head.

'I remember now, sir. *The War-dog* was battling against the water, trying to make headway, then it disappeared into the gloom. I saw bursts of light, then a great dragon surged across the water. The lights on *The War-dog* faded. The dragon drew closer. I believed it must have eaten *The War-dog*, swallowed it whole.'

'You can't have seen that.'

'Master, I am simply telling you what I tell others. *The War-dog* left the quayside.' Madcap used his hands to describe what had happened. 'Bobbing it was! Bobbing into the dark. Then its lights, burning on both poop and stern, went out and the dragon surged on.'

'So this dragon crushed the battle-boat?'

'Yes, it devoured it.'

'So why do we have no fragments, no crumbs from this nightmare banquet?'

'Because the dragon swallowed it whole.'

Corbett gazed in exasperation at Kynaston, who just pulled a face and shrugged.

'Very well.' Corbett handed over the coin, which Madcap grabbed with a cry of triumph.

'See,' he screeched, 'I see everything at night, even the Immortal.'

'What?' Corbett rose and grasped the man by his shoulder. 'Whom did you see?'

'The Immortal, standing beneath the sign of the Twilight.'

'How did you know it was the Immortal?'

'Because I have seen him before, on Broken Wharf, where he and his coven gather. Dresses in purple, he does. Oh yes, he does. As I said, they would assemble at Broken Wharf until you found those three corpses and brought them back here. Now I think the Immortal has gone away.'

'Where to?'

'Only the devil knows.'

'You saw him under the tavern sign?'

'Yes, yes, I did. Just after you hanged Sarasin.' Madcap tapped the side of his scabby nose. 'Not as fey as you think, eh, royal clerk?'

'And he was standing under the sign dressed in purple?'

'As you say. Now can I go?'

'No, first tell me what happened.'

'He was just standing there staring up. Then he turned, following the high curtain wall. I scampered after him, but when I rounded the corner, he had vanished and so had the lantern he carried. Gone like the mist before the sun. And now so must I.'

Madcap turned, almost knocking Kynaston aside. Ranulf grabbed him by the front of his jerkin, pulling him very close.

'Do you have anything else to tell us, Madcap?'

'Nothing, nothing more. Now let me swim away, because that's what I am doing. Swimming towards heaven.'

'Then go, my friend,' Corbett declared. 'But I stand

by my first judgement. You are not as mad as people think or you pretend.'

Ranulf pushed Madcap away for Kynaston to take downstairs. Corbett sat half listening to the clatter fade. Kynaston returned, bustling in to grab his cloak and war belt. He promised he would continue the search for anything that would solve the mystery of *The War-dog*'s disappearance. Corbett thanked him.

For a while after the admiral left, Corbett just sat, eyes half closed, reflecting on what Madcap had said.

'Sir Hugh.' Malfeson broke the silence. 'What should we do? We seem to be making no progress.'

'I sit, I watch and I listen,' Corbett replied. 'But we have no loose thread in the tangle confronting us. I wish we did. But remember, monseigneur, some of these matters affect the power of France as well as the honour of the Capets, your saintly royal family.'

'True,' Malfeson agreed, ignoring the thin veil of sarcasm in Corbett's last words. 'But Hugh, there are other matters, other issues. I have seen and heard about the preparations your king is making. He plans to take the royal array across the march and into Scotland to confront and utterly annihilate Robert the Bruce and his host.'

'And your King Philip is determined to bring Flanders under his writ, if not discreetly then by other means. Philip plans, or so we have heard, an invasion to bring to battle and destroy the Flemish war host.' Corbett wiped his lips on the back of his hand. 'I do think,' he added, 'that all this turbulence in the body politic has some bearing on this game of kings. Now there's one loose thread I would love to find and pull.'

'Let me make it very clear,' Malfeson declared. 'Philip of France sees your king as a friend and ally as well as his son-in-law. He means well. Consequently, we are not pleased to see you continuing to trade with the Flemings. One of their great war cogs, *The Basilisk*, is anchored further down Queenhithe. A large vessel, armed and ready for battle. We would like to see such cogs banned from all your ports and harbours.'

'Unfortunately for you and your master,' Corbett replied, 'my king does not want any break with Flanders at this moment in time. The Flemings need our wool and we need their gold. Surely you've heard the saying "Money, even when it whispers, is heard above all other sounds"?'

Malfeson laughed, nodding in agreement. 'I will go and look at *The Basilisk*,' he declared, 'then return to sup with you, my friends.'

'I would prefer you to stay, monseigneur.'

'Why?'

'Because our work continues.' Corbett paused. 'This investigation is different from any others I have undertaken. I work for my king and my queen, but I am also aware that the shadow of France looms over what I do. We have touched on this before, but the significance might become more obvious. However, until then, Monseigneur Malfeson, I need your help, your skill, your knowledge and, above all,' he smiled, 'what your sharp wit and keen mind unearths.'

'In which case, Sir Hugh,' Malfeson spread his hands, 'I am at your service.'

'Good. However, before we begin to list and describe the challenges confronting us, let us have words with our resident chaplain, the Black Robe, the Benedictine, Brother Ricard, who lodges here at the Twilight. Ranulf,' Corbett tapped the top of the table, 'search out Brother Ricard and ask him, ever so courteously, to join us here.'

Ranulf left, and returned very quickly with the Benedictine, who, leaning on his walking cane, gently lowered himself onto the chair Corbett pulled close.

'Sir Hugh?' The Black Robe cocked his head and smiled at the clerk. 'I did wonder when you would send for me. Indeed, I was waiting.' He laughed sharply. 'If I had waited any longer, I would have come searching for you myself.'

'Why?'

'Don't play games.' Ricard's smile widened. 'You are as sharp and as keen as a hawk on the wing. While I am simply a Black Robe, a Benedictine with a damaged knee.'

'And a wit as sharp as anyone else,' Corbett retorted. 'You must see things here at the Twilight. So please tell us what you know, what you have observed and what you suspect.'

'Very little,' Ricard replied. 'I have my chapel with its sacristy, a chamber for my own use. I helped Malling with his accounts and his two daughters with their horn book. I also move among the customers ready to give advice, pray for someone or dispense absolution when I shrive them at the mercy pew. I lead the times of prayer and, of course, I celebrate my dawn mass here.' He pointed at Corbett. 'I can guess very much what you'd like to know. However, I cannot, under pain of instant excommunication by the Church, tell you what I have learnt under the sacramental seal. Nevertheless, what I can say is that I have heard very little to explain the mysteries and dire occurrences here.'

'Very well,' Corbett replied. 'So, let us turn to that fateful occasion when Sarasin murdered Rahmel, the French clerk. What do you know about that?'

'Again, very little,' the Black Robe replied. 'Rahmel and Sarasin met here. The riffler chieftain was immediately recognisable. He was a man to be feared. No one dared accost him. He and the French clerk would meet and sit well away from others in some window enclave. No one would bother them except for the taverner's two daughters, Rachel and Rebekah. Both young ladies were most sweet over Master Rahmel.' The Benedictine grinned. 'So much so I did wonder if their heavy flirting would end in one bed for all three.' His smile widened. 'Oh, Sir Hugh, believe me, I have heard of much worse things.'

'What did Sarasin make of all this?'

'I can't say. God knows, Sir Hugh, I could see he came here to conspire – yes, that's the right word – and that he needed Rahmel. But again, God knows what he was plotting, because I certainly don't. All I could deduce was that he was fervently urging Rahmel to join him in some enterprise; mischief, I suppose. Murderous malevolent mischief, as befits one of London's leading rifflers. On the other hand, Rahmel seemed to grow increasingly reluctant. I wasn't there when the fatal encounter occurred. I was in my chapel and heard the screams and yells. I hurried into the taproom, Sarasin had fled, or so I was informed. The dagger play had been most sudden and violent. Apparently Rahman shouted at the riffler to leave him alone, edging away from his erstwhile friend. Then Sarasin struck. He stabbed Rahmel and fled.'

'And Rahmel?'

'He was lying on the floor, blood pumping from two wounds: one in the belly and the other on the side of his neck. I knelt beside him and administered absolution. I could see he was past all human help.'

'Did he say anything?'

'Yes, but it was mere babbling, almost drowned by the cries and screams of Rachel and Rebekah.' The Black Robe rubbed his face. 'I had to yell at Malling to take his daughters away. No sooner had he done so than Rahmel grabbed the front of my robe.' He turned to stare at Malfeson. 'I am sorry, monseigneur, but this actually happened . . .'

'What did?' Corbett demanded.

'I don't know what Rahmel was babbling about; it was only after I gave general absolution for all sins committed—'

'What did he say?' Corbett insisted, trying to curb his impatience.

'He said the queen should be careful, especially of

her own kind. Malfeson in particular.' The Benedictine shrugged. 'At the time, I dismissed this as one piece of babbling among many. But now that I have your acquaintance, sir, I must tell you what Rahmel said about you.'

'What did he mean?' Corbett glanced at the French clerk, who had remained as calm and unruffled as ever.

'I don't know,' Malfeson replied. 'Those around the queen don't like me. They know I am the special envoy from her father. Indeed, my dispatch to England testifies to my position and status. It is also,' he shrugged, 'a snub for those whose task it is to serve and defend our queen. Philip of France believes his beloved daughter needs extra protection, and that is why I am here.' He paused. 'As you know, I tried to help Rahmel break from Sarasin. I did my best. He did respond, because he was desperate. However, in the end I suspect he came to resent me, hence his dying remark. He wanted to weaken my position with the queen. I am here to protect her and, with all due respect, the events that have occurred only prove the need for my presence in England.'

'In which case,' the Benedictine declared, 'I am sorry I had to say what I did.'

'No, no,' Corbett countered. 'I believe it's nothing more than the usual politicking, to be found in any court under the sun. Brother Ricard,' he urged, 'do continue. Tell me what you saw and heard after the killing.'

'Well, as you know, Sir Hugh, Malling and his two daughters turned king's evidence. Sarasin was caught, tried and hanged. At first, everything in the Twilight seemed to be prospering. Sarasin's execution truly removed the deep shadow he had cast over this tavern, at least for a while.'

'Brother Ricard,' Corbett interrupted, 'my apologies, but did you converse with Sarasin?'

'On his way to be hanged, I asked him if he wanted to be shriven, but he replied that he would see me in hell.' The Black Robe pulled a face. 'I don't think he was at all concerned about his immortal soul.' He sighed. 'Perhaps he changed his mind after meeting Christ in judgement.'

'And the consequences that same week? You claimed that the dark shadow Sarasin cast over the tavern disappeared, but only for a while. What did you mean?'

'Sir Hugh, I can't say much about that. Malling became fey witted with hysteria; his daughters disappeared, allegedly visiting relatives in Faversham. Sir Robert Swinton and Elias Poulter were no better than minehost. I offered help to all three men, but it was futile. Swinton and Poulter bolted themselves away in their chambers, deeply suspicious of anyone who tried to approach them.'

'And you don't know of any reason for this mysterious change in mood?'

'None, Sir Hugh.' The Black Robe licked his dry, bloodless lips. 'Though listening to scraps of chatter and gossip from around the taproom, I did wonder if all three men truly believed Sarasin had survived his hanging. Or if not, was he striking back from beyond the grave? We now know what happened to all three and to those two hapless young women. Someone or something, Sir Hugh, prowls around this tavern intent on death and destruction.'

'And the disappearance of the battle-boat *The War-dog*?'

'Again, Sir Hugh, why should I know anything about that? God bless those poor archers, and Malachi, their captain. Of course, I saw them, but just in passing, nothing more. The same is true about the death of your prisoner, or should I say his murder. I've heard the gossip about what Matilda the milkmaid saw and how Stigand the watchman zealously guarded that entrance into the garden. However, for what it's worth, I do suspect – though I have no real proof – that there was something secretive in the relationship between Malling, Appleby and Stigand. They enjoyed a common secret, but do not ask me what that might be.' The Benedictine sighed and clambered to his feet, leaning heavily on his walking cane. 'Sir Hugh,' he tapped his stick on the floor, 'my joints are stiffening. I have no more to tell you.'

'And I have no more to ask, but Brother, please think, reflect, and if you remember anything, let me know.'

Corbett exchanged the kiss of peace with the Black Robe, then ushered him out of the room. He'd hardly closed the door when Malfeson sprang to his feet.

'Sir Hugh!' he exclaimed.

'Sit down, my friend.' Corbett patted the French clerk on the shoulder. 'The queen trusts you, I can see that clearly enough, and what she decides is good enough for me. For the moment, never mind such gossip. I need to dictate, so let us prepare. I also need to visit the jakes, wash my hands and face and try to assemble my thoughts. We will begin,' he peered at the hour candle, 'when the next red circle is reached.'

Ranulf and Malfeson left Corbett to his ablutions. Once he had finished, he prepared the chancery table for his two companions. As he did so, he reflected on what the Black Robe had told him. His brain teemed with thoughts, scraps of conversation, things he had glimpsed, morsels of what he'd heard.

'It's time to impose order,' he murmured to himself, 'and God willing, I shall.'

He knelt on the prie-dieu before a wall painting depicting Christ the High Priest and prayed for guidance. Just as he finished his prayer with a Gloria, Ranulf and Malfeson knocked on the door. Corbett let them in and waited until they were comfortable and ready. For a while he just paced up and down before taking his chair at the table facing his 'learned scribes', as he called them.

'So, let us begin. Let us regard the mysteries that challenge us as separate entities as much as we can. Each is like a folio stacked on a shelf in a library, yes?'

'If you say so,' Ranulf replied.

'The first folio concerns the Templars. They were a military order dedicated to driving the Turks out of Outremer. They failed miserably. Twenty years ago, Acre, the last Christian stronghold in the Holy Land, was stormed and taken. The Templars retreated into Europe, dedicating themselves to commerce and banking. They lost their vocation so they lost their way. They grew fat on grants of estates, manors and an entire range of generous privileges.'

Corbett drew a deep breath. 'Monseigneur Malfeson, you will not like what I am about to say, but I believe it to be the truth. The Templars became rich, but they also became lazy. The kings and princes of Europe watched and waited, eager for an attack on them, which would bring them great profit. Six years ago, Philip of France led that assault. He issued decrees demanding the immediate arrest and imprisonment of all Templars, and his great lords followed suit, as did the other princes of Europe, including my own master, King Edward. All these rulers desperately needed money, and none more so than Philip of France. He had to collect money for a great chevauchée against Flanders, which undoubtedly has already been plotted. He also had to provide a suitable dowry following his daughter Princess Isabella's marriage to Edward of England some five years ago.'

'True, true,' Malfeson murmured.

'Philip, however,' Corbett continued, 'tried to justify his seizure of the Templar wealth. The Chambre Noire—'

'Some individuals in the Chambre Noire, not all,' Malfeson interrupted.

'Very well,' Corbett agreed. 'A group of Philip's ministers drew up a lengthy bill of indictment against the Templars. They accused the order and all its members of a long litany of heinous crimes against God and his Church.' He paused, inviting Malfeson to reply, but the French clerk just shrugged, as if what Corbett had said was of little importance to him. 'The Templar leaders in France,' Corbett continued, 'under their Grand Master, Jacques de Molay, have endured torture and interrogation; this will only end when these men break and confess to crimes and sins they have never committed. Once they have, they will be burnt alive on some island in the Seine. The office of the Secret Seal has collected enough evidence to indicate what Philip will do. Certainly, in France the Templar order will simply cease to exist and all its treasures will find their way into the royal coffers at the Louvre. I believe a great sin is being committed for which someone will one day have to atone. Oh, by the way,' he gestured at Malfeson, 'would Rahmel have had anything to do with the persecution of the Templars?'

Malfeson shook his head. 'No, he was a ladies' man, more interested in court dalliance than affairs of state.'

Corbett tapped the table. 'Whatever Philip and the Chambre Noire might say,' he continued, 'I don't believe one word of the accusations levelled at the Templars. And nor do I believe they are behind the present threat to our queen.'

'Why do you say that?' Ranulf interrupted.

Corbett emphasised his argument with his fingers. 'First, why should the Templars threaten Isabella? It only worsens and weakens their cause and their plight. They will make few friends or allies by threatening to burn a young queen mother and her child. Second, Isabella is very well protected. Third, why not choose more fitting prey. Men who played a key role in the destruction of the Templars. Ministers such as de Nogaret and de

Marigny? Fourth, why publish what they intend to do? Any successful ambuscade depends on both surprise and speed, which they have certainly lost.'

'Are you sure?' Malfeson demanded. 'Sir Hugh, look at the evidence. First two priests were warned about the danger to Isabella. Threats delivered on the same day, around the same hour, in both Paris and London. We all know the Templars have followers in both cities. They certainly have the means to issue threats in such a manner. Second, two attempts have been made: the candle that toppled in the queen's quarters and that dastardly attack in the Jerusalem Chamber. Admittedly, the candles may have been an accident, but what happened in the Jerusalem Chamber certainly wasn't. Any doubt about the alleged perpetrator was resolved when those Templar seals were discovered scattered about. Nevertheless,' Malfeson threw himself back in his chair, 'although there is enough evidence to make me think the Templars are guilty, deep in my heart, Sir Hugh, like you, I don't believe they are responsible. Not for one second, one heartbeat.'

'Then who is, and why?' Ranulf exclaimed.

'Lord have mercy on us all,' Corbett retorted. 'I cannot answer either question.'

'I am the same,' Malfeson declared. 'I just wonder if all of this is a diversion; a pretext for something else. It must be.'

Corbett stared hard at the French clerk. He knew very little about this powerful envoy, trusted so implicitly by the queen.

'Sir Hugh,' Malfeson spread his hands, 'you are studying me as if you are seeing me for the first time. I appreciate you have not known me for very long, while you are not completely au fait with the sinister policies of the Chambre Noire or its devious trickery.'

'Such honesty demands an honest reply,' Corbett declared. 'I take what you say about a diversion; a pretext. In our analysis we must not forget those long, twisted skeins of treachery that run through both the English and French courts. We must be wary of these. God knows who is really responsible for the attacks on the queen. Who can we trust?'

'I agree,' Malfeson replied, 'but on one matter I will not negotiate. Namely, my loyalty to Queen Isabella, my princess, the most beautiful daughter of the King of France. I am her man both body and soul, in peace and in war.'

Corbett nodded, then turned away to hide the surprise in his face. Malfeson's passionate declaration was like to that for a woman he deeply loved and cherished. Was there more to his relationship with Isabella? Corbett sensed there was, but this was not the time or the place to probe further.

'Master, the hours pass.'

'They certainly do, Ranulf, so we move to the second folio on our shelf. The mysterious happenings in the Twilight. Now, we know that Sarasin and Rahmel met here. We have also learnt from you,' Corbett pointed at Malfeson, 'that Sarasin pandered to Rahmel's lust for soft flesh, be it male or female. The riffler was prepared to use that in blackmailing Rahmel into cooperating with him. You also informed us that Sarasin was involved in some conspiracy to seize our Queen Isabella. Why this was being plotted, or by whom, we do not know. Rahmel realised that he had become deeply enmeshed in Sarasin's scheme. He fiercely objected, so their friendship turned sour. There was a quarrel in the Twilight, Sarasin drew his dagger, killed Rahmel, then fled. Our riffler lord thought he was untouchable, that nobody would go up against him. He was soon proved wrong. Our taverner's two daughters, Rachel and Rebekah, were smitten with Rahmel, and they, along with their father, turned king's evidence. So Sarasin paid the price for his crime.

'Now . . .' Corbett sipped at his blackjack of ale, 'Sarasin was executed, hanged from the tavern signpost, so that should have been the end of it all. However, within a week of his execution, matters turned dire, as if some avenging demon had swept into the Twilight and unfurled its banners. A pall of deep fear engulfed the tavern. Swinton and Poulter retreated to their rooms, hiding behind locked and bolted doors. They refused to see anyone, and yet they must have done eventually. Let us imagine that the assassin approached Poulter's chamber first and somehow inveigled him to open the door. We are not sure what exactly happened then, except that this visitor was such a dreadful sight that Poulter's heart failed him. So, we have this paradox,' Corbett continued. 'Poulter is reluctant to accept visitors such as Brother Ricard but opens the door to the assassin who literally terrifies him to death.'

'It must have been as you say, Sir Hugh,' Ranulf declared. 'Something happened that made his heart fail. Perhaps that was not difficult to achieve. Poulter was heavy and obese, big bellied and cumbersome. Shock can kill a man like that. I have seen similar happen in the royal array when the banners are unfurled and battle is imminent.'

'True, true,' Corbett agreed. 'But whatever it was, Poulter now lies dead. Our sinister assassin then approached Swinton's chamber. Again the intended victim was compliant. Swinton didn't drive his visitor away; in fact, he opened the squint gap. Outside, the assassin simply released the catch on his small hand-held arbalest and the bolt smashed Swinton's face into a shower of blood, brain and bone. So who was that killer? How was he able to approach his victims when Brother Ricard was barely tolerated? It certainly is a mystery. Was it someone in the tavern, or a stranger? However, nobody reported suspicious strangers prowling the premises, or anything else that might help our investigation.'

'And Malling's daughters, Rachel and Rebekah?'

'Well, Ranulf, we now know that they certainly did not go to Faversham; that was Malling keeping up some pretence. Both young women were abducted, and their captor then issued both a warning and a punishment to their father: the severed ring fingers of his two daughters. In truth, an act of sheer cruelty, which tipped Malling into the madness we witnessed. He deeply regretted being involved in the capture and execution of Sarasin, so he lashed out, provoking his own death. The only evidence we do have is that small roll of parchment found hidden in the waistband of an item of clothing belonging to one of those young women. There is not much there: just two ill-formed words, "calcul" and "cucul". What these fragments actually mean is beyond me.'

'They must have some significance,' Ranulf mused. 'Why scrawl two half-formed words then hide them in a piece of clothing? All we can assume is that one or both of those young ladies were desperately trying to leave a message that would help identify their abductor.'

'I agree, Ranulf. But there again, we do not even know the circumstances of their abduction. When, where and how did it occur?'

'So,' Malfeson spoke up, 'within days of Sarasin's execution, all those involved in his capture, trial and execution, with the exception of us three, were murdered in retaliation. Malling, his two daughters, Swinton, Poulter and the hangman Magpie.'

'So it would seem,' Corbett murmured, 'and we three are undoubtedly marked down for death. A dangerous challenge we must confront. But come, we are not yet finished with our folios. Let us pass to the next one.' He cleared his throat. 'We took that riffler prisoner, we locked him in a shed well away from the tavern. True, I concede, I should have left a guard. However, the prisoner was sorely injured, held fast in a garden outhouse with a soaring curtain wall surrounding it. There was no other entrance to that garden except through the door being closely guarded by Stigand. He informed us who went in: the prisoner, then Appleby accompanied by the leech Thirston, and finally Matilda the milkmaid. Now she claims to have seen a mysterious purple-clad stranger who declared he was the Immortal, a title we have touched on before.'

'I wonder,' Ranulf exclaimed, 'if we know the full truth about who went into that garden. Brother Ricard believes Appleby, Stigand and the lately deceased Malling share some secret.'

'Whatever that signifies,' Corbett replied. 'However, let's leave that for a while and move to our fourth folio – the disappearance of the battle-boat *The War-dog*. We know what happened before it left the quayside. Nothing extraordinary or surprising was noted. Brother Ricard confirms this. It departed from Queenhithe and simply disappeared into the mist. The only evidence we have is the ramblings of Madcap about a dragon swallowing the vessel, along with seven archers and one navigator. Gone! Vanished!' He clapped his hands. 'Disappeared without a trace. Now I would wholeheartedly vouch for those Tower archers, as would Ap Ythel. Good men and true. As for the navigator, I have asked Appleby to cast about to find out who he was, but so far with no success. Our tavern steward informed me that such men are in the main single and itinerant, looking for work up and down the Thames. Ah well, gentlemen, these are the folios of murder, torture, treason and robbery. God save us all.'

More murderous mayhem was being planned in the ruins of the Moabite, a derelict ancient tavern that stood in a desolate ruined village north of the city wall. Ravaged by one of those malignant infections that periodically swept the city and beyond, the village was now shunned. No one went there even during waking hours. Many claimed it was haunted, a haven of ghosts and malignant spirits. Little wonder the journeymen, tinkers and traders avoided it. The outlaws and wolfs-heads who wandered the wasteland were equally wary. They talked of dark shapes floating through the ruins. A cohort of ghosts was allegedly glimpsed searching for something or someone. Nonetheless, the Immortal and his legion of followers regarded the Moabite as ideal for their midnight meetings. Orders were issued, and the Immortal's adherents were instructed to keep all approaches to the derelict village under close scrutiny.

The Immortal had convened this assembly to deliver judgement, and his followers had been summoned to the tavern to watch their lord and master at work. He held court behind a sturdy buttery table, which had been moved onto a dais so it now dominated the well-lit taproom. Two prisoners crouched on the floor before the dais; in between them stood an iron-hooped barrel, which served as a table for a powerful lanternhorn that bathed both men in a glowing pool of light.

The Immortal, garbed in purple, a mask of the same

hue covering his face, framed by a deep ermine-lined cowl, supped from a bejewelled goblet burgled the previous evening from a merchant's house in Poultry. Now and again he helped himself to a cube of freshly cut venison specially grilled by a cook formerly of the royal household. The man had once served the king's uncle. He had been patronised and favoured by his master until he was caught pilfering precious plates from the kitchen treasury. He had escaped with his life, but had been put to the horn by special proclamations posted at the Standard in Cheapside and the Great Cross in St Paul's Churchyard. Now he was busy serving his mysterious new master in this taproom where the fumes and smoke from his oven mingled with the stench of sweat and leather.

The Immortal raised a hand for silence. He then pointed to the far corner of the room, where a blood-soaked corpse lay, the legacy of a violent affray earlier that night. He snapped his fingers, and his henchmen, following his direction, hurried to remove the offending cadaver. Once they had done so, the Immortal rose to his feet.

'So let us begin,' he declared in a ringing voice, pointing at the two prisoners. 'Madcap, stay where you are, but, my beloveds, bring a chair for Brother Walter here. He's our friend, aren't you, Walter?'

He paused as a riffler brought forward a narrow leather-backed chair with a cushioned seat. Brother Walter was ordered to sit, and a deep-bowled goblet of wine was thrust into his hands. The prisoner grinned in a fine display of yellow peg-like teeth.

'A man of substance is Brother Walter,' the Immortal went on. 'A close friend of Brother Robert Plancton, hanged by Corbett on the scaffold just outside the abbey gate. Corbett, God damn him, did not care for benefit of clergy or the status of a Black Robe. Walter, however, escaped; fled for his life, but later came back! Creeping back, I'd say, yes, Brother Walter? Oh yes.' He answered his own question. 'I know all. I see all. I hear all.'

There was an ominous silence that smothered all noise in the taproom.

'Some say,' the Immortal went on, pointing at a now terrified Walter, who had put his goblet on the barrel and sat grasping the arms of his chair, which glistened with sweat. 'What do they say about you, Walter? That you are not an upright man? Some claim you turned traitor, became a villain, a royal approver bartering your life for those of others, such as Brother Plancton. How you supplied the cunning Corbett with names, occasions, hiding places and other such valuable information.' He paused. There was no sound in the taproom except for Madcap sobbing quietly to himself. 'However,' he raised his own goblet and toasted Brother Walter, 'I don't believe that. Do you hear me, Walter? I don't believe it. Not one jot, not one tittle.'

Brother Walter visibly relaxed, sagging in the chair. He eagerly grabbed the goblet from the table beside him and noisily gulped the claret.

'And you shall prove your innocence,' the Immortal

proclaimed. 'You are to kill. You are to carry out the execution of Sir Hugh Corbett for his many crimes against me and mine.'

The declaration was greeted with shouts and acclamations, which reverberated through the ancient tavern. Even Walter, at first shocked into silence, joined in the chorus of cheering salutations to the Immortal and to himself. In truth, he felt liberated. No longer would he live under the dangling sword of suspicion. His past would be forgotten and, as far as he was concerned, the sooner the better. He would become a trusted henchman of his great leader. He felt a surge of excitement as he raised his goblet in toast to the company.

At last the salutations faded away as the Immortal shouted for silence. 'And now we come to Madcap. That garrulous monkey who scampers along the Thames. He takes note about matters on which he really should keep silent. But not Madcap, oh no! He is patronised by the great and the good. No less a person than Miles Kynaston, the King's Admiral in the south, a man well known to all of you.' His voice rose. 'Kynaston should also be here on trial for his crimes against us. Heaven knows, he has tried hard to hang most of you. If he had his way, you would all be decorating the gibbets along both banks of the Thames. Anyway, he will have to wait, at least for a time.'

Once again, his words were greeted with shouts of approval and bloodcurdling threats levelled at the admiral.

'But even worse,' the Immortal continued, 'Master

Madcap was also ushered into the presence of that common crow, the villainous Sir Hugh Corbett, Keeper of the King's Secret Seal, with whom we have so many, many grievances to settle.' He clapped his hands, got to his feet and strode forward to grab Madcap by the throat. 'So, monkey man, what did you tell Corbett? Was Kynaston present? And that soft-headed Black Robe Brother Ricard, eh? And there'd be others, such as Ranulf-atte-Newgate. All our enemies, but none more so than Corbett.' He shook Madcap like a lurcher would a rat, then let him fall to the floor.

'I told him nothing,' Madcap shrieked, rubbing at his bruised throat. 'Nothing at all.'

'We shall see, we shall see.' The Immortal turned, snapping at his cohort of henchmen to draw closer. 'Toast him,' he rasped. 'Let him do the fire dance.'

Madcap must have suspected what was going to happen. He screamed and struggled as he was hoisted on top of a barrel, his arms tied tightly to his sides and the other end of the rope secured around one of the beam hooks. The barrel was then removed, and one of the Immortal's henchmen pushed a wheeled brazier forward so that the fiery coals were only a few inches below the prisoner's feet. Madcap twisted and turned, screaming in agony as the heat increased. Eventually, sobbing and crying, he was cut down and propped against one of the taproom pillars.

'So,' the Immortal crouched before him, his eyes glittering behind his purple mask, 'what did you tell Corbett?'

'That I saw the dragon devour *The War-dog.*'

'Do you know what that means?'

'No, master. It's just what I thought I saw through the shifting mist.' Madcap shook his head. 'I do not know,' he protested. 'I swear I do not realise the significance of all this.'

'Anything else? Tell me, for I will get to know everything. I will know if you are lying.'

'I told Corbett I had seen you once.'

'Oh, did you? When, where?'

'Beneath the tavern sign of the Twilight. I told him that I followed you around the curtain wall but that you mysteriously disappeared.'

The Immortal drew his long stabbing dirk and pressed the tip against Madcap's throat.

'Anything else?'

'No, no,' Madcap spluttered.

'In which case, go in peace.' The Immortal twisted the dagger around and deftly slit Madcap's throat. Madcap trembled, eyes popping, spluttering and coughing as he choked on his own blood. He continued to shudder and jerk for a while, then fell still. 'Only the devil knows what he really told Corbett. And worse still, what Corbett made of it all. Now, it's time we dealt with that conniving clerk.'

'An attack on the Twilight?' one of his henchmen asked.

'No, not that way. Let's first see what Walter achieves and then we will speak to the brethren. And send

Madcap's corpse back to Kynaston as a warning of what happens to those who meddle in my affairs.'

Corbett left the Twilight just as a sickly dawn soured the sky. Broken clouds drifted. A stiff breeze swept back and forth across the river. The thaw had set in deeply, only to pause as the melting snow turned to ice, which sloped and slipped from eaves, sills and ledges. He walked carefully, following Ranulf, who helped Chanson lead the horses. Eight Tower archers protected them, weapons at the ready.

Corbett stared around. Walking along the dark runnels and alleyways of London reminded him of wall paintings he'd seen in the ancient churches of Rome: garish yet vivid portrayals of the human condition. London's streets were a shifting tableau of citizens thronging out either to shop or just to wander and gape. Everyone and everything seemed to be on the move. The scaffold carts clattered by, three in a row, bearing the mutilated torsos and severed heads of criminals. These had been taken down from the poles where they had been exhibited after execution, and were being transported to the great burial site near St Mary atte Bow, where they would be thrown into the lime pits. The feral dogs that prowled the streets, their appetites sharpened by the cold, were tantalised by the smell of rotting flesh. They closed in around the execution carts, leaping and yapping. One of these mongrels collided with a dancing bear being taken to its stockade. The bear lunged, swift as a snake, and hit the dog so hard it crashed into a stall selling pewter dishes. A shouting match erupted between the bear keeper and the pewterer. The latter appealed to Corbett as a witness, but the clerk just shook his head, telling his escort to move on.

The noise was now intense. A hellish cacophony created by crashing wheels, tolling bells and the slamming of doors and shutters. Beneath all this, the continuous hymn of the streets, made up of so many sounds. Jesters, troubadours and minstrels trying to divert the crowd and so earn a coin. Corpses on carts, barrows, sleds and hurdles clattering to some parish church for burial. Priests, garbed in copes, carrying the viaticum to the sick and dying. These men of God were jostled by the night-walkers and dark-dwellers, who saw such priests as easy prey. City bailiffs had emptied the jails. All those indicted during the great freeze were now to suffer public punishment, their arms, hands and fingers twisted in the vice-like grip of the stocks and pillories.

The air was rich with gusts of competing smells, be it the rank stench from the open sewers or the mouth-watering fragrance of fine pieces of meat being toasted over a grill. Corbett would have loved to close his eyes, rest from all this clamour. However, he had to prepare for an audience at which he had very little to report. Nonetheless, he believed it was important to meet with the queen and discover if she had matters to raise. He had already dispatched Malfeson ahead of him to prepare for his arrival. After that, he must visit Admiral Kynaston, who had sent a peremptory message asking Corbett to meet him.

He pulled his cowl closer about him, then sighed with relief as they turned into the royal precincts at Westminster. They were met by chamberlains who escorted them deep into the labyrinthine palace, nothing more than a collection of buildings linked by galleries and passageways. At last they reached the royal quarters, where Malfeson was waiting. He served them morning ales, bowls of kissing confits from the larder and freshly baked bread from the pantry. Once they had finished, he took them into the Jerusalem Chamber, which had been richly refurbished after the recent mysterious fire. New turkey rugs covered the floor, while the wall tapestries and triptychs celebrating the history of the Holy City had been cleaned and replaced. Corbett noted with wry amusement how all the braziers were firmly capped, though these still provided warmth, as did the fire roaring merrily in the hearth.

He took his seat at the top of the table, to the right of the king and queen's throne-like chairs. Malfeson continued to scurry about doing this and that, including a regular inspection of each brazier. Corbett shifted his gaze, his attention drawn by the mantled hearth carved in the shape of a snarling dragon's mouth. He studied the intricate sculptures as he recalled Madcap's description of how a dragon had swallowed *The War-dog*. He was still reflecting on this when a chamberlain entered the room to announce the imminent arrival of the king, the queen and the Countess Marguerite.

A short time later, preceded by trumpeters and heralds, Edward, holding Isabella by the hand, the other grasping that of the countess, entered the Jerusalem Chamber and took his seat at the head of the table, flanked by his two companions. The three royals were swathed in thick pure wool, purple robes lined with the most exquisite ermine, while the light constantly flashed on the many rings, bracelets and pectorals they wore. For a while, all was noisy and busy, with much coming and going, but at last order was imposed. The officials of the royal household withdrew, and the king and those he had summoned sat silently around the polished oval council table.

'Well, well.' Edward broke the silence, tapping his fingers against the tabletop. 'Hugh, what have you brought us?'

'To be blunt, sire, nothing.'

'Nothing at all?' Countess Marguerite rasped. 'Your queen is threatened, her clerk slain, her jewels filched, Templars lurk deep in the shadows around us, yet—'

'Enough!' Isabella intervened. She stared at Corbett, then quickly winked, her face creasing into a brief smile. Corbett smiled back and sketched a bow as Malfeson lifted his hand to speak.

'Your Grace,' the French clerk declared, 'I have worked alongside Sir Hugh. What we face is a tangled mystery at the centre of a truly devious maze.' He gestured across the table at Corbett. 'Sir Hugh can, like any craftsman, only work with what he has, and as regards this situation, it is not much.'

'All I need,' Corbett added, 'is one loose thread, and the tangle will break free and tumble.' He stared around the council chamber. 'I can say this here, locked away in the king's own quarters: the sons and daughters of Cain prove to be extremely arrogant, which makes it easier for God and his angels to bring them to account.'

'And are you one of the angels, Sir Hugh?'

'No, my lady countess, I simply work for them.'

The countess forced a smile, while the king and queen burst out laughing, the merry sound easing the tension in the chamber.

'Hugh,' the queen spoke up, 'some people advise that I move formally into sanctuary. From here to the abbey, where I will be protected by both Crown and Church.' She let her cloak slip, rubbing her right shoulder for warmth. Malfeson, ever watchful of his queen, hurried to put more logs on the fire. Corbett waited until he retook his seat, then pointed at Ranulf, who sat shaking his head.

'What say you, my friend?'

'Sir Hugh, I disagree. With all due respect, your Grace,' the Clerk of the Green Wax looked at the queen, 'I urge you not to move. The wolfsheads we now confront are wild beasts, wicked souls who tortured two innocent young women. Such sinners have no love for God nor man. They will assault you . . .' He paused as the fire in the hearth abruptly burst out in a flurry of flaring flames and gusts of scorching heat.

Fragments of fire showered the floor, scorching the turkey rugs and nibbling greedily at the rush mats. Edward sprang to his feet, even as Corbett grabbed him and thrust him away from the hearth. Malfeson and

Ranulf seized the queen and the countess and shielded them from the flickering sparks that cascaded down. Ranulf's shouts of 'To the king, to the king!' alerted the guards outside. Corbett, however, yelled at them not to come in, fearful that any draught might turn the fire into an inferno. He gently pushed the king into a window seat; Ranulf and Malfeson followed, escorting the queen and Countess Marguerite. Corbett then hurried to the door, opening it just wide enough to admit Ap Ythel, his archers and a few frightened chamberlains. Dust covers, used in the chamber when it was recently cleaned, were quickly found. Ap Ythel's archers used these to beat the flames and smother the fire. At last order was imposed. Chamberlains took Isabella and the countess out of the chamber. Edward watched them go, then strode towards Corbett, his face twisted in fury. He grasped the royal clerk by the shoulder and squeezed hard.

'My lord,' Corbett murmured, 'take your hand off me.'

The king's cold, hard stare softened. He released his grip and tapped Corbett gently on the cheek, then shook his head.

'Here we are,' he declared, 'in the very heart of my palace, the centre of my power. How dare they!' He jabbed a finger at Corbett. 'Find them, Hugh, find them. Rip off their masks, then hang their torn corpses as a warning to others about what happens to those who threaten their king.'

Once the king had left, Corbett sat in a window seat watching Ranulf, Malfeson and Ap Ythel clear the chamber. 'Fire ghouls!' he murmured to himself. 'That's what my mother called a fire out of control. Thank God that didn't happen here.'

'Master?'

'Nothing, Ranulf, just the Keeper of the King's Secret Seal talking to himself.' He rose and crossed to the hearth, where he stood staring down at the blackened debris. 'Ap Ythel, I want all these fragments, be they burnt to a cinder or not, taken to some empty storeroom. And have a pair of gauntlets or gardening gloves ready for me. I shall need them to sift through the remains.'

'Sir Hugh?' Malfeson called out.

'Yes, monseigneur?'

'I must leave. I must see the queen.'

'Of course. Give her my best regards. Tell her that I will be continuing my hunt for the wolfsheads. She must be assured I will trap them.'

Malfeson promised he would and hurried out. Ranulf and Ap Ythel also left. A short while later, Ranulf returned to collect Corbett, and led him along empty corridors and galleries into an enclosed garden containing a small summer house all cleaned and cleared ready for the spring. Ap Ythel had arranged lanterns, lamps and sconce torches, which now cast a shifting light over the spent charcoal taken from the hearth in the Jerusalem Chamber. Corbett put on stiffened gardening gloves and began to sift among the ashes, watched by a bemused Ranulf and Ap Ythel. He picked up pieces of charcoal and examined them closely. At last, he paused, holding up the remains of a charred log. Drawing his dagger, he used it to poke through the gap down the centre of the log. He got to his feet, placed the log on a wall ledge and beckoned his two companions over.

'Look,' he explained, 'this is a small fire log brought in by the hearth or spit boys. They split the log in two and hollow out the centre of each half, into which they cram sweet-smelling herbs. The two halves are then lashed together. During the course of the evening, the flames will eventually reach these logs. They split the wood and burn the perfume, and so the fire exudes both warmth and sweet-smelling aromas.'

'Then what?'

'Look at this log, Ranulf, or what's left of it.' He turned it over, pointing to the blackened groove and tapping what looked like a scrap of leather. 'Believe me, this is not your usual thin oilskin-type leather. No, this pouch, and others like it, is fashioned out of thickened reinforced leather like that used in the production of war belts or sheaths for a blade.'

'Or even a battle harness.'

'True, true, Ap Ythel. So,' Corbett put the remains of the log down, 'our would-be assassin either fashioned or bought small purses or pouches of thickened boiled leather. He or she poured oil into these and tightly secured the neck of each. For the first attack our assassin simply arranged for these oil pouches to be thrust into a number of braziers.'

'And the second?'

'In the second, Ranulf, the pouches were placed in certain logs brought in by the servants. One or more of these would eventually catch fire, and the flames would flare.'

Ap Ythel spoke up. 'Oil is a very dangerous weapon. Once fired, it has a mind of its own.'

'Malfeson tended to the hearth,' Ranulf interjected.

'True, Ranulf, but that could prove his innocence. After all, putting those logs on the fire was very hazardous. One of them could have split to create a small fire storm around our French clerk.'

'So how do we discover the *ignifer*, the fire-bringer. What is he trying to achieve?'

Corbett shook his head and lifted his hand to his nose. He sniffed, then sniffed again. 'Interesting,' he whispered.

'Master?'

'Oils have their own individual odour, Ranulf, and this one is no different. Oh yes.' Corbett pointed at the door. 'Ranulf, Ap Ythel, discreetly now, find out who is the queen's washerwoman, the one who deals directly with Isabella. Ask her to meet me in the Jerusalem Chamber. Tell her it's for her own great profit. Be gentle.'

The two men, though surprised by Corbett's request, left the summer house, while Corbett returned to the Jerusalem Chamber. He stood over one of the braziers, warming his hands, wondering if what he had discovered might be a loose thread. Ranulf and Ap Ythel soon returned, accompanied by a short, squat lady covered from neck to toe by a leather apron, a beaver hat pulled tight over her greying hair. She peered at Corbett, her rough, grubby face twisted in annoyance.

'You wanted me, sir?' she demanded sharply. 'You are a lord of the soil, so I had no choice but to come. You need something washed? Laundered?'

'No,' Corbett replied, holding up a silver coin. 'I want to give you this.'

His offer seemed to transform the woman's demeanour in the twinkling of an eye. 'Why, sir?' She stretched out her hand, but Corbett shook his head.

'Not yet. Tell me, what is your name, your title?'

'Ursula, sir, principal washerwoman in the queen's household. I defer only to the queen and the Keeper of the Wardrobe. No one else. Dirty clothes are my concern.'

'I am sure they are, Ursula.' Corbett glared at Ranulf, who was trying hard not to laugh. 'I asked to meet you because I have a task for you. Now, you launder the queen's clothing? Her linen?'

'Yes, I do it for her and others of the royal household, including the king, as well as any of their guests.'

'Good, good,' Corbett declared. 'Then my request is this. I want you to go through all the clothing given to you in the last ten days and scrutinise it carefully. This includes their Graces' garments as well as those of their honoured guests.'

'What am I looking for?'

'Anything that really should not be there.'

'Such as?'

'You will know when you find it.' Corbett spun the

coin and Ursula caught it deftly. 'Find something and there will be a second coin. Now, mistress,' he bowed, 'I bid you adieu.'

Corbett left Westminster some time afterwards, accompanied by Ranulf and Malfeson. The weather had not changed and the world seemed to be locked in an icy greyness that chilled the body and dulled the spirit. Chanson led the horses, and Corbett, following the advice of his Clerk of the Stables, decided not to ride, as underfoot was icy and dangerous even for their sturdy-footed garrons. They followed the river path past the various quaysides. Reaching Queenhithe, they continued on to Dowgate, where Admiral Kynaston had his chambers in the Beacon, a large, sprawling hostelry overlooking the Thames.

The admiral, grim faced and taciturn, met them in the buttery. He served them goblets of mulled wine, telling them to drink deep and quickly before braving the freezing weather outside. Once they were ready, they left the tavern. The harsh cold made them shiver, while a rolling sea mist stung their faces. Kynaston led them to the edge of the quayside and pointed across the river. Corbett glanced at him questioningly.

'Patience,' murmured the admiral. 'Be patient.'

As they stood there, the rolling bank of river mist abruptly parted, and Corbett caught his breath at the magnificent bearing of the great two-masted war cog riding at anchor.

'*The Basilisk*,' he whispered.

'Oh yes,' Kynaston replied. '*The Basilisk*. The pride of the Flemish fleet. In truth, it's a floating fortress.'

Corbett murmured his agreement. He had heard about this splendidly fearsome engine of war, but he was still surprised by how truly powerful it looked: the sweep of its lines, its lofty stern, broad midships and elevated prow, which ended in the carved face of a snarling basilisk.

'It looks heavy,' Kynaston went on, 'yet under sail it's swift enough.' He pointed to the hoists ranged along the deck. 'It can carry war horses and heavy supplies.'

'Why are you showing me this?'

'Because as you must know, Hugh, the Flemings are very interested in the presence of French envoys at Westminster, the Countess Marguerite in particular. They wonder if the French are turning our king's heart against Flanders. They fear that Edward will side with Philip and so persuade his father-in-law not to give aid to Bruce and the Scots.' He paused. 'The French threaten us with hints that they might support Bruce and the Scots so we English retaliate by hinting that we will use Flanders against the French. This game has been played for decades. Welcome to the chess board of princes! There is one other matter. On the night *The War-dog* disappeared, I reported that nothing out of the ordinary occurred. Well, in a way, it did. A matter of petty significance, perhaps.' He gestured towards *The Basilisk*. 'According to my source, a river reeve, the cog left its moorings along the quayside and went out into midstream. A short while later, it returned.'

'Why do you suppose it did that?'

'I did ask its master, Luytens, the same question. Of course, he would not let me on board, but he assured me that the manoeuvre that evening was to test the cog's rudder.' Kynaston shrugged. 'It's common enough for a cog to leave the quayside and sail into midstream to check on something. Why, Hugh, do you think *The Basilisk* had something to do with the disappearance of *The War-dog*?'

'Just a thought, my old friend, just a thought.'

Kynaston stamped his feet against the cold. 'Hugh, for the love of God, let us return to the Beacon.'

Once they were comfortably ensconced before a roaring fire, Kynaston slurped his hot wine before toasting Corbett with his cup.

'Hugh, tell me your thoughts on *The Basilisk*. Do you really suspect it was involved in the disappearance of that battle-boat?'

'Is it possible,' Corbett replied, measuring his words, 'that *The War-dog* and *The Basilisk* could have encountered each other?'

'That would be a nonsense,' Ranulf declared.

'I agree.' The taciturn Malfeson shook himself free from his self-imposed silence. 'I agree,' he repeated.

'Then let us hear the arguments to support what you say.'

'Well first, master, the crews of *The War-dog* and *The Basilisk* had no reason for enmity. Indeed, the opposite. The Flemings would not want to spoil their relationship with our king, nor do we English have any desire for conflict with Flanders.'

'Very true, Ranulf,' Corbett breathed. 'And?'

'Well,' Malfeson dried a drop of spilled posset with his finger, 'if there was any encounter between the battle-boat and the cog, there would be proof enough of a clash. The sound of conflict, of a fierce battle breaking out, would provoke interest all along the river: there would be a host of witnesses to such an encounter.'

'And the same can be said of a mishap or an accident.' Ranulf spoke up again. 'Sir Hugh, I know the river, it would reveal the detritus of a clash, be it corpses or wreckage.'

'I agree.' Corbett drained his cup. 'There is no evidence whatsoever linking *The Basilisk* and *The War-dog*.' He got to his feet. 'Miles, show me a battle-boat. I have seen the likes before, in Wales, but let me refresh my memory.'

They left the Beacon swathed in their cloaks, bracing themselves against the hideously cold mist. The admiral led them further along the riverside to where a broad trench had been dug into the quayside, spanned by a bridge. Other, narrower trenches led off either side of this. He explained how the Thames would flood these trenches and so cleanse the craft moored there before they were taken out for use along the river. He added that this facility was only for smaller vessels, such as bum boats and fishing smacks. There were also a number of battle-boats moored there. Corbett, trying to ignore the blistering breeze, clambered down the iron rungs and stepped into one of these. The others joined him, chattering among themselves and cursing the icy weather.

Corbett stared around. He had once served in a battle-boat and knew a few of its details, but now he stood midships scrutinising every aspect. The vessel was long and slender, almost a smaller version of a war cog, with its high jutting sweep both fore and after. The stern was like a small castle; the prow jutted aggressively. Midships was slightly broader and housed six benches for the oarsmen, three on either side, though some battle-boats, as Corbett remembered, were a little larger and needed eight oarsmen. Battle-boats were like dagger blades; silent and swift, they would come alongside larger craft. Their crews would then clamber up the side of enemy vessels on both port and starboard. Once on deck, they would harass the crew into surrender and so take the vessel out of the fight to be held, both craft and crew, for ransom.

Corbett cautiously walked forward. There were two great wooden bolts driven into both sides of the prow. There would be two more of the same in the stern. These bolts would be very tight when the battle-boat was on the river. However, they'd be loosened when the vessel was docked in the shallows so the water could rush in to cleanse the dirt and detritus, swilling the bilges so the boat would be lighter and easier to row.

'Are you finished?' Kynaston called. 'I have something else to show you.'

Corbett said he was done. They left the battle-boat

and walked further down the paved side of the trench, passing enclosures where small boats were docked. Some of these needed repairs; others as Kynaston explained, had been found drifting on the river.

'This one will interest you, Sir Hugh.' He grasped Corbett's arm and pointed down to a squat bum boat with a canvas covering. Corbett glimpsed a naked foot thrust from beneath the tar-soaked sheet.

Telling him to wait and watch, the admiral climbed down the iron rungs and pulled back the covering. Beneath it sprawled a gruesome torso soaking in a thick puddle of its own blood. This had poured from the severed neck as well as the decapitated head thrust on a nearby pole. Corbett crossed himself, covering his mouth and nose against the nasty stench of corruption. The face of the corpse was twisted in the fearsome grip of sudden death, blotched and sagging. Nonetheless, it was recognisable as the coarse-featured Madcap.

'In God's name!' Corbett breathed.

'A warning?' Kynaston asked. He leant down and plucked a small pouch from the dead man's hand. In it was a scrap of parchment, its message scrawled in black ink. He handed this to Corbett, who read the bleak warning aloud.

'"Vengeance! I, the Immortal, swear horrid vengeance. Those who have sown the tempest will reap the whirlwind."'

Ranulf, standing quietly beside him, glanced at his master. 'Sir Hugh?'

'He can threaten and bluster, my friend,' Corbett

replied, 'but in the end he will have to do business with me, and that will end in his death.'

Corbett and his companions returned to the Twilight, where they broke their fast. Afterwards, Ranulf questioned Corbett about what he made of the day's events.

'I don't know, Ranulf. I really don't.' Corbett tapped the side of his head. 'Images, thoughts, theories and ideas course about like scattered leaves. So far, I can detect no pattern whatsoever. No loose thread I can pull. All I can do is wait and watch.'

'And the Immortal's warning?'

'Another tumbling collection of malicious menace, and yet, if I am honest, I also detect fear. The Immortal views us as a real and dangerous threat, and that is comforting. Something I shall cherish in the hours to come.'

The next morning, Corbett rose as usual. He stripped, washed at the lavarium and dressed in fresh linen. As he did so, he wondered about Ursula the washerwoman and what she might find. When he had finished dressing, he peered through the arrow-slit window filled with thick mullioned glass.

'A day of grey ice and blood-chilling cold,' he whispered to himself. 'God have mercy on all poor travellers. Keep them safe, keep them warm.'

He pulled on his boots, strapped on his war belt and, with his military cloak over his arm, made his way down to the taproom. The tavern was slowly wakening, the air sweetened by fresh cooking smells. A spit boy, his face heavy with sleep, came into the taproom and answered his query about what was cooking, informing him that the kitcheners were preparing brisket in a rich herbal sauce. The boy left, and Corbett made his way up to the small chapel. It was lit by lanternhorns carved in the shape of vine-encrusted pillars, as well as a row of spigots holding the purest beeswax candles.

He knelt on the prie-dieu before the glittering bronze tabernacle. As he crossed himself, he caught the mirror-like sheen of the tabernacle as well as the dark shadow that flittered across it. He immediately threw himself to the right, even as he heard the rasp of a crossbow bolt cutting the air above him to smash into the wall. He turned, dagger out, crouching like any street fighter. His assailant had now dropped the small arbalest and drawn both knife and sword. Corbett waited, shifting like a shadow against the wall. He tensed, and was about to spring forward when he heard a sharp crack. His assailant groaned, hands going out, sword and dagger dropped in a clatter. The would-be assassin sank to his knees, lurching forward, blood spurting from the back of his head like wine through a cracked barrel.

Corbett clambered to his feet and raised a hand in welcome to Brother Ricard, who now stood resting on his cudgel-like walking cane.

'God save you,' he rasped. 'I was about to enter the chapel when I saw this.' He gestured at the fallen assailant. 'I glimpsed him slip in just after you. He must have been lurking there. As for the rest.' He raised his cane and tapped its bulbous hand grip. 'Just as lethal,' he murmured, 'as any mace or war club. Now,' he sketched a quick blessing over the fallen man, 'let us see whom we have sent to God.'

Corbett crouched and turned the body over. He felt for a blood beat in the throat and against both wrists: there was none. He then pushed back the blood-soaked cowl, peeled off the thick cloth visor and stared down at his dead assailant. He noted the podgy face with its half-open mouth and heavy-lidded eyes now dull and sightless. Memories stirred. He was sure he had met this man before. He pushed the head to one side, then paused as Ranulf and Malfeson burst into the small chapel.

'Walter Mappe!' Ranulf declared, pointing at the corpse. 'I'll never forget his ugly face. Do you remember him, master? Allegedly one of Puddlicott's henchmen. However, there wasn't enough evidence to hang him alongside his brother on the gallows outside the abbey.'

'Ah yes, Master Mappe.' Corbett nodded. 'A man who really wanted the best of both worlds. He ranked high in Puddlicott's cohort, enforcing whatever mischief his masters wanted. He turned king's evidence and received a pardon for that. However, we were not sure exactly where his true loyalties lay. Probably with himself and no one else. Ah yes.' He stared down at the dead face. 'Master Mappe must have heard about the chaos and confusion both here and at Westminster, so plotted to use it to settle matters with me. He would have done so if it wasn't for you, Brother Ricard.' He extended his hand, which the Benedictine clasped.

'God be thanked,' Ricard intoned. 'And God be thanked for my cudgel stick. Now,' he breathed out noisily, 'I'll go through his wallet and purse and see what I can find.' He quickly searched the corpse, but found nothing but a few coins, which Corbett insisted he keep.

'Ranulf,' Corbett beckoned his henchman, 'have Appleby call the sheriff's men. He is to order them to gibbet Walter's corpse.' He kicked the booted foot of the fallen man. 'And the sooner the better.'

'Gibbet, master? Where?'

'On Queenhithe quayside, so all can learn from the proclamation nailed to his skull: how traitors to the Crown and those who dare raise their hand against a king's man suffer dire penalties.'

Corbett thanked Ricard again, then crossed himself and returned to his own chamber. Once there, he locked himself in, sat on the edge of the bed and let the tears flow.

'So swift,' he whispered, 'so sudden, so deadly. Lord, I do not fear death but only its consequences. Maeve and my children . . .'

He sat drawing in deep breaths. Then he dried his face and went to stand by the window, pulling the shutters back so he had a clear view of what was happening in the ice-covered yard below. He felt the warmth seep back through his body. Out there, he reflected, deadly assassins lurked, sloping like wolves through the murk.

'Oh, and I'll be waiting for you,' he whispered. 'I will wait as I always do, to trap, capture and destroy each and every one of you.'

PART FIVE

They are raised up on high so that their fall be greater.

egotta was concerned, deeply so, about Corbett. She had heard, without betraying herself, the chatter in the taproom at the Twilight. Corbett had asked her to wander both the Twilight and the Tabard. News about the assault on him had swept along the river like a stiff breeze, and in turn, this gossip had spread across the various quaysides. Megotta had learnt that it was a solitary assassin, but she didn't believe that. There had to be others involved, there had to be! The roisterers in the taproom were certainly all agog with speculation about such an audacious assault on a high-ranking king's man. She was determined to learn more about it as she passed from one table to the next, hips swaying, lips all carmined, with a dirty gold wig pulled over her own hair. She had perfected all the mannerisms of an experienced whore and she used these as she moved around the taproom.

All sorts of folk assembled there. The cold had forced

them into the warmth, especially the men from the boats, as well as tinkers, traders, chapmen and street vendors. At first, Megotta learnt very little, until she passed one table where a group of fishermen were playing a desultory game of hazard against two ratcatchers, who, she was certain, were using heavily loaded dice. She had fastened on the mumbled conversation of one of the ratcatchers. He claimed he had seen the navigator of *The War-dog* the day after the battle-boat had disappeared. She could hardly believe her good fortune at such a discovery. She'd learnt, like everyone else, that the navigator had disappeared along with the rest of the crew. Perhaps not so.

She watched that table like a hungry cat would a mousehole, waiting for the right time to lunge. At last, she could. The game ended and Megotta, all smiles, closed with her quarry as he sat counting his winnings. She slid onto the bench beside the ratcatcher, all flirtatious and eager to please.

'You are Spikenard,' she declared. 'I have heard of your reputation.'

'As what?' Spikenard retorted, gazing lecherously at her ample thrusting bosom.

'Oh, that you are a hungry man, all hot and lustful as any spring sparrow.'

'And so I am,' Spikenard declared, his hand going out to cup one of Megotta's breasts, but she coyly knocked it aside.

'I understand that you saw the gubernator . . .' she deliberately stumbled over the Latin word, 'the navigator who was on board *The War-dog*. I've heard you saw him the day after *The War-dog* disappeared. I need to know,' she continued in a rush, 'because I was sweet on Conway, one of the Tower archers. I used to let him . . .' She chattered on, feeding Spikenard's greed and lust. She eventually paused to sip at his blackjack. She made a face. 'How do you know that the man you saw was the navigator on the battle-boat?'

'Oh, very easy,' Spikenard spluttered, determined to impress this whore who had taken such an interest in him. 'You see, mistress,' he wiped dirty fingers down the front of his battered leather jerkin, 'I am a ratcatcher. The port reeves hire the likes of me to keep the teeming vermin in check. If they swarm too much, they eventually move onto the vessels docked along the quayside.'

'So you hunt them?'

'Oh yes, I put down poisoned bait as well as clear away the corpses. Dead rats rot quickly. They are not a pretty sight, while the smell is like Satan's own farts. Anyway, I saw the crew of *The War-dog* assemble outside and go to the battle-boat waiting there. I glimpsed the navigator. He was trying to pull his leather hood more firmly against the biting breeze.' Spikenard spread his hands. 'And then they were gone. God knows where.'

'And the day after?'

'About the same hour, I was busy ratting along the quayside when I heard voices and footsteps.' Spikenard suppressed a shiver. 'Quaysides at night can be dangerous places. Very dangerous! So I slid into an enclave waiting for whoever it was to pass on. I glimpsed five men clambering into a barge. They were merry and boisterous. One of them turned and, in the light of the lanternhorn placed high in the stern of that barge, I saw the same face I had seen the day before. He had a scar here,' Spikenard tapped his right cheek, 'a savage welt, a true dagger wound. Anyway, he and the others settled into the barge, then they cast off and slid into the darkness. I did wonder then about the truth of what had happened to *The War-dog*.'

'Why didn't you report what you had seen?' Megotta demanded. 'After all, the port reeves, harbourmasters and the rest were offering rewards for any information.'

Spikenard just laughed and dug his face deep into his blackjack, slurping noisily until he gaspingly shoved it away.

'Woman,' he slurred, 'you are stupid. Along the river you keep yourself to yourself. Or at least I do. You hide in the shadows.' His gap-toothed grin faded and he glowered at Megotta. 'You seem to want to know a lot about *The War-dog*.'

'I couldn't give a rat's turd about *The War-dog*,' she retorted. 'All I am interested in is Conway. I want to know what happened to him. Do you have any more to tell me?'

'No, but I would love to swive you.' His hand went out again to squeeze her breast. 'Come now, my pretty.'

'Not here.' Acting all flirtatious, Megotta gently pushed away his hand. 'I can get something more comfortable than a freezing alley wall or a rutted track-way.'

'Well that's what I want,' Spikenard declared. 'A good rut.'

'But not here,' Megotta repeated, getting to her feet. She leant down, her lips only a few inches from his face. 'A nice warm garret chamber,' she whispered. 'I have an understanding with minehost. Let me go and prepare, then I shall return to show you something that will take your breath away.'

Spikenard could only gaze lecherously. Megotta quickly kissed him on the brow, then hurried off, pushing aside greedy hands and ignoring the litany of salacious offers customers made. She reached the corner staircase, climbed to the first gallery, then slipped through the gloom to Corbett's chamber. She knocked on the door. Ranulf answered and ushered her in. Corbett was sitting on the side of the bed, already dressed for sleep.

'Megotta!' he exclaimed. 'What is it?'

She told him about Spikenard. Corbett quickly shook off his brooding mood.

'That loose thread. At last I have one. Ranulf, go down to the taproom. Bring Master Spikenard here.'

Ranulf returned a short while later, dagger drawn, pushing Spikenard into the chamber. The ratcatcher was now all nervous, bleating and pleading, until Corbett calmed him down, making him sit on a cushioned stool with a goblet of wine. He also twirled a silver coin before the ratcatcher's eyes, promising him more if he cooperated.

'So,' he declared, 'tell me what you told the lady here.'

Spikenard did so. Corbett listened intently, now and

again whispering to himself. Once the ratcatcher had finished and pocketed the coin, the chamber fell silent. Megotta sat tense on a wall bench. Ranulf, narrow eyed, watched Corbett, who seemed deep in thought.

'Master?'

'Ranulf, I suspect the navigator our friend here has described is dead.'

'Why?'

'I now reckon the Immortal may well have been responsible for the disappearance of *The War-dog*. He would want all those involved in that mystery to remain very low and very quiet. Our good friend Spikenard, however, glimpsed the navigator meeting with the Immortal's escort. Is that true?' The ratcatcher nodded. 'And they were all laughing and talking?'

'Yes, sir.'

'So,' Corbett continued, 'the Immortal, or whoever organised the disappearance of *The War-dog*, would be furious that the navigator hadn't remained in hiding. Accordingly, he dispatched four of his worthies to settle the problem once and for all. They would meet with our navigator, all friendly and cheerful, entice him into the night and cut his throat.' He got up and began to pace the chamber. 'What I now believe,' he continued, 'is that the navigator played a crucial part in this mystery; so important was he that he could never be taken up for questioning. What we must now discover is what his role was in the disappearance of that battle-boat and its cohort of archers.'

'Master, we need proof for all of this,' Ranulf retorted.

'Well, let's test my theory. I wonder if we can find some evidence. At least let us try. Ranulf, you and I will take Spikenard up into the city, to the great mortuary at St Mary atte Bow. We will look among the dead so we can help the living. Megotta, you have done very well, thank you. Now seek out Malfeson and tell him what has happened. He can stay here with you, waiting and watching for anything of interest. Ranulf, take Master Spikenard to your chamber while I dress against the night.'

Within the hour, Corbett and Ranulf, with Spikenard between them, left the Twilight with a cohort of archers and made their way towards St Mary atte Bowe. Thankfully it was not too far. The night was bitterly cold, though the sky was cloud free, promising that the sun would rise to finish the thaw once and for all. The ground underfoot had turned into a filthy slush, the hunting run of rats, mice, feral cats and dogs; it truly was like passing across the landscape of hell. Beggars, false or otherwise, whined for a coin. A wandering pig had been caught and gutted, its carcass stripped of anything that could be roasted by the itinerant cooks. The air was foul and fetid with a host of rank smells.

Strange creatures slipped through the dark. Corbett glimpsed a cohort of deer people; a noisy pack of men and women, faces painted white, lips carmined, with antler horns adorning their heads. He had heard of these and their secret ceremonies in lonely churchyards or on the wild heathland north of the city. As far as he was concerned, they had not been accused of anything illegal. Others, just as sinister in appearance, their faces masked, sloped through the night, nothing more than a gaggle of shadows. Torches spluttered, their leaping flames giving off a shower of sparks around those who carried them. The guild of dung collectors had built heaps of rubbish and set them alight. The glow and the warmth of these bonfires attracted the dark-dwellers to revel in the heat as well as scorch the scraps of meat they had collected.

At last they reached the great ornamental lychgate leading into God's Acre, the wasteland that ringed the brooding mass of St Mary's. This was the cemetery of lost souls; the last resting place of the soon to be forgotten. Corbett knew it was a place that was never quiet, never still. Even in the dead of night it was lit up by raging fires, which pierced the darkness and illuminated row upon row of burial pits. Naked corpses found in the city and unclaimed by anyone were tossed into these pits, lumps of dead flesh to be covered with lime.

Corbett, exercising his authority, strode into the church and up the main aisle into the Great Hall of the Dead. Here he was greeted obsequiously by the bald-headed, ugly Keeper of the Dead, attired in jet-black robes, a pomander in one hand and an asperges rod in the other. He listened attentively to Corbett, then led them into the Purgatory, a long room with row upon row of shabby pallets covered with canvas cloths soaked in pine juice. He explained that all the corpses brought in by his minions, the Seekers of the Dead, would be exhibited for five days; then, if unclaimed, they would be consigned to one of the lime pits. Corbett told the man he was searching for a certain corpse, probably delivered over the last few days and in all likelihood the victim of an assault. The Keeper of the Dead nodded and led them to a cordoned-off area where, he declared, the victims of violence, be it murder or accident, were on display. Spikenard went around the tables, a pomander thrust against his mouth and nose. He pulled this away as he stared down at one of the corpses.

'This is the man, Sir Hugh,' he called out. 'His head shaven, with a dagger cut close to his right eye, though when I last saw him,' he sniffed at the pomander, 'his throat was not opened from ear to ear.'

Corbett went across to the table and stared down at the river-soaked corpse, eyes all glassy and protuberant, mouth slack and ringed with dirt, a hideous jagged cut across his scrawny throat.

'Where was this one found?' he demanded.

'Oh, floating like a leaf off Queenhithe,' the Keeper replied, studying his leather-bound ledger on a lectern near the great hour candle. 'No one has yet claimed the corpse, so it will be the pits for him.'

'Master Spikenard,' Corbett declared, 'are you sure it is he?'

'Sir Hugh, I'd swear to it. The scar so close to the right eye is what I particularly glimpsed.'

'Good, good,' Corbett murmured. 'So let us re-enter the land of the living.'

Once they had left the precincts of St Mary, Corbett

led Ranulf and Spikenard into a narrow-roomed ale-house. He gave Spikenard another silver coin and strongly advised him not to say a word to anyone. Spikenard, overjoyed at his new-found wealth but clearly frightened, promised that he would be gone from the city for many a day. He then made his farewells and disappeared into the night. Corbett and Ranulf made their way back through the darkness. The hour was now very late, and the Twilight was empty. Appleby and Stigand were closing up, locking doors and securing shutters.

'Listen, Ranulf,' Corbett whispered once they reached the first gallery. 'I realise it is late and you are probably as tired as I am . . .'

'Master?'

'At first light, take those same archers who trailed us to St Mary's and back and search out Admiral Kynaston. Ask him to meet me here and have a battle-boat at the ready. I need his advice.'

Corbett awoke the next morning as the city bells began to toll for the call to the dawn mass. Feeling much better, he dressed hurriedly and attended Brother Ricard's recitation of the divine office, followed by an equally swift mass. Afterwards, the Black Robe excused himself, saying he had urgent business at the abbey. Corbett wished him well, then broke his fast in the buttery on a bowl of shredded spiced beef. He'd hardly finished when Ranulf and Malfeson joined him. Corbett sat reflecting on the conclusions he had reached. He hoped he was correct. He had found more than just one loose thread.

When Kynaston arrived along with two burly hench-men, Corbett and his companions greeted them, then strapped on their war belts, swung their cloaks about them and followed them out into the freezing-cold day. Corbett took some comfort from the cloud-free sky and the deep red glow strengthening in the east as the darkness receded. They walked in silence down to the quayside, where the admiral, taciturn as ever, gestured at the steps leading down to the battle-boat berthed there. Corbett carefully boarded it, followed by his henchmen, while Kynaston's escort remained on guard along the quayside. Corbett sat down in the stern, the others on benches facing him.

'Sir Hugh?'

'Thank you all for coming. Now listen to what I propose. On that fateful evening, *The War-dog* prepared to leave Queenhithe. Malachi waited for the navigator. He needed him so as to thread the Thames, turbulent and dangerous at the best of times, even more so during freezing midwinter. Now Malachi did not know that the man had been bribed and was party to what was being plotted; the navigator would have told him some tale about being hired by Malling or Appleby or even by you, Sir Miles. An agreement, like many other such agreements, of little worth to anybody else.'

'Very true,' Kynaston declared, 'especially on a dark, cold winter's evening. People moving about cowled and cloaked against the cold.'

'So the stage was set,' Corbett continued, 'for the murderous masque. The battle-boat casts off. The archers row it across into midstream; they too are all hooded and cloaked against the cold. The darkness deepens. However, they are not alone. *The Basilisk* has also, quietly and with little fuss, slipped its moorings. The cog is shrouded by the night, with most of its lights dulled or extinguished. It slowly approaches. On board *The War-dog*, however, matters have suddenly turned nasty. The navigator explains that there is a leak, a breach, with water seeping into the vessel. There is no such breach. In truth, he has undone or loosened the sluice bolts, probably those two in the prow.'

'But the navigator would have been in danger as well,' declared Kynaston.

'No, Sir Miles, he knew exactly what he was doing and the effect of what he was intending. The navigator was probably a professional sailor, a river man. However, the rest of the crew on *The War-dog* were archers; young men from Wales with little experience of rivers, seas, currents and all the terrors of the deep. All they can see is water slapping about their boots, and of course they trust the navigator implicitly. Malachi probably tells him that they all want to be safe on dry land, or whatever else is closest. He and his archers don't really care about anything except getting safely off that boat. In truth they were in no real danger. The navigator could reinstate or tighten the sluice bolts. However, salvation of a different kind was close at hand.'

'*The Basilisk*?'

'Oh yes, Sir Miles. The Flemish war cog and its crew were party to this plot. So *The Basilisk* comes floating out of the murk. The navigator insists that *The War-dog* seek its help. The crew of the battle-boat agree. The Flemings respond. *The War-dog* closes with *The Basilisk*. Nets and rope ladders are lowered. The archers climb up, desperate to get away from the threatening danger. Malachi also arranges for the treasure chest to be lifted aboard, then he follows it up. The archers, of course, are very grateful for all the help. The treasure chest is stowed away, while the master of *The Basilisk* goes further. He will also take *The War-dog* into his care. His crew use the cranes and hoists aboard the cog to raise the battle-boat. No one objects. The crew of *The War-dog* still view *The Basilisk* as their saviour. Everything has been done under the cover of the darkness and a rolling river mist. Only one person sees *The War-dog* being hoisted up.'

'Madcap, the lunatic, his wits all fey.'

'Yes, Sir Miles. In Madcap's turbulent mind, a soul profoundly touched by the moon, *The Basilisk* is the dragon swallowing *The War-dog*. He was, in fact, edging towards the truth, so much so that the Immortal – whoever he is and whatever he intends – ordered his murder.'

'And now what?'

'Sir Miles, I don't really know. I think *The Basilisk*'s seizure of *The War-dog*, its crew and treasure is definitely linked to Puddlicott's attempt to steal the Crown Jewels from Westminster Abbey some ten years ago. Many of the items in that treasure chest were part of what was stolen during the great robbery. Consequently, was the seizure a deliberate mocking insult?' Corbett shrugged. 'I cannot say. I also think *The Basilisk* is connected to a plot, touched upon by Sarasin in his dealings with Rahmel, to seize our queen and hold her for ransom.'

'Never!'

'Yes, Sir Miles, there is something very dark gathering close by. We now enter the game of kings and the clash between the lords of power, but I need more information; more hard evidence for my theories.'

'And those poor archers?'

'God knows, Ranulf, God only knows.'

Corbett climbed out of the battle-boat and led his companions back to the Twilight. The buttery was empty, so he took it over, ordering goblets of hot spiced wine from an anxious-looking Appleby. He assured the taverner that all was well, and what they needed from the Twilight at the moment was hot drinks and some freshly cooked food. Appleby visibly relaxed. He scurried around bringing in platters and jugs before leaving Corbett to his own devices.

Once they were alone, the buttery door guarded by Kynaston's henchmen, Corbett tapped the table. 'So,' he murmured, 'what do we have here? Well, we now know that *The Basilisk* undoubtedly played a part in the mischief boiling around us. However, we have very few details: scraps of evidence, nothing more.'

'All sizzle,' Ranulf agreed, 'and no sausage.'

'As I have said,' Corbett declared, sipping at his goblet, 'the master and crew of *The Basilisk* are in some unholy alliance with our self-proclaimed Immortal. Both undoubtedly contributed to the disappearance of *The War-dog* and its crew.'

'An unholy alliance,' Ranulf agreed, 'and a secret one. The navigator, whoever he was, threatened that secret. Somehow, somewhere . . .'

'Indeed,' Corbett replied. 'He may have talked to someone, or failed to carry out an order from the Immortal, so he paid the price: his throat slashed and his corpse tossed into the Thames.' He sighed deeply. 'To get more evidence, we need to board *The Basilisk*.'

'Very difficult,' Kynaston warned. 'And highly dangerous. Any attempt to force our way onto that cog will be viewed as an act of war. Our king would not want that. We do know that the master runs a very tight ship. He does not even allow his crew to disembark. Any approach will be challenged. *The Basilisk* leaves its moorings now and again. It patrols the river and the estuary, ostensibly to keep a sharp eye on French ships as well as those of the Count of Flanders and his allies. True, it's a ship of war and it's in our waters, yet it still has the right to refuse to allow anyone to board. Sir Hugh, I warn you. Force is not the answer to this problem.'

'Knock on the main door.' Malfeson spoke up.

'I beg your pardon?'

'Sir Hugh, the cog is one of the mightiest in the Narrow Seas, yes? It is permitted to sail up and down the Thames.'

'Of course,' Kynaston intervened. 'It sought licence from our king to do just that and he could not refuse.'

'Then why not visit it?' Malfeson replied. 'Perhaps on the pretext of a formal welcome by our king, who is delighted that the greatest cog in the Flanders fleet is gracing the Thames.' He paused at the laughter his proposal provoked. 'Let's row out to *The Basilisk* unarmed, with a small cask of the best Bordeaux, as well as a platter of the sweetest marchpane from a local pastry shop. Ask to board and see what happens.'

'Bravo, bravo!' Corbett laughed, patting Malfeson on the shoulder. 'But not you, my friend. You cannot board that ship. You are a subject of King Philip and you are vulnerable to a power such as Flanders. I don't want anyone pointing a finger at you, or worse, seizing you. It would be best if Ranulf and I accompany Sir Miles, together with Ap Ythel and some of his archers.'

'When?'

Corbett pushed back his chair. 'As soon as I can collect a small tun of the best Bordeaux from Master Appleby.'

Within the hour, Sir Miles, accompanied by his escort, climbed into a royal barge under the command of its own liveried navigator. The barge pushed off from Queenhithe quayside and cut across the Thames to where *The Basilisk* was riding at anchor. The day was cold, but a clear sky provided some comfort. The whipping breeze had softened, while the Thames, though swollen and swift, posed no danger. A bank of thick mist hovered midstream. They passed through this, the six oarsmen battling the rising swell, until they came within clear sight of *The Basilisk* and its ornately carved prow.

Corbett had insisted that the barge should be adorned with stiffened pennants displaying the gorgeous royal coat of arms of King Edward. Ap Ythel, standing in the prow, also held an unfurled banner, which snapped noisily in the breeze as it loudly proclaimed the status and authority of the vessel and its crew. Ap Ythel carried a huntsman's horn, on which he now blew a series of braying calls notifying the Flemings of their approach. Corbett wondered if they would be accepted. The taffrail of *The Basilisk* was crowded with men, while the master and his officers clustered on the high stern watching the royal barge surge towards them. No opposition was offered. Ap Ythel blew more rasping calls on the hunting horn before proclaiming in a powerful, carrying voice that the envoy of the English king, no lesser a person than the royal admiral, Sir Miles Kynaston, wished to board *The Basilisk* to formally greet and welcome its captain and crew on behalf of his royal master.

'You are most welcome,' a voice replied, ringing across the water separating the two vessels.

Corbett relaxed. Sections of the taffrail were now being moved as the cog prepared to receive its visitors. Rope ladders and netting were thrown over the side of the ship. Ap Ythel rapped out an order, and the royal barge turned so it rested against the side of the cog, held secure by knotted cords. Once it was steady, Kynaston went first, with Corbett closely following him. The Keeper of the Secret Seal had seen battle at sea, but climbing up the side of that vessel, which rose, sank and strained at its ropes, provoked a deep, clammy fear.

Once Kynaston, Corbett and Ranulf were safely on board, Ap Ythel and two of his archers followed to stand either side of the King's Admiral. A voice shouted fresh welcomes, and a slender whippet of a man with a weather-beaten face and close-cropped hair approached, seeming openly pleased to greet his visitors.

'My name is Louis Luytens, master of *The Basilisk*.' He gestured at the two sailors who flanked him. 'These are my henchmen.'

Further introductions were made. Ap Ythel had brought up a small tun of the best wine and a silver platter of marchpane. Kynaston presented these to Luytens with a brief but pretty speech on how pleased he was to board this formidable war cog.

Corbett stared around as he tried to steady himself against the shifting deck. The cog was truly magnificent. It housed hoists and winches along each side, as well as trebuchets and mangonels built specifically to fit within the ship's armaments. There were bowls for fire and tar, with catapults standing nearby. The crew looked well trained and confident, all armed, even now. If the Flemings were perturbed by Kynaston's visit, they certainly hid it well. Luytens was all charm and welcoming. He insisted on showing them his ship from prow to stern, beneath deck and above it. At last he ushered his visitors, or at least Corbett and Kynaston, into the stern cabin. The chamber was cramped but cleverly crafted. It housed a table with a bench either side, as well as a cot bed that could be lifted up against the bulwark. He waved them to a bench, then sat opposite.

Corbett watched him closely, staring at the Fleming's rugged face and sharp watery blue eyes. He's laughing at us, he concluded to himself. He knows the real reason for our visit. However, we cannot detect a shred of evidence to prove that *The Basilisk* was involved in the disappearance of *The War-dog* and its crew.

Luytens continued his show of bonhomie as he broached the cask of Bordeaux and served them generous goblets. Corbett decided he'd seen enough. He drank his wine faster than he should have done, then turned to Kynaston. 'Sir Miles, I have enjoyed my visit but I have urgent business ashore.'

Kynaston took the hint and, a short while later, they returned to the barge, which cast off for an uneventful journey back to Queenhithe. Once they were ensconced in Corbett's chamber in the Twilight, the Keeper of the Secret Seal gave vent to his frustration. Kynaston concurred, but Ranulf spoke up.

'Sir Hugh, I believe Luytens was too clever by half. Please, you must talk to Ap Ythel.'

The captain of archers, waiting outside on the gallery, was invited in. He sat on a stool, opened his belt wallet and took out a medallion the size of a coin. At first Corbett thought it was a pilgrim's badge, but it was fashioned not out of pewter but from some hard metal. He rubbed it between his forefinger and thumb, then held it up to the light to make out the face of a hallowed saint as well as a prayer etched around the rim, pleading for the protection of the famous Franciscan St Anthony of Padua.

'That was Malachi's,' Ap Ythel declared. 'He had a passionate devotion to Anthony of Padua. At one time he thought he had a vocation to be a Franciscan, but hard knocks and the need to support his mother and others led him along the path of war. Nevertheless, his dedication to St Anthony remained. He would take that medallion out and rub it between his fingers as you did, Sir Hugh, but he would never have dropped it. He has sent us a message.'

'Explain.'

'Malachi wore the medallion on a chain around his right wrist. He must have somehow left it deliberately for anybody who came after them to notice. He had a total belief in St Anthony. He would have said a prayer that the medallion be found, and it has. Sir Hugh, Ranulf has informed me of your conclusions on this matter. This medallion demonstrates that Malachi and his men became prisoners, held fast where I found it thrust between the deck planks. I repeat, he left it there deliberately. I know he did. I went aboard that cog looking for something he would have left, and I found it.' Ap Ythel swallowed hard. 'I am sure,' he continued, 'there are other items, but I found only one.'

Corbett stared at this master bowman, deeply upset at the loss of his men, and quietly cursed himself. The crew of *The War-dog* had disappeared, yet he had not even acknowledged the grief of their comrades. Caught up in this business, he had overlooked men who would gladly lay down their lives for him, for Isabella and the king.

'Ap Ythel?'

'Yes, Sir Hugh?'

'When this is all over – and one day it really will be – we shall mourn our dead, yes?' Ap Ythel smiled and nodded. 'We shall gather in the chapel at my manor at Leighton and sing the requiem. Afterwards we shall toast those who have stood shoulder to shoulder with us in the shield ring.' Again Ap Ythel nodded, wiping away the tears welling in his eyes.

'Sir Hugh,' he murmured, 'Malachi is dead, I know that. There is little we can do about it.' He tried to compose himself as he continued. 'I have discussed this with Ranulf and he agrees. When we were on board *The Basilisk*, its master was only too delighted to show us his ship and prove that it carried no trace of *The War-dog* or its crew.'

'I would concur,' Corbett declared.

'Sir Hugh, Luytens was arrogant. He made a most dreadful mistake. He showed us around the cog both above and below deck. Didn't you notice that all the water barrels, not to mention the flasks of Flemish ale, were apparently filled up, frothing at the rim, while fresh meat hung in nets from the rafters waiting to be cured?'

'Oh ye heavens!' Corbett exclaimed. 'Sir Miles?'

'God knows I wish I had noticed that,' the admiral admitted. 'What Ap Ythel has described is very pertinent. Now, we already know that Luytens does not allow his men to go ashore, and no merchant boats are permitted to approach the cog.'

'So he must be reprovisioning somewhere else,' Corbett concluded.

'No,' the admiral replied, 'not a place, but another ship. Oh yes,' he continued excitedly, 'I receive reports on all ships that enter the estuary, especially foreign vessels. Now there's a merchantman flying Flemish colours, *The Hirondelle*, that visits the occasional harbour or port. I strongly suspect that it buys purveyance there. Then, on an agreed date and hour, the two ships meet and *The Basilisk* receives fresh supplies.'

'And *The Hirondelle* takes what Luytens wants to get rid of.'

'Precisely, Sir Hugh.'

'So what do we do?' Corbett murmured. 'Leave it for a while? Watch and wait? Or do we storm both vessels? But that . . .' He trailed off, lips moving soundlessly.

'Master,' Ranulf declared, 'you are beginning to talk to yourself.'

'A sure sign that I should retire, reflect and respond.' Corbett smiled. 'You know all my ways. My friends, for the moment we are finished.'

The meeting broke up. Once he was alone, Corbett took a sheet of parchment and wrote down the names of all at Westminster and elsewhere who were in some way involved in the matters under investigation. Those at the palace included the queen and Countess Marguerite, while de Craon and the d'Aunay brothers – the 'Squires of the Glove', as Corbett thought of them – lurked in the shadows. He paused in his writing, recalling those exquisitely fashioned gloves. 'So strange, so very strange,' he whispered to the darkness. 'Those two knights don't have a pair each, just one glove both the same. Ah well.'

He continued with his listing before moving on to the Twilight, which housed Appleby, Stigand, Brother Ricard and Malfeson. 'Now,' he went on to himself, 'we have the names. What have they said? What have they done? What have they not said and done? What motivates them?' He wrote swiftly, using a cipher known only to himself. Eventually he felt heavy eyed, so he lay down on the bed and slept until a sharp knock on the door roused him.

'Sir Hugh, it's Megotta. You must come down to the taproom.'

He hastily made himself ready and went out onto the gallery. Megotta had disappeared. Corbett waited for a while, then went downstairs. He stood in the doorway and stared around. Megotta was flirting with a huddle of fishermen, but most of the customers were the noisy spectators of a tournament of taunts; a game where two opponents shouted abuse at one another. The victor was the one who never stumbled or halted in his spate of salacious insults. Ranulf was deeply involved in this, openly confronting the tavern blacksmith.

'Snake tongue,' the latter bawled.

'Froth and scum,' Ranulf yelled.

The slurs flew backwards and forwards.

'Baseborn.'

'Whore's offspring.'

'Dunghill villain.'

'Shit pot.'

'Viper vile.'

'Tickle brain.'

The taunting was swift and steady until Ranulf shouted, 'Slack arse.' The blacksmith stuttered and stumbled before lapsing into the chorus of laughter that signified his defeat.

Ranulf caught sight of Corbett and sauntered across the taproom, sipping at a blackjack of ale.

'All the glory to the victor. Is that why I am here?' asked Corbett.

'No, Sir Hugh,' Ranulf whispered. 'Never mind the taunts. Look behind you, in the shadows of that window seat.'

Corbett glanced across the taproom and felt a prickle of apprehension. There was something quite dangerous in the way the stranger lounged behind the table, his war belt rolled around his sword scabbard. He was tapping the hilt of the dagger he had placed within easy reach. He sipped at his goblet while staring around, ignoring Corbett, who stood studying him carefully.

'Undoubtedly a warrior,' Ranulf hissed.

'And one who's served in Outremer,' Corbett added, scrutinising the stranger's sallow clean-shaven face, his steel-grey hair and beard all neatly cut. 'Well, well, well, let us meet our new guest.'

The two clerks walked across. The stranger made ready to greet them, moving both his cloak and war belt out of the way. He gestured at the empty seats, but Corbett shook his head.

'Who are you?' he demanded.

'Who am I? I am Giles Fitzalan, a distant kinsman of the powerful Arundel family, though,' he half laughed, 'they would not welcome me with any great affection.'

'You are a swordsman, a mercenary?'

'Among other things, Sir Hugh.' Fitzalan extended a hand, which Corbett clasped, as did Ranulf. 'Gentlemen, do sit,' he urged. 'You now know me as I do you.' He pointed a finger. 'You are Sir Hugh Corbett, Keeper of the King's Secret Seal, loyal henchman of Queen Isabella, and your companion is the red-headed Ranulf-atte-Newgate, senior clerk in the Chancery of the Green Wax. I also believe that the wench Megotta is a member of your household, but I can never get a fair description of her.'

'Few people do.'

'True, Sir Hugh, she could be any one of the whores who throng about here. Those others are more recognisable.' Again the half-laugh as Fitzalan gestured to where Malfeson, Appleby and Stigand stood staring fearfully across.

'In heaven's name, what is wrong with them?' Ranulf exclaimed.

'Sir Hugh, of your kindness, can I ask that we meet in your chamber together with those three worthies over there.' Fitzalan held up a hand. 'I swear I am no threat to anyone here, but we need to speak on matters of life and death.'

'Ranulf,' Corbett replied, 'take our guest to my chamber, and myself and the three worthies, as you call them, will join you shortly.' He turned and walked across to Malfeson and the others. 'You stand there,' he said, 'like conies caught out in the open by a hawk. What is it you fear? Our visitor seems to know you and apparently wishes to renew his acquaintance with you. So come. I recognise this type of man. You cannot escape him, so it is best if whatever business he has with you be done here and now.'

He walked off, confident that the three men would join him, and they did so, climbing the stairs like felons mounting the scaffold. They entered Corbett's chamber, and he seated himself at the chancery desk with Ranulf sitting behind him. Fitzalan took a stool while the other three sat on a wall bench to Corbett's left.

'Shall I begin?' asked Fitzalan.

'Please do.'

'My name is Giles Fitzalan. I am a preceptor in the Order of the Temple, a Templar through and through. I have managed to survive despite the clutching, bloody hands of the so-called Holy Inquisition. Not to mention the agents of Philip of France. My task is to seek out, encourage and protect those Templars who remain after the outrageous attack on our order. I carry warrants and letters, signed and sealed by Jacques de Molay, Grand Master of our order. As you may know, de Molay now languishes a tortured, broken man in the Châtelet prison in Paris. You want to inspect those letters and warrants, Sir Hugh?'

'No, I do not. Please continue.'

'I wander Europe. Over the years I have built up a comitatus of former Templars. They form one battle group, though they move in cohorts no bigger than three or four men. We have a system of couriers, as well as a widely flung net of places we can stay, shelter, reprovision and refresh ourselves. We also fix times and places when our comitatus comes together as a whole.'

He paused to thank Ranulf, who had got up and filled a goblet of wine. He sipped this appreciatively, then raised it in toast to Corbett. 'Sir Hugh, as I have said, I search out our former brothers who may be hiding or have put themselves beyond the law. A number have been proclaimed *utlegatum* – outlaws, wolfsheads who can be killed on sight. I also seek out others who have built a new life: prosperous men who hide behind a screen of respectability that protects them from any questioning about their previous life as Templars.' He pointed at the three men sitting on the wall bench. 'Men such as these. Monseigneur Guillaume Malfeson, senior clerk in the Chambre Noire, placed there by his father, King Philip, who does his level best to protect his baseborn son. Philip tried to hide him among the ranks of the Templars, then whisked him away when our order was attacked. Oh yes, Guillaume was well protected and patronised.' Fitzalan grinned. 'Talk about having friends in high places.

'Then we come to the Englishmen now calling themselves Stigand and John Appleby.' He clenched his fist. 'Two good sturdy Saxon names for two Englishmen who certainly escaped the eye of the storm. Both men were part of the garrison around the Temple church along the Strand in London. Stigand was a professional porter as well being a custos or guard in the treasury there. Appleby, as he calls himself, proved to be a superb quartermaster. No one could equal him in the purchase of purveyance and his preparation of food for the table. When the storm broke and engulfed our order, both men fled for pastures new. They were lucky, successfully escaping as well as taking a goodly portion of gold and silver from the Temple treasury. Once they had spent some months in hiding, they emerged into the full light of day and Appleby handed over his treasure to . . .'

'Henry Malling.'

'Precisely, Sir Hugh. Malling used the money to improve, enlarge and enhance this magnificent hostelry.'

Corbett stared at the men sitting on the wall bench like three scholars lined up for a beating. Malfeson moved his head and just for a few heartbeats Corbett caught a fleeting expression that seemed to indicate the French clerk was not as cowed as he pretended to be.

Fitzalan gestured at Appleby and Stigand. 'I am not here to punish or to reclaim lost monies. Quite honestly, I would prefer that you and any brothers have part of the treasure rather than it be lying in the coffers of the Exchequer at Westminster or some arca housed deep in the Louvre Palace.' He put down his goblet. 'As for you, Malfeson, it is always good to have a friend, an ally, a former comrade so close to Philip's tangled web. And it is tangled, yes, my friend?'

Malfeson nodded as he stared unblinking at Fitzalan. All three men had become visibly more relaxed.

'Strange,' Corbett declared. 'Brother Ricard thought there was a connection between the three of you, and he was correct. Now we know what it is.'

'You certainly do, Sir Hugh.' Fitzalan leant forward, staring hard at Corbett as if assessing his true worth.

'What is it?' Corbett demanded. 'Do remember that I could have all of you arrested. My king has withdrawn his love for the Templar order.'

Fitzalan spread his hands. 'Very good, Sir Hugh, go ahead and try. I will resist, as will those with me, and a few good men will die. You do not want that, I am sure. You have a reputation for honesty and integrity. I know, as does my order, that you did not believe in the scandalous allegations levelled against the Templars and our Grand Master, the litany of heinous lies: the celebration of the midnight rites; kissing Lord Satan's arse and releasing unclean spirits to haunt and hurt this kingdom. All nonsense, Sir Hugh, absolute nonsense, a farrago of lies. Anyway,' he sighed noisily, 'I need to speak to you.'

'Then speak.'

'Just you alone, Sir Hugh. Well, Master Ranulf may stay. I must advise you that what I have to say, and I have proof, will be of great benefit to your king and queen.'

'If you say so.' Corbett gestured at the three former Templars. 'I have no problem with who you are now or who you once were. Indeed, I can safely assert that the Crown has little interest in the same. So, gentlemen, please leave us to our guest.'

Malfeson and his two companions left the chamber, anxious to be away from Fitzalan, who, Corbett suspected, was a man to be greatly feared. A master swordsman who had probably performed military service in foreign parts. He also suspected that although Fitzalan appeared to be by himself, the Templar would undoubtedly have a comitatus hidden somewhere in one of the many taverns along Queenhithe.

Corbett waited until the sound of footsteps faded. Fitzalan sat back in his chair as the royal clerk gestured at him. 'I am listening.'

'I am sure you are,' the Templar replied. 'Now, God only knows what you are involved in, Sir Hugh, but I understand it is quite delicate and dangerous. We have heard about the sudden attacks against you, in the Twilight and beyond.'

'Such attacks are now common knowledge.'

'I am sure they are. However, I must assure you that none of mine have been involved in any threats or violence against you or your kin.'

'You must have heard about the fires in the palace and the Templar seals found in the chamber where the fires broke out?'

'Oh yes, but again, I assure you, we had nothing to do with such nonsense. Be it the sudden fires or the various threats levelled against Philip of France, God judge him, and his beloved daughter Isabella.'

'So who is responsible?'

'Sir Hugh, I don't know, but it's not the work of the Temple. I do have my suspicions, but they will have to wait for a while. Let us return to the Templars. Some former members of our order, such as Appleby and Malfeson, have blended in to normal life most successfully. They were fortunate. But many others, especially the older knights, have found it very difficult. Some of them turned to outlawry, be it in the open countryside or deep in the darkest shadows of this city.' He raised his goblet. 'Oh yes, Sir Hugh, former Templars can even be found among the ranks of the rifflers. Yet at the same time, their allegiance to our order still holds.'

'And?'

'And, Sir Hugh, some of those former Templars hiding deep in that landscape from hell that you call Whitefriars have informed me that some nasty soul is preparing to attack you at the Twilight.'

'They have tried before, as you are aware. I have a bodyguard, a comitatus . . .'

'Oh, I know you have, Sir Hugh. However, these assassins will not come streaming into the tavern. They know that you and others will be waiting for them behind a wall of sharpened steel. Oh no, we have heard the rumours, the whispers. A more fearsome pack of assassins, who call themselves the Brethren, prowl the city, and you are their intended prey. Good coin has been spent to remove you once and for all.'

'And the hirer?'

'Some say the Immortal, whoever that may be. Now let me inform you. The Brethren do not strike in the taproom or the forest glade. No, they will attack you when they think it's appropriate. They will first try to mislead you before they launch their ambuscade. They are very cunning, very patient and they manifest themselves in different guises.'

'And what is your stance in all this?'

'Sir Hugh, I wish to show my goodwill. I will stay here at the Twilight. Master Appleby owes that to me and our order. Now that I have warned you against a deadly foe, let me remain with you to strengthen your defence. I put my sword at your disposal for what will be a most bloody affray. Now, I think it's time I saw Master Appleby, but please heed my warning. Be on the alert. The leader of these assassins is like a prowling, ravenous lion, seeking whom he may devour. In this case, you and yours.'

'Let him try,' Corbett retorted. 'And God willing, I shall be ready with both net and sword.'

'Good, good.' The Templar made to leave.

'Fitzalan?'

'Yes, Sir Hugh?'

'Would you trust Malfeson?'

He leant forward, right hand raised as if taking an oath. 'I would trust him with my life. Malfeson was a good Templar and a most skilled clerk. Rest assured, Appleby and Stigand are gone – no longer Templars – but Malfeson? Oh, we have great hopes for him.'

'Meaning?'

'Meaning that when the time comes, he will play his part in our order's affairs. For the time being, he clashes with others in the Chambre Noire. Now that is something I must also discuss with you, once I have gained your trust.'

'You have that.'

'Let us see, let us see.'

Corbett reflected on his meeting with Fitzalan as he and Ranulf planned and plotted their next move. They agreed with Admiral Kynaston, now a regular visitor, that it would be pointless to board and seize the Flemish cogs. So far, they had no evidence to warrant this, while any attack on a foreign ship might well be construed as an act of war. Moreover, news from Westminster was not good. Edward and Isabella were growing restless, Isabella in particular. She was now publicly referring to a possible journey out of London, down to Dover and across the Narrow Seas to meet with her esteemed father. Corbett learnt of this with growing trepidation and wrote letters begging her to stay calm and keep herself well protected in the royal enclosure at Westminster. Malfeson also promised he would do what he could, and he was true to his word. The queen's letters became less acerbic and more appreciative of what Corbett and others were trying to do. Corbett and Ranulf also considered what defence they could mount against the Brethren without alerting the assassins, who would simply wait for another occasion. Corbett was determined on meeting this enemy and utterly annihilating it.

Fitzalan eventually returned, but he had no fresh

news. He brought with him two sturdy former Templar sergeants, who joined Chanson in the warm comfortable stables. Fitzalan himself had been provided with a chamber on the first gallery, close to Corbett.

Corbett eventually summoned what he called his household: Ranulf, Malfeson, Stigand and Appleby. He instructed them to keep a sharp eye on all visitors, even the journeymen now passing through the Twilight. The weather had changed for the better, on the verge of producing the first shoots of spring. Consequently the tavern became even livelier and noisier, a real distraction for Corbett. Matters became even more trying with the arrival of the Fellowship of St Thomas of Canterbury. This guild of pilgrims – six men and four women, along with three boys and a little girl who never stopped screaming loudly – proclaimed how they were making their way to venerate their patron saint's shrine in Canterbury. Appleby and Stigand searched them all, as they did every visitor, but all they found was an axe for cutting wood and the usual battered belt dagger. The youngsters had the run of the place, racing upstairs and down chanting a doggerel verse: 'Not last night but the night before, three dead men came knocking at the door.' They recited this time and again the length and breadth of the tavern.

'I wish they would go,' Corbett grumbled.

'Master,' Ranulf replied, 'they soon will. They say they have to be in Canterbury by the twenty-ninth of January, the anniversary of Becket's murder in his palace there.'

Corbett was only half listening, but he froze, a prickle of fear that cleared his mind of everything except what Ranulf had just said.

'Repeat that,' he demanded. He fought to keep calm as Ranulf did so.

'Master, what is it?' his clerk asked.

'Go down to the taproom or outhouse, wherever the pilgrims are camped. Draw them into conversation. Be subtle and sly, but ask them to repeat what you have just told me. Don't alarm them. Wrap it up cleverly.' Corbett waved a hand. 'Some pretext for your curiosity.'

Ranulf left. Corbett sat listening carefully, now alerted to the possibility of a deep danger lurking very close by. Ranulf returned.

'Sir Hugh, I asked them again for the date and the place under the pretext that my mother hopes to be in Canterbury to venerate the saint. I tried to keep the matter light. However, once their leader replied and I tried to explain, I caught a sudden shift in his eyes . . .'

'I'm sure you did. We may have alerted them.'

'To what?'

'Ranulf, those pilgrims proclaim themselves dedicated to the memory and saving grace of Thomas à Becket, or Thomas of Canterbury, this kingdom's greatest saint and most holy martyr. Archbishop Becket opposed the king at that time, which led to his murder, not on the twenty-ninth of January but the twenty-ninth of December in the year of Our Lord 1170. In addition, Becket was not murdered in his palace but in the cathedral. For the love of God, here is a group that proclaims itself the Fellowship of St Thomas of Canterbury, yet it doesn't even know the correct date and place of his famous martyrdom.'

'A silly mistake?'

'Ranulf, I once besieged a fortress in Wales. It was well fortified, its defenders all buckled for war under a famous Welsh captain, yet I took that fortress easily.'

'How?'

Corbett laughed. 'Someone left a door open and in we charged. Now, as regards this, the leader of these mysterious pilgrims may have had his suspicions alerted. So if they are who I believe they are, they will strike very soon.'

'Whom do we confide in?'

'Ap Ythel, Fitzalan, no one else. We cannot be certain about the others keeping silent. It's best if we four prepare ourselves. In the meantime, we can only deal with the matters in hand.'

Corbett continued his drafting, only resting when he joined Ranulf in the buttery. His henchman assured him that he had spoken to the other two and they would be ready. Corbett returned to his chamber; darkness fell. The tavern grew quieter as customers left. Ranulf joined Corbett in his chamber. Once again he assured his master that Ap Ythel and Fitzalan were ready. He then helped Corbett prepare their defences. The door to the chamber was both locked and bolted, while each clerk had two arbalests primed, ready and within easy reach. Corbett felt distinctly troubled: a deep unease that recalled his war days in Wales, where the danger was equally pressing. He'd be riding through some empty snow-carpeted valley or warming himself before a fire in a shadow-ringed clearing and this same deep feeling would disturb his humours. Ap Ythel claimed that soldiers were like animals. They could eventually develop and hone a sense of approaching evil, of imminent danger, of some threat lurking deep in the darkness around them. Corbett certainly felt this now. The silence seemed more profound, broken now and again by the creak of the tavern's timbers.

He tried to relax, taking out his Ave beads and praying for Maeve and their children. He smiled to himself as Ranulf, despite his vow to be vigilant, sank into a deep sleep, his gentle snoring disturbing the silence. Corbett reflected on what both he and his henchman had to face. Who was behind the murders here at the Twilight and elsewhere? He also accepted that the game of kings was being played out around him, but for what purpose? He recognised that Isabella and, more importantly, her infant son had changed the game. For the first time ever, an English prince had been born who would not only inherit the throne of England but could also lodge a compelling claim to that of France. True, the present French king had three sons, Louis, Philip and Charles. Corbett, however, had learnt a great deal about these princes, including the rumours rife at the English court that all three might be incapable of fathering a child. The king's sons, so reports claimed, led dissolute lives, and rumours were rife about the licentiousness of their courts, held far away from the hawk-like gaze of their prudish father.

Corbett sighed, got up and peered through the shutters. The first grey light of dawn was mingling with the dark. He returned to his comfortable chair and began to recite another Ave, before slipping into a deep sleep . . .

'Not last night but the night before,' a deep voice chanted, 'three dead men came knocking at the door.'

'In heaven's name,' Ranulf exclaimed. 'At this late hour?'

Corbett, also jolted from sleep, rubbed his face and stared around.

'Don't do anything, Ranulf, just listen.'

'Not last night,' the voice repeated, 'but the night before, three dead men came knocking at the door.' This was followed by three loud bangs along the gallery outside.

'Sir Hugh?'

'I know what they are plotting. Ranulf, keep your arbalest at the ready. Now, silent as you can, draw back the bolts, unlock the door and move swiftly away.'

Ranulf did so. He'd hardly retreated to his post when there were three knocks on the chamber door, followed by that infernal chant.

'Now,' Corbett breathed, 'be ready.'

Abruptly the door to the chamber was kicked open and two crossbow bolts whirred through the air.

'Loose!' Corbett shouted, and both he and Ranulf released the catch, their bolts speeding towards the shadows sliding into the chamber.

Loud cries and screams confirmed that both barbs

had found their target. Two of the shadows crumpled to the floor while the third turned and fled. Corbett and Ranulf crouched beside the two fallen assailants. One was already dead; the bolt had shattered his forehead. The other, mouth bubbling blood, was grievously wounded in the chest. He could only moan, eyelids fluttering.

'You knocked on the wrong door,' Ranulf rasped, before drawing his dagger and giving his enemy the mercy cut, slicing open his throat.

The two men rose, primed their arbalests and cautiously made their way down the stairs towards the sound of fighting, steel scraping on steel, the air riven by shouts and curses. These abruptly abated, the noise fading like a grumbling storm to lapse into silence. In the taproom, servitors, shuddering with fear, had lit torches, lanterns and candles. Appleby was serving wine to anyone who wanted it, even as he cried, the tears sliding down his face.

'Stigand is dead,' he called out to Corbett. 'Killed immediately as the attackers came through the garden. They must have rapped on the door of his closet chamber.'

'And when he opened it?' Corbett declared. 'The bolt was loosed?'

'Yes, his head and face all shattered, Sir Hugh.'

'They tried the same on me.'

Fitzalan came out of the shadows, cleaning the blood from his sword blade with a rag. He tossed this onto the fire the servants were building up. Brother Ricard arrived, a white-tasselled stole around his neck.

'I have visited our dead,' he intoned. 'Poor Stigand, an ostler and one of the spit boys.' He sat down on a stool, mopping his brow. 'All dead, but all blessed. And the enemy? How many of them were cut down?'

'From what I understand,' Fitzalan replied, 'two died outside Corbett's chamber. I killed the two that visited mine.'

'I am sure I wounded one,' Brother Ricard declared. 'I smashed his head as he stole into my chamber, but I was unable to pursue him.' He stared around. 'Where's Monseigneur Malfeson?'

'He left shortly after darkness fell,' Appleby replied. 'Claimed he had urgent business with her Grace.' He shrugged. 'I believe he had a royal barge waiting.'

'Let it be, let it be,' Corbett declared. 'Malfeson will have to wait. We must impose order here. I will leave that to you, Appleby. Ap Ythel, have your archers scour the outbuildings and the paths leading to the Twilight.' He paused. 'Oh yes, what happened to those assassins who survived? Did they escape?'

'Yes, through the garden,' Appleby replied.

'And their weapons?' Ranulf demanded. 'They were bereft of any armament when they arrived here. All who enter the tavern are rigorously searched.'

'God knows that,' Corbett retorted. 'Master John,' he pointed to Appleby, 'have the corpses moved to the mortuary at St Mary's. Tell the Keeper of the Dead to forward all costs to the Exchequer at Westminster.'

Other customers came down to the taproom all agog with curiosity at what had happened, offering to help put the tavern back to order. Corbett crossed to Ap Ythel and grasped him by the arm.

'Follow me,' he whispered.

He led the captain of archers out through the half-open garden door into the ice-cold frostiness of a strengthening dawn.

'Sir Hugh?'

'Yes, my friend?'

'Why did the assassins alert us with that chant? Others have asked the same.'

'Ap Ythel,' Corbett replied, as they slipped and slithered towards the garden house, 'you're an archer. Now, remember when the children of that murderous group used to chant their refrain to the mounting annoyance of us all.'

'Yes, I certainly do. Oh, by the way, Sir Hugh, I believe they moved the children out late last night before they began their attack. I suspect those little ones were taken from some orphanage or even just hired off the street. They certainly were very annoying.'

'They were indeed,' Corbett replied. 'So when we heard that refrain being chanted by adults as they climbed the stairs, this would deepen our annoyance and frustration. They would have expected me or Ranulf, as many would, to fling open the door, to shout our protests or discover what was happening.'

'Of course!' Ap Ythel exclaimed. 'Anyone who did so would stand defenceless against a background of light, a perfect target. Who taught you that, Sir Hugh?'

'You and yours did.' Corbett grinned. 'One of the

lessons I learnt fighting in Wales. Now,' he drew Ap Ythel closer as if they were examining the ice-bound summer house, 'let us find out how the assassins entered the tavern.'

'But they were here already, pretending to be pilgrims.'

'I agree, but they were joined by others who brought in weapons and probably took away the children. However, it is not really the garden I am interested in. Ap Ythel, I want you to scrutinise the curtain wall of this large, sprawling hostelry.'

'What am I looking for?'

'Something you did not expect to find. You will recognise it as soon as you see it. My friend, I know the weather is biting cold, but let's hope we can throw some light on the darkness confronting us.'

Corbett returned to the tavern, where Malfeson, still cloaked and booted, was warming himself before the taproom fire.

'Ranulf has already informed me,' he declared, clasping Corbett's hand, 'about events here. I am sorry I missed the murderous affray, but I understand you fought them off.'

'And you?'

'I went to see the queen at Westminster. She is a little sweeter, but I do sympathise with her. She feels cramped and caught, imprisoned by the danger confronting us all. The king is insistent she must go nowhere without an escort.'

'Have there been any more fires?'

'No, thank God. Every chamber the queen visits

is now vigorously searched. Every brazier or fire is raked and turned. The king fears, however, that his beloved wife is growing increasingly intolerant of this. Isabella is impetuous and as you know has a hot temper. Edward, God bless him, worries she may even try to run away.'

Corbett sighed noisily. 'Is that,' he asked, 'what the queen's enemies truly want?'

Malfeson shrugged. 'I went to Westminster to counsel the queen and help her calm down. I am not sure how effective I was. Anyway, for what it's worth, Sir Hugh, she sends her love and blessings. She desperately wishes to converse with you.'

'And so she shall . . .' Corbett broke off as Ranulf approached.

'Sir Hugh, you have a visitor. She is in my chamber.'

Ursula the washerwoman, shrouded in a heavy cloak and hood, made to rise as Corbett entered the room. He invited her to sit and asked her if she required anything to eat or drink. She shook her head, her small, pebble-like black eyes never leaving this royal clerk who seemed to put the fear of God into everyone.

'My lord,' she stuttered, 'I cannot stay long, I must return as quickly as possible.'

'You have found something?'

'Yes, my lord.' She undid the folds of her cloak and brought out a thin leather bag. From this she pulled a folded linen smock, the kind a lady of quality would wear when she was in her private quarters. It was snow white, undoubtedly new, which only emphasised the dark stain on both sleeves.

'I know stains, my lord. These are oil stains, quite expensive oil, I would say.'

'Could it be part of some beauty treatment?' Corbett offered. 'High-born ladies like to rub creams and oils into their hands and faces.'

'Possible, my lord, but come, smell it.'

Corbett and Ranulf both did so, and both clerks caught the tainted smell of cooking oil.

'Perfumes and ointments,' Ursula proclaimed loudly, 'are fairly easy to remove, otherwise such ladies would not use them.'

Corbett grunted his agreement. The lady Maeve was insistent that any powders and potions to be used were those that could be easily washed off any costly item. He again scrutinised the stains and pronounced himself satisfied.

'And who does this linen smock belong to?'

'To Countess Marguerite of Burgundy.'

Corbett closed his eyes and whispered a brief prayer of thanks.

'My lord, are we finished?'

'Yes.' He opened his eyes and smiled down at the washerwoman. 'Ursula, you may go, but do so swathed in cloak and cowl from head to toe. Greet no one and tell no one of what has passed between us.' He took two silver coins from his belt purse and pushed them into her callused hand. 'You haven't done so already, have you?' Ursula, all fearful, shook her head. 'Do not mention it to anyone, or you could die.' She quietly moaned. 'No, don't worry, we will keep you safe, but you must play your part. Silence is your best defence.' He held up the smock. Ursula took it and folded it away, then left.

For a while both clerks sat in silence reflecting on their meeting.

'Well, well, well,' Ranulf exclaimed. 'The queen will be furious.'

'She will also plot.' Corbett fell silent at a sharp knock on the door.

'Who is it?' Ranulf asked, picking up his arbalest all primed and ready.

'Fitzalan.'

Ranulf admitted the Templar, who sank gratefully into a chair and accepted a deep-bowled goblet of mulled wine.

'*Pax et bonum* to both of you.' He lifted his cup in toast. Corbett and Ranulf responded. 'So,' he began, 'I was right. The Brethren did attack, and mercifully we fought them off.'

'It's a pity we didn't kill them all,' Ranulf declared.

'Yes, but we wreaked hideous damage on a very dangerous coven. Clever, eh, using children as a pretext. And of course, they came without a weapon in sight.'

'So who armed them?'

'Heaven knows,' Fitzalan replied.

'I think I do,' Corbett retorted. 'The Immortal must have planned all this. Anyway, Ap Ythel is now busy searching for the truth, a piece of evidence I am sure he will find.' He leant over and tapped the Templar on the arm. 'And what will happen to the Brethren?'

'Oh, they'll disappear for a while,' Fitzalan replied, 'and probably vow to leave Sir Hugh Corbett and his entourage well alone.' He fell silent, staring into his wine cup.

'It is good to see you,' Ranulf declared. 'But why are you here?'

'To negotiate.' Corbett spoke up. 'That's why you're here, isn't it, Fitzalan? You proved your worth to us and now you wish me to respond.'

'Very much so, Sir Hugh. I will be blunt and brief.'

'Please do.'

'I lead a comitatus of about fifty Templars. Note that I talk of Templars, not former Templars. We are who we are until death. As I have said, my comitatus usually moves in small groups. However, this spring, around Lady Day, the Feast of the Annunciation, I want to gather them in the shadow of Alnwick Castle in Northumberland.'

'The Percy stronghold.' Corbett half smiled. 'A powerful family in the north-east who vehemently opposed the king's seizure of the Temple and all its assets.'

'True, Sir Hugh. Now, travelling to Alnwick will be relatively easy once winter has passed and the ground underfoot is good for riding. We will shelter with the Percys for a while, then move further north. You can guess where we are going?'

'Ah,' Corbett sighed, 'I certainly can. You are going to enter Scotland, and your difficulties will surface along the Scottish March. English troops are massing there. Castles and strongholds are being fortified and provisioned. Most of the troops are veterans, skilled in war. They will certainly challenge any group of armed men they encounter. So, how do you intend to avoid such a danger?'

'You guess most accurately, Sir Hugh. If you were to furnish me with letters and licences duly signed and sealed by the English king's principal clerk, his Keeper of the Secret Seal, no one would dare interfere with us. We would have permission to move and pass without any obstruction from anybody. We would then be able to buy supplies, horses,' Fitzalan waved a hand, 'and so on.'

Ranulf whistled beneath his breath. Corbett rose and moved to the window. He pulled back the shutters and stared out. The weather was bleak. In the yard below, servants and ostlers slipped and slithered across the cobbles. He stood, eyes half closed, as he reflected on what Fitzalan had told him. The Templar had spoken the truth. If he tried to cross the Scottish March, which teemed with English troops, he and his comitatus would certainly be challenged. A convoy of fifty men would not deter predators, who would envy the Templars' horses, harnesses, armour and whatever else they possessed.

He broke from his reverie as he heard his name called. He turned. Fitzalan had moved to stand beside the lectern, which held a book of the Gospels. The Templar placed one hand on the book and held the other up as he intoned the words of a sacred oath that what he said was the truth.

'Which is?' Corbett demanded.

'You said I was here to negotiate, and so I am. I will tell you the truth as far as I know it. What you do with that information is up to you.' Fitzalan paused. 'We are,' he began, 'and I mean the Templars, very much aware of the powerful Flemish war cog *The Basilisk*, which goes up and down the Thames and into the estuary to meet its supply ship, *The Hirondelle*. Oh yes,' he paused at Ranulf's exclamation of surprise, 'we move quietly in the shadows until we become part of the shifting darkness. We know all about Luytens, master of *The Basilisk* and close henchman of the Count of Flanders. He is allegedly in the Thames and Narrow Seas to protect Flemish shipping. That is both logical and understandable. The Narrow Seas are fast becoming a battlefield where English, French, Flemish and Spaniards, not to forget the Hanse, vie for trade. Violence can break out quite quickly, so *The Basilisk* is there to defend Flemish interests. However,' Fitzalan rested against the lectern, 'let us move from the cog for a while to Queen Isabella. She is a powerful figure in her own right. She is on the verge of fulfilling Philip's vision of a Capet, a grandson, wearing the Confessor's crown at Westminster, while a possible second grandson would be granted the wine-rich English province of Gascony.'

'A separate duchy?'

'Yes, Ranulf, a separate duchy.'

'Which would make it easier for it to be absorbed into the French Crown, to be part of their patrimony.'

'I would certainly agree with that. However, as I have

said before, the Chambre Noire is divided. Some of its members espouse Philip's dream, but others point to a possible nightmare: what, they argue, would happen if none of Philip's sons produced a male heir, so clearing the way for the young prince born of Isabella and Edward to claim the throne of France and so wear the crowns of both kingdoms.' Fitzalan tapped the book of the Gospels. 'Isabella is truly feared because of who she is and the rights she and others might assume. In a word, those who oppose Philip's vision would love to see the queen and her son removed, and that is why *The Basilisk* stands so close to your shores.'

'What?' Ranulf exclaimed.

'Oh yes, Ranulf, Flanders is very much part of a far-flung conspiracy to abduct Queen Isabella.'

'And then what?'

'Hold her to ransom?' Fitzalan shrugged. 'Heaven knows.'

'It's true,' Corbett spoke up, 'that there are many strands here. What you have told us accords with what we already know. I believe that Countess Marguerite initiated this plot.' He smiled at Fitzalan's look of surprise. He then told the Templar what he and Ranulf had discovered.

Fitzalan heard him out. 'I agree with your conclusions,' he said when the royal clerk paused for breath.

'Marguerite of Burgundy wants the queen removed for a myriad of reasons,' Corbett went on. 'Jealousy, envy, but above all the threat Isabella and her son pose to herself and her husband, who is heir to the French

Crown. However, his claim, without a male child, is weakening.' He collected his thoughts. 'To further her design and those who conspire with her, Marguerite journeyed to Westminster. She has the resources for those warnings to Isabella issued in London and Paris. And thus the game began.'

He pointed to the hearth. 'Those eruptions were easy to stage. The toppled candlestick was the first. Next the fires caused when pouches full of oil were thrust into a brazier. It would take some time for the flames to reach them and thus cause the conflagration. The same technique was used with those hollowed logs. I believe Countess Marguerite organised all this personally. We now know the effect of her plot. Isabella is deeply frightened and Edward equally concerned. Isabella is the light of his heart. She has made him the proud father of a lusty little boy. The queen, however, feels imprisoned. Matters are certainly worsened by the sombre warnings, the fiery eruptions, the lack of any real resolution of the threats confronting her. It all takes its toll.'

'And eventually she will break free,' Fitzalan declared. 'That lies at the heart of the plot. Once she does, the conspirators will strike. They'll seize the queen and her son, hustle them into a barge then onto *The Basilisk* before Edward and his court realise what has happened.'

The chamber fell silent as all three men reflected on the conclusions they had reached. Corbett eventually got to his feet.

'For the moment,' he declared, 'we are done here. But come, Ranulf, let us break our fast in the taproom before adjourning to my chamber, which has probably now been restored. I have certain letters and licences to draft, sign and seal. Yes, Fitzalan?'

'One further matter,' the Templar replied. 'Sir Hugh, please retake your seat.' Corbett did so, indicating that Ranulf follow suit. Fitzalan continued. 'Everyone has heard about the so-called secrets of the Temple. We have been depicted as magicians, the keepers of all kinds of startling secrets. I wish it was so. However, you may not believe what I am about to tell you. Have either of you ever heard the story of the Wandering Jew?'

'I have,' Corbett replied, 'but the details are now vague.'

'Then let me refresh your memory. In the year of our Lord 1099, the Crusaders stormed and captured Jerusalem. One of the leaders of this Crusade was Hugh de Payens, who later founded the Templar order. Now, the Crusaders fought their way ruthlessly into Jerusalem and up into the Temple Mount. Believe me,' Fitzalan crossed himself, 'it was a bloodbath, with people slaughtered to left and right. No one was spared. The blood ran like a river through the streets of Jerusalem. Anyway, the Crusaders, God forgive them, reached the Temple Mount and discovered cavernous chambers where all kinds of treasures were hoarded. Not just gold and silver, but precious relics such as the Holy Shroud that purportedly clothed Christ's body after it was taken down from the cross. Then there was the Mandylion, which covered his face and left a miraculous image of our Saviour's features.

'However, what was most surprising was the man Hugh de Payens found chained and manacled in one of the dungeons. He had him freed and given every comfort, and this individual, who called himself Cartaphilus, began to tell him the most compelling story, declaring how he had been born a Jew but later converted to Christianity. De Payens asked him when this conversion had taken place, and Cartaphilus replied that he had been converted over a thousand years earlier, just after Christ's death. How he had met the living Christ and all who consorted with him, including Peter and the Apostles. He declared that he'd wandered Jerusalem before it was destroyed by the legions of Rome, and claimed that he had maintained the same age of thirty for the last eleven hundred years.'

'Never!' Ranulf exclaimed. 'A madman surely?'

'No, according to de Payen's secret chronicle, Cartaphilus was perfectly lucid and rational. He was also a living fount of all kinds of knowledge about matters such as the Empress Helena finding the True Cross, and the conversion of her son, Constantine, to the Christian faith.'

'Did others get to know about Cartaphilus and what he claimed?'

'No, Sir Hugh. De Payens was very cunning, astute and sharp as is becoming of our founder. Indeed, the Great Wanderer, as Cartaphilus described himself, begged him to keep silent on all matters, to which he agreed. He and Cartaphilus became close comrades. Indeed, Cartaphilus encouraged de Payens to found our order and helped him draw up its rules and other documents.'

'But who was he really?' Ranulf demanded.

'Oh, that lies at the heart of the mystery. Cartaphilus claimed he had encountered Christ during our Saviour's trial before Pilate in the Antonine Fortress in Jerusalem. On that same day, before the Sabbath, Cartaphilus helped Christ, manacled and chained, as he was moved from one place to another. He was part of Christ's military escort. However, he became impatient at our Saviour's laboured walk. Christ, of course, had been scourged, beaten and abused, and walked as a truly wounded man. Cartaphilus, however, anxious to have the prisoner dispatched before the Sabbath, cruelly pushed him, shouting at Jesus to hurry up. He kept repeating this until Christ turned and stared fixedly at him. "I shall not hurry up," he declared, "and neither will you, Cartaphilus. You shall stay as you are until I come again, this time in glory, at the end of time."'

'Impossible,' Ranulf spoke abruptly. 'Nonsense! I have heard similar fanciful stories from our wandering troubadours and minstrels.'

Fitzalan waved a hand. 'I simply describe what I have learnt. But please hear me out. At first de Payens was just as sceptical as you are, Ranulf. He refused to believe Cartaphilus. Nevertheless, he kept this startling, strange individual in luxurious seclusion in a house in the Holy City. In the meantime, Cartaphilus continued to make astonishing statements about the past. One day, he offered to take de Payens out to Masada, a fortress built by Herod the Great overlooking the Dead Sea. It is in fact an eagle's eyrie and was regarded as impregnable until Rome's armies besieged and attacked the last great stronghold in the Jewish revolt. The journey was perilous. They had to climb almost up to the sky to get into the ruined fortress. Masada was deserted. Only the vultures nested there. To cut to the chase, once they arrived, Cartaphilus unearthed a casket containing documents. One of these gave detailed descriptions of our Wandering Jew, emphasising the birthmark beneath his left eye. The documents were signed and sealed, as was the casket, the hardened wax providing a date hundreds of years earlier.'

Ranulf whistled beneath his breath.

'And the relevance of all this?' Corbett demanded.

'Oh yes, the relevance, Sir Hugh, is this. Cartaphilus helped found and organise the Templar order. He was there as it began to flourish, becoming rich and powerful. He also promised to assist it over the coming years.'

'But he could not prevent the dissolution of the Templars under Philip of France's persecution?'

'Indeed, Sir Hugh. However, from the very beginning he warned de Payens that the order would grow so prosperous and powerful it would provoke the jealousy and envy of the great lords of the soil.'

'It certainly did,' Corbett replied. 'And?'

'Cartaphilus promised he would do what he could to help. He also promised that he would pursue and punish those who abused the Templar order in a way that the world would marvel at.' Fitzalan shook his head.

'I know from those who work in the prisons of Paris where Jacques de Molay and the other Templar prisoners were confined and tortured that our Grand Master was visited by Cartaphilus. The Great Wanderer disguised himself in the black and white robes of the Dominican order, claiming to be a member of the so-called Holy Inquisition. He demanded private speech with de Molay. The details were later passed on to me by someone in my pay, an officer at the Châtelet.

'De Molay was confined to a stone-flagged cell but one with a spyhole cleverly built into it. My protégé,' he grinned, 'as I like to call such creatures, overheard scraps of conversation. De Molay protested his innocence of all the heinous charges against him, while his visitor promised vengeance if Philip of France continued his persecution of the order, which he certainly has. De Molay will not be allowed to walk free. He will be racked and savagely tortured until he confesses to whatever Philip wants. This will end in blood. The Templars will be destroyed and, if so, heaven help the House of Capet. In a word, gentlemen,' Fitzalan got to his feet, 'I believe that Cartaphilus, whoever he may be, is preparing to wreak vengeance on Philip in his palace at the Louvre, and on Bertrand de Got, also known as Pope Clement V, cowering like a rabbit in Avignon. More than this I cannot say. Now I must bid you adieu till we meet formally to take our leave tomorrow morning.'

'Fitzalan?'

'Yes, Sir Hugh?'

'Do you believe Cartaphilus's story?'

'When I study the history of my order, I do detect a moving hand. Someone secretly guiding us at the behest of the Holy Spirit.'

'But a man who never dies?'

'I suspect his title and calling are true. Perhaps it's just a role held within a certain family and passed from one generation to the next like a birthmark. That's what I think, Sir Hugh. Nevertheless, he is bent on vengeance. One further matter overheard in the Châtelet was de Molay's question about how vengeance would be carried out, and against whom. His visitor replied that poison was the Queen of Murders and that was all he would say.'

'Was Isabella mentioned?'

'Not in the context of being included among the Great Wanderer's intended victims. Apparently de Molay and Cartaphilus agreed to leave her to her own devices, whatever that means. No, they were in agreement about who should be punished: Philip of France, his creature Pope Clement V and the French king's henchmen and sons.'

'How?'

'God knows, Sir Hugh, though, as I said, poison was mentioned. I do wonder how Cartaphilus will get close enough to mingle venom into whatever his victims eat or drink. All I can say is that the thunderstorm is still far off, but it will break soon enough and blood will flow.'

PART SIX

Thus the thorn turns into a lily,
rust into iron, dross into gold.

The following morning, just after daybreak, Fitzalan and his retainers made their farewells to Corbett and his henchmen. They met in the stable yard, Fitzalan still holding the leather chancery satchel containing the letters and licences he had asked for. He gave this to one of his companions so he could clasp hands with Corbett and exchange the kiss of peace. He then mounted his destrier, its hooves scrabbling on the cobbles as the Templar stared down at the royal clerk.

'*Pax et bonum*, Sir Hugh. God protect you. I would have loved to stay, but . . .' He raised his hand, turned his horse and, with his escort following behind, rode out of the tavern yard. Corbett watched them go.

'Do you think our paths will cross again?'

'Possibly, Ranulf, though it might be on the battle-field. Fitzalan and his ilk are seasoned warriors, who seek the protection of Robert the Bruce. He in turn will ask for their support. So when our king – and he surely will – moves across the Scottish March to decide who rules Scotland, Fitzalan and his comitatus will follow Bruce. But that is for the future. Now I am going to walk this tavern. I want to ensure that there is nothing left here that might help us.'

'Are you attending mass?'

'No, Ranulf, not today.'

Corbett raised his hand and walked back into the tavern. Despite the death of Stigand, Appleby was desperately trying to rectify matters and bring the place back to its usual comfortable security. Corbett was greeted as he moved along the galleries and passageways. He went into various chambers and eventually reached that of Malling's daughter Rachel. He sat on the bed and stared around. He'd seen the same in Rebekah's room.

'Definitely a lady's chamber,' he whispered, and smiled as he recalled his own daughter's room at their manor at Leighton. The chamber was adorned with colourful ribbons, and housed a small chancery desk and a painting of a lady, possibly Guinevere. Corbett stared around and glimpsed a horn book on the bed: pieces of parchment cut into squares and fastened with chancery twine. He picked it up and leafed through the stiffened pages. One entry, the last, caught his eye, and he paused, stomach clenching in excitement. He had not expected to see this, but it was there, so easy to read. Grasping the book, he got to his feet and returned to his own chamber.

There, he took out his record of all that had happened

since he'd arrived at the Twilight. Ranulf knocked on the door and came in. He sat for a while, watched his master and realised it was useless to stay and talk. He knew the signs as of old. Corbett the hawk was on the wing, ready to plunge. He was preparing an indictment, drawing up his conclusions, drafting and redrafting his thoughts, making them match the evidence available, bringing in what he'd first dismissed but that now proved very relevant.

Corbett worked into the night. He summarised, scrutinised and drafted again. He snatched a few hours of sleep, woke and quickly washed at the lavarium. He then broke his fast on bread and meat along with a cup of red wine taken from a freshly broached hogshead. Ranulf and Chanson joined him. They ate in silence and, when finished, went out into the yard, where Ap Ythel and six of his archers were waiting to escort Corbett to Westminster. Earlier in the day, he had dispatched a messenger to the king and queen telling them that he desperately needed to see them on a most urgent matter.

Once he had arrived in the royal precincts, a knight banneret hurried to take him and Ranulf along to the Jerusalem Chamber, where Edward and Isabella were waiting, agog with curiosity about what their Keeper of the Secret Seal wanted to say. Ranulf was equally curious. Corbett, however, refused to be drawn. He asked Ranulf to stand guard outside the chamber, adding that he would not be long. Deeply curious, Ranulf leant against the door and strained his hearing, surprised to hear the king's heavy-bellied laugh followed by a more sedate one from the queen. Apparently matters were soon settled, and Corbett, with a look of deep satisfaction on his face, left the chamber, tugging at Ranulf's sleeve as he led his henchman away.

'Sir Hugh?'

'Ranulf, the king is going to visit the Twilight tomorrow evening.'

'And the queen?'

'No, no, just the king. Isabella will stay here, well guarded and protected. Now we must hurry back to prepare for his visit. He is eager to escape the shadows of Westminster.'

'Why the Twilight?'

'Oh, his Grace simply wants to visit a tavern that has played such a dramatic part in recent events. He also wants to thank you, me and all his loyal subjects in and around the Twilight.'

Corbett repeated the same message when they returned to the tavern, and his words truly stirred the community there. Appleby, all aflutter, sent his minions out to the markets to buy the purveyance they needed. Then the taverner, who seemed highly anxious and nervous, drew up the menu, claiming it would be second to none. The planned banquet would include the finest wines, shoulder of pork, white broth, mutton and lamb cooked in a tangy lemon juice, as well as platters of various sweetmeats. Other dishes were added. In the meantime, the taproom was truly transformed. Tables were pushed together and covered with cloths of snow-white linen worked in damask with flowers, knots, crowns and fleurs-de-lis. Precious vessels were taken out of the tavern's arca, the strongbox hidden deep in the cellars – goblets of ivory as well as silver gilt, platters and other precious utensils – and the air was sweet with the smells of spices and herbs, stewed beef, capon, baked pastry, venison, blancmange fritters and other indulgences. Corbett felt slightly guilty at the work he had created, but it was necessary, just as it was that he dispatch urgent messages to Admiral Kynaston.

The next morning, Corbett attended a mass celebrated by Brother Ricard in his small chapel. Afterwards he took the Black Robe aside. Hand on his shoulder, his mouth almost brushing the Benedictine's ear, he whispered how it was not the king who would descend on the Twilight that evening, but the queen and a number of her household maidens. Ricard stared bemusedly back.

'So why inform me, Sir Hugh?'

'Because I want you to celebrate mass in your chantry chapel, a service of thanksgiving. Her Grace will arrive here as the bells toll for vespers, her journey hidden beneath the cloak of darkness.'

The Black Robe promised he would join Corbett in welcoming the queen. He was sworn to silence, then left claiming he had urgent business with his lord abbot.

Corbett returned to the preparations. Appleby had been instructed to close the tavern for the day under the pretext that urgent repairs needed to be carried out, though everyone knew the real reason. Corbett had also dispatched Megotta and six of Ap Ythel's archers to Westminster. As for the rest, he informed Ranulf, they could only wait and see. Ranulf murmured his agreement, though in truth he was totally bemused by what was happening. The Clerk of the Green Wax was deeply suspicious that the preparations were only a charade concealing something else. He tried to question Megotta before she left, but she was equally bemused. She informed him that she would only discover why she and the archers were being sent to Westminster when they arrived in the royal precincts.

The day drew on. Darkness fell. The hour of the bat. Preparations at the Twilight were finished. The great taproom was now fitted out like any royal hall with costly tapestries adorning the walls and thick turkey rugs covering the floor. Beeswax candles glowed. Braziers spluttered. The light of fire and flame danced in the silver and gold supper ware. A horn brayed. Corbett went out into the main porch as if to welcome the small procession making its way across the tavern yard. In the glow of sconce and cresset torches, the riders dismounted from their gaily caparisoned palfreys. There was a little confusion to begin with, but then, preceded by two of the archers, the procession wended its way towards Corbett. He bowed, then knelt to kiss the glinting silver rings before rising and leading the party into the taproom to take their seats behind the high table. Brother Ricard, dressed in a milk-white chasuble, came hurrying across full of questions about the mass. Corbett just shook his head.

'No trouble, Father, just go back to your chapel for the moment.'

Once the Black Robe was gone, Corbett ensured that his guests were comfortably seated. The taproom was now held in a strange silence. Appleby and his servitors stood clustered in the doorway to the great kitchen, waiting for instruction. Ap Ythel and his archers took up position either side of the hearth, while Ranulf slouched in a window seat wandering what on earth was happening. He'd asked Corbett about the whereabouts of Malfeson, but his master had just smiled and shook his head. He'd then recalled that the French clerk had left the previous evening with messages for Kynaston and the Constable of the Tower.

Corbett stood staring down at the floor, head slightly turned as if he was straining his hearing. Sounds echoed from outside. He looked up and snapped his fingers at Ap Ythel.

'Quick as you can,' he urged. 'I want a fire arrow loosed up above the tavern.'

Ap Ythel hurried out. Corbett bowed towards his guests, seated as silent as statues behind the high table.

'In a while,' he murmured. 'In a while.'

Ap Ythel returned to report what he'd done. Corbett thanked him and walked closer to the door so he could listen to the bells of the city pealing out the end of vespers. The ringing had scarcely stopped when the silence was shattered by the main door being kicked open and the sound of mailed feet. Corbett thrust a hunting horn into Ranulf's hand then walked across to the door of the taproom and waited. There was a sharp rap. He opened the door and a cohort of armed men, all buckled for war, surged into the room. Ap Ythel and his archers made to resist, but Corbett, who had stumbled against a table, shouted that no one was to move. He got to his feet as the intruders, about twenty in all, fanned out across the taproom, arbalests at the ready. They reeked of leather, sweat and the stink of the river. Their leader stepped forward and took off his war helmet.

'Well, well,' Corbett exclaimed, 'Master Luytens has come to the feast.'

'Shut up, Corbett, and remain as you are. You will be safe, even though I have orders to kill you as well as your red-haired familiar.' Luytens gestured at Ranulf. 'Stay calm, clerk,' he urged. 'Do not even think of resisting.'

He then approached the table and bowed.

'Your Grace?'

'No queen here, Master Luytens,' Corbett sang out. 'Oh no, instead please meet Megotta the Moon-girl, Daughter of the Sun. She will now reveal herself so you can look upon her and marvel.'

Megotta pulled the thick, heavy-veiled headdress from her head, followed by the gold-coloured wig beneath. She bowed mockingly towards Luytens as she gestured at those sitting either side of her.

'And here they are, sir. Nothing prettier than a cohort of Tower archers, eh?'

The headdresses of her escort were now removed, together with the costly gowns and cloaks that had concealed the leather harnesses beneath.

'I sincerely hoped that you would not study the booted feet too closely. Sir Hugh, we are ready to leave now.'

Megotta and the archers made to rise, but Luytens, beside himself with fury, screamed at them to remain seated. He then returned to his own escort, now not so threatening as they realised the trap they had stumbled into. Luytens, his narrow face all flushed, shouted at his comitatus to remain alert. Corbett, ignoring the Fleming, walked over to Ranulf and tapped the hunting horn he had thrust into his hands just before the intruders arrived.

'Three blasts,' he ordered.

'What is this?' Luytens strode across, sword drawn, its point only inches from Corbett's throat.

Corbett simply shrugged, turning away to confront Luytens' comitatus.

'Listen!' he bellowed.

'Shut up!' Luytens screamed.

'Let him speak.' One of the invaders, a swaggering rogue, lifted his hand. 'You have hired me and mine, Master Luytens. We are rifflers, we take our orders from the Immortal.'

'And one of those orders was to obey me.'

'Ah, true,' the riffler replied, 'but come, sir, matters have truly changed. On our crossing here we were assured that we would be abducting the Queen of England, but all we have is a moon-girl.'

'A true lady of high quality,' Megotta riposted. 'Far too exalted for the likes of you.'

The riffler grinned and blew her a kiss, which she acknowledged with an obscene gesture.

'Be that as it may . . .' Luytens was desperately trying to maintain his authority.

'Gruffeld is correct,' another of the rifflers called. 'Let the man speak.'

'We do not have the queen,' Gruffeld shouted, pointing at a window. 'Only hell knows what is waiting for us outside.' His words were greeted with cries of approval.

'You are right,' Corbett declared. 'Now listen. You may know me. I am Sir Hugh Corbett, Keeper of the King's Secret Seal. I am here to offer you life or death; the choice is yours. You will never abduct our gracious queen, nor will you leave this place alive if you try to resist. Already two royal war cogs, *The Sentinel* and *The Paladin*, stand alongside *The Basilisk*. Whatever crew were on board *The Basilisk* are now either prisoners or dead. The same is true of *The Hirondelle*. The war barges and battle-boats you arrived on are now in the hands of royal men-at-arms. In addition, all approaches by land and sea into Queenhithe lie under the closest watch. In a word, gentlemen, you are trapped. If you resist, you will be slaughtered. Those who survive will suffer the most excruciating death at Smithfield or Tyburn.' He paused. 'As I have said, the choice is yours.'

'Accepted,' Gruffeld bawled. He loosened his war belt and put this and his arbalest on the floor. The others swiftly followed suit.

Once they had disarmed themselves, Corbett had the doors opened and royal men-at-arms, hobelars and archers flooded the taproom. Luytens asked to speak with him, and Corbett agreed provided that the Flemish captain be manacled and chained. Then he walked over to him.

'Well?'

'Sir Hugh, on your oath, you swear that me and mine will be spared? If so, I can help you.'

'I have already given my word. I might even make matters easier for you.'

'Very well.' Luytens moved in a clatter of chains, staring as some of his men were dragged to their feet. The prisoners were quietly cursing their surrender as well as the way their captors were helping themselves to their weapons and personal possessions.

'I can make things a little more comfortable,' Corbett declared. 'So just tarry here.' He walked to the doorway, calling for Ranulf and Ap Ythel to join him outside, where he gave them strict instruction about what should happen to the prisoners and their possessions, as well as other urgent matters. Once satisfied that both henchmen would carry out his orders immediately, he returned to face Luytens. 'Very well,' he declared, 'let us be brief and blunt. So, who hired you?'

'Marguerite, Countess of Flanders.'

'Yes, I thought as much.' Corbett smiled thinly at the surprise on the captain's face. 'Oh yes, Master Luytens, we know a great deal. Do continue.'

'The countess opened secret negotiations with the Count of Flanders, who agreed to assist.'

'Why did she make that request? What did she want?'

'I was not privy to that. I was simply given sealed orders to take *The Basilisk* into the Thames estuary, sailing back and forth as if keeping a close eye on Flemish shipping.'

'And the Immortal?'

'When we first arrived, Sarasin the riffler chieftain came aboard. He explained that he would try to create an opportunity to seize the Queen of England, together with her son if possible, and abduct them. He said he would keep me closely informed of developments.' Luytens pulled a face. 'Of course, he then killed that clerk, for which you hanged him. I thought that might be the end of the matter.' He shrugged. 'As you now know, it certainly wasn't. Indeed, matters took a more urgent pace. I received an envoy from someone calling himself the Immortal.'

'Do you know who that is?'

'Sir Hugh, how could I? I did ask for his true name. I received the reply that his name was the Immortal and that it was not my concern who he was or what he did. For a brief while I truly wondered if Sarasin might have survived the hanging, but,' he shook his head, 'I came to accept that he was well and truly gone.'

'And this envoy?'

'He reported how the queen was both anxious and fearful because she believed someone close to her was lighting fires.'

'Who?'

'I suspect the Countess Marguerite, or an important official of the household. I was also informed that the queen might move here or there. The Immortal said he would pounce when the time was right.'

'Which was tonight?'

'So we were told. We were encouraged to see it as easy as plucking a rose.'

'But you ran into the sharpest thorns. Anyway, if you had succeeded, what then?'

Luytens shook his head. 'We would have taken the queen to Flanders. Once that happened, we were no longer needed.'

'Let us turn to another matter,' Corbett said. 'The treasure chest and the disappearance of the battle-boat.'

'Oh yes, the Immortal's envoy explained how treasure and other precious items are moved from one palace to another. I was informed that a chest containing such would cross the Thames in a battle-boat manned by archers. A navigator would accompany them so they could safely thread the shallows and currents. He would be chosen by the Immortal, who would also supply the time, date and place. The navigator would convince the archers that the battle-boat had got into difficulties, and so they would bring it alongside *The Basilisk*; that happened as planned. They were only too willing to leave their vessel and swiftly climb the netting. I then used our cranes and hoists to raise the battle-boat and bring it aboard. I'll be honest, Sir Hugh, it all went very smoothly.'

'Yes, yes,' Corbett murmured. 'It's all logical enough. The Immortal leads the rifflers, who undoubtedly have adherents in the Tower. One of these informs him about a treasure chest being prepared and loaded onto a cart. Such information could be easily bought with no questions asked.'

'I believe the same, Sir Hugh.'

'And the treasure, where is it now?' Corbett asked abruptly.

Luytens gave a sharp bark of laughter. 'It's still on board *The Basilisk*, or nearly so. You will find the chest wrapped in the strongest netting you can find, on the starboard side of the cog, just below the prow. It's safer there than if you had it chained and padlocked in the hold.'

'And the crew of *The War-dog*?'

Luytens swallowed hard.

'The crew?' Corbett repeated. 'The archers, what happened to them?'

'Sir Hugh, I will take any oath, and you can interrogate my men. We first went out into the Northern Seas and tossed the battle-boat, heavily weighted, down into the deep. Then we sailed back into the estuary to make our meeting with *The Hirondelle* and transferred the crew to them. They had all been well fed and properly treated on board *The Basilisk*, I promise you that. The plan was to create a deep mystery about how the battle-boat had disappeared: a mystery that would hopefully last for months. Of course, by then we would be far away.' He took a deep breath. '*The Hirondelle* was to take the archers north to some small port along England's east coast, Scarborough or even further. They would be put ashore to make their own way home. By the time they returned to London, the business in hand would be finished. Naturally the English Crown would object, but we could act all innocent. We would claim to have helped *The War-dog* in its difficulties, rescued the crew and handed them over to *The Hirondelle*, who would argue that they had urgent business in the north but again gave the required assistance!' Luytens shrugged. 'As for the treasure, we would ask what treasure? However, matters turned out so different! Sir Hugh, I swear those archers, although prisoners, were hale and hearty enough when they were transferred to *The Hirondelle*.'

'And their captors?'

'Not Flemings, but Frisian pirates whom the Count of Flanders had hired.'

Corbett closed his eyes and groaned. 'Frisians!' he exclaimed. He opened his eyes, stared at Luytens and poked him in the chest. 'Frisians,' he repeated, 'the very dregs of hell. God have mercy on those poor men. Now, Luytens, on your oath, is there anything else?'

'No, Sir Hugh. We made a mistake. We were misled. We were informed that the royal entourage would be leaving Westminster Palace for the Twilight. All we had to do was cross the river, ring the tavern and abduct whomever we wanted.'

'Who told you that?'

'Again, an envoy from the Immortal, but he too was tricked. You've trapped the bastard, haven't you, Sir Hugh?'

'The good Lord delivered him into my hands. Luytens, you and your men should really hang.' Corbett saw the alarm flare in the Fleming's eyes. 'But I believe you acted honourably enough. I do not think you are a man to ill treat prisoners.'

'So what will happen to us?'

'Well, the English Crown is now the proud owner of a magnificent war cog. It will make a useful addition to the king's fleet. As for you, I understand the Count of Flanders has imprisoned English seamen here and there. We will trade you for them. So, one last time, is there anything else you can tell me?'

Luytens shook his head, and Corbett ordered the guard to take him to join the rest being herded along the riverside to the Tower. He then hastily dictated a message to Kynaston and dealt with a flurry of other matters. Eventually he announced himself truly exhausted, and retired to his chamber.

Corbett rose just before first light and decided he would wait before he prepared himself for an audience with the queen at Westminster. Instead, he went down to the petty buttery, where Appleby served ladles of piping-hot potage. Corbett apologised for his deception over the king's purported visit, but added that the Crown had needed to settle certain important matters. Once it was all over, Appleby and the Twilight would be lavishly rewarded. The taverner should have been delighted. However, he still seemed agitated and highly nervous. Once he had served Corbett, he hurried away. A short while later, Ranulf, Kynaston and Ap Ythel arrived. All three delivered their reports on what had been achieved since Corbett had issued his instructions the night before.

'So,' Corbett turned to Kynaston, 'you used *The Basilisk* to take *The Hirondelle*?'

'As easy as slipping off a step, Sir Hugh. We were aboard before they even realised what was happening. Some of the crew resisted and were cut down, their corpses tossed overboard. The captain and four of his henchmen survived.'

'And *The Basilisk* was just as easy?' Ranulf demanded.

'Of course, my friend,' the admiral replied. 'It had been virtually stripped of its crew and armament in preparation for the so-called abduction. Luytens left his house open and we occupied it.' He paused. 'Sir Hugh, we also have the treasure chest. It was where you said. However, as regards our captured archers, we closely questioned Brasov, the captain of *The Hirondelle*, but he refused to answer. We did a thorough search but found nothing, then we reached Queenhithe and Ap Ythel came aboard.'

'I searched that ship from prow to stern.' The captain of archers' voice was shot through with a profound sadness. He paused to rub the tears welling in his eyes. 'I found a clothes chest. Admiral Kynaston had seen the same but thought the clothing belonged to the crew of *The Hirondelle.*'

'I was wrong,' Kynaston intervened. 'Ap Ythel searched among the garments folded there, as well as the war belts and swords stacked in a corner, a small armoury. He recognised both clothing and weapons as belonging to Ensign Malachi and his archers.'

'That's the truth,' Ap Ythel declared. 'I then closely examined some of the clothing, but I found no bloodstains.'

'So what happened to them?'

'I suspect, Sir Hugh,' the captain of archers again dabbed at his eyes, 'that they were stripped, still manacled and chained, then thrown over the side.'

'In this weather they would not have survived long. God save them.' Corbett rubbed his face as he tried to control the anger welling within him. He knew these archers. Welsh lads from the valleys. Superb bowmen and yet almost childlike in their innocence, be it singing or telling each other the most outrageous tales. He took his hands away from his face. 'The crew of *The Hirondelle* are *utlegatum*, wolfsheads who have attacked royal troops and committed the most heinous murders. This will not take long. Bring them in.'

He moved to sit behind the high table, still positioned on the dais, and watched as Ranulf laid out his war sword, a book of the Gospels from his chamber and the usual documents, signed and sealed in the royal chancery, giving him full power to deal with all matters affecting the Crown. The Frisian pirates were herded in: five men dressed in a motley collection of women's clothing, their fingers, wrists and necks adorned with cheap jewellery. They looked what they were, Corbett thought, men bound for hell, with their cruel faces, sly eyes and slobbering mouths. They did not beg for mercy, and when he questioned them, they simply grinned and glanced away. Brasov, their grey-haired, scar-faced leader, pretended he couldn't understand Corbett, who eventually shrugged and raised his right hand as a sign that he was delivering judgement.

'You offer,' he declared, 'no defence against the charges I have levelled against you. Ap Ythel, Ranulf, hang them from the tavern sign and the gallows close by. Make it as protracted and as painful as you can. Ah,' he pointed at Brasov, 'you now have something to add to the proceedings?'

The Frisian gathered spittle in his mouth, but then thought better of it when Ranulf grasped him by the chin, not letting go until Brasov had swallowed what he had gathered.

'Corbett,' the pirate grated, 'we are as guilty as sin. After all, it's obvious what we've done, except,' his voice rose, 'we did not kill the archers for sport, for fun or because we are blood-drinkers, killers born and bred. Oh no, search out the bastard who preens himself as the Immortal. He dispatched a message delivered by fishermen who brought their herring boat alongside. It was quite simple: "No witnesses."' Brasov moved in a rattle of chains. 'We simply made sure there weren't.'

Corbett gestured to Ranulf and Ap Ythel sitting to his right. 'Let us continue, if there isn't anything else.'

'There's nothing,' Brasov retorted.

The prisoners were hustled out, Ranulf calling for the archers to help them. Corbett sat listening to the clamour fade. Appleby shuffled in and, at Corbett's request, cleared the judgement table. The Keeper of the Secret Seal ignored him as he continued to sit reflecting on the coming confrontation. Then he sighed, rose and went up to his chamber. Appleby had left the items he had cleared from the taproom outside the door. Corbett, still lost in his own thoughts, placed them on the bed. As he threw the sword down onto the thick counterpane, he abruptly paused as it clinked against some metal object. He carefully removed everything from the bed and pulled back the coverlet, then caught his breath as he stared down at what he had uncovered. Twelve miniature caltrops, each comprised of four sharp spikes jutting upwards from a flat stable base. He picked one of these up and studied the wickedly pointed razor-sharp tips.

'Who put you here?' he murmured. 'Surely not Appleby! No, he is locked, as he should be, in his own deep fear, desperately trying to avoid his coming confrontation with me. This is the great killer's work, one last lunge at me. I was meant to come in here exhausted and depleted. I would throw myself on the bed and these would be waiting.' He turned, fetched a candle, then crouched by the door, scrutinising the lock as well as the freshly dug cuts around it. 'So simple,' he murmured. 'You picked the lock. Another of your criminal skills. Well, you are going to need all your cunning to escape the closing trap.'

A short while later, having washed and changed, Corbett met Ap Ythel and Ranulf in the stable yard. The weather had broken. The cold was no longer so intense, while a gentle breeze made the corpses of the hanged Frisians scrape against the tavern sign. Five black shapes turning and twisting. The archers who now accompanied Corbett had stripped the corpses of anything of worth, and the dark-dwellers had crept out to see if anything had been left for them. When they realised that there was nothing to be had, they had slunk away, leaving the witches and warlocks to their usual vigil. Such creatures were fervent in their belief that the corpses of hanged men had properties that could be used in their midnight rites. These scattered as Corbett and his companions galloped down the now iron-hard trackway towards Westminster.

They arrived at the appointed hour. Malfeson was waiting for them. He exchanged the kiss of peace with Corbett and his two henchmen, then led them along the labyrinthine corridors and galleries stretching down to the royal precinct and the closely guarded Jerusalem Chamber, where Queen Isabella was waiting. Corbett and his companions made their obeisances, then sat at the council table either side of the queen. Isabella promptly declared that her husband had delegated matters to her while he dealt with other urgent business. She thanked Ap Ythel and Ranulf for their attendance before turning to Corbett, sitting on her right.

'Hugh,' she smiled, 'the doors are closed and secured. Knights from my household patrol the corridors and galleries. So, begin. Tell me what conclusions you have reached.'

'Your Grace, I am not sure how much you already know, or how much our comrade here has told you.' Corbett gestured at Malfeson. 'First, your Grace, you are a woman of contention. Your father,' he hurried on, spurred by Isabella's troubled look, 'sees you and your infant son as the foundation of a new order in Europe under the Capet imperium. Be that as it may, others argue that your son could be the catalyst for a disastrous future.' He paused. 'Your Grace, let me spell it out. If, in the fullness of time, none of your brothers produce a male heir, Prince Edward of England could claim the French throne as his right, and there would be consequences.

'Of course, this is the game of kings, where others can intervene, and they certainly have. Mysterious messengers recently appeared in London and Paris. These self-confessed Templars issued warnings against you, my queen, about how you and your family must atone for your father's persecution, as they put it, of the Templar order. They warned that you would be harmed by fire. Such nonsense was undoubtedly the work of your sister-in-law Marguerite, Countess of Burgundy. She had the means and the influence to arrange these sombre warnings. She initiated these during her state visit to London.' Corbett waved a hand. 'Your Grace, we now know how the burnings were planned and carried out. Oil was poured into boiled leather bags. Some of this oil seeped out, staining the countess's clothing.'

'Yes, yes,' the queen whispered, waving a hand. 'Malfeson informed me of this.'

'Matters then turned murderous,' Corbett continued, 'a twist in all this villainy. I believe Marguerite also opened secret negotiations with one of London's most powerful riffler leaders.'

'Sarasin?'

'Yes, your Grace, Sarasin. Heaven knows how this was arranged. Countess Marguerite is a princess. I cannot see her traipsing through the London mud to some dingy tavern in Whitefriars or elsewhere. She probably used the d'Aunay brothers, whom I call the Squires of the Glove.'

'Wait!' Isabella exclaimed. 'Why do you call them that?'

'Because, your Grace, on one occasion when they approached me, each had an exquisitely designed glove on the table before them. One glove for Philippe and the other for Gautier.'

'Are you sure of that, Hugh?' Malfeson declared. 'Would you go on oath to describe what you saw?' The French clerk leant against the table staring fixedly at Corbett, then turned to the queen. 'More evidence, your Grace.'

'What is this?' Corbett exclaimed. 'Why are these gloves so important to you?'

Isabella stretched out and patted Malfeson on the arm.

'Tell him, Guillaume. Tell him what you know.'

'Sir Hugh,' Malfeson drew a deep breath, 'I am the Lady Isabella's most fervent royal retainer at the court of her father, King Philip. I watch out for her; I always have. However, I soon realised the princess was the object of great spite from her three sisters-in-law, Marguerite, Blanche and Jeanne – three princesses married to King Philip's sons, one of whom, our king constantly bragged, would produce a male heir to the

French throne. Everybody knows that, it's no great secret. Anyway, around midsummer last year, I was boating along the Seine. To keep matters succinct, I spied our three princesses arriving at the Tour de Nesle, an old watchtower built over the river. My glimpse only lasted a few heartbeats, yet I was certain of what I saw. I became very suspicious.'

'Why?'

'Well, Sir Hugh, I wondered why three princesses of the blood were visiting a derelict, desolate river tower? I decided to set up close watch. Nobody else was informed. Sure enough, I became aware that such visits were fairly frequent. More importantly, the princesses were joined by the two d'Aunay brothers.'

'And you suspect these meetings were part of an adulterous affair between the brothers and the princesses, all possible mothers of a future French king? In heaven's name,' Corbett exclaimed, 'Philip of France would tear them apart for such a crime.' He glanced at Isabella. 'Are you going to inform him? Will you make your own accusations?'

'Eventually I must,' Isabella replied. 'However, at this moment I do not have enough evidence against them. Continue, Guillaume.'

'I was very zealous in my watch,' Malfeson continued, 'but I made a mistake. On one occasion, I am sure – perhaps there was even a second one – Marguerite of Burgundy glimpsed me, a hurried glance when she noticed me as I did her. I tried hard to hide this error. Nevertheless, I continued to watch. I quickly realised that Marguerite and her two accomplices were deeply infatuated with the d'Aunay brothers. I have studied all three princesses, Sir Hugh. Marguerite is supremely arrogant. She would never acknowledge any mistake or weakness in her behaviour. Nevertheless, she began to suspect that Queen Isabella of England knew a lot more about her than she should.'

'Marguerite did not decide to come to London,' Isabella intervened. 'I invited her in order to watch her as well as those two knights of her household.'

'My mistress,' Malfeson added, 'believed we might learn more during such a visit.'

'Instead,' Corbett replied, 'Marguerite decided to use the visit to wreak revenge on a woman she hated. She also wanted to silence you, your Grace, and what you might suspect.'

'Precisely, Sir Hugh. I watched closely, as did Malfeson, but so far, the only mistake they've made involves those gloves. Describe them, Hugh.'

Corbett did so, and Isabella clapped her hands like a child.

'Yes, yes, they are the ones I gave Marguerite. She in turn gave one glove as a token of her affection to each of her paramours, a courtly custom in Paris between a mistress and her knight. Marguerite and her two arrogant lovers have made a dreadful mistake. I am, as yet, not fully certain that she is an adulteress along with my two other sisters-in-law. Nonetheless, I must confront the harsh reality that all three threaten the legitimacy of succession to the French throne. If one of them did become pregnant, what proof would we have that such a child belonged to one of my brothers and was not the by-blow of one of the d'Aunays? All three princesses are ruining their chances of ever becoming a mother to the next French king. They are also bringing my father's court and crown into hideous disrepute. I doubt very much,' Isabella continued, 'whether our two pride-puffed knights informed Marguerite of what you have just told me. They were just showing off, proof that they were being adorned with the favour of a future queen.'

'True,' Malfeson agreed. 'And while they were displaying their trophy, Marguerite was planning to silence you, my queen.'

'Continue, Hugh.'

Corbett rubbed his face. 'It's so difficult,' he confessed, 'to believe what you have just told me.'

'We would have done so eventually,' Malfeson replied. 'But we had to wait for your conclusions, which again are accurate.'

'Such a stupid mistake,' Corbett murmured. 'Those gloves were on the table in front of them, and when I commented on them, they snatched them away and hid them beneath their cloaks.'

'Come.' Isabella leant forward and patted the back of Corbett's hand. 'Let us hear your conclusions in full.'

'Marguerite searched out Sarasin and told him what she wanted,' Corbett continued. 'Our dearest queen abducted and shipped to foreign parts, where God knows what might have happened. I suspect they would also have tried to snatch your son, though I have little evidence for such an allegation.' He paused as the queen filled his tankard with morning ale and poured small cups for herself and Malfeson. She lifted hers in toast.

'Sir Hugh, we listen.'

'Sarasin must have been offered a fortune. Greedy, eager to be wealthy, he cultivated your squire Rahmel. We all know what happened then. Rahmel was murdered by Sarasin, who paid for his crime on the scaffold.' Corbett cleared his throat. 'For a few days after the riffler's execution, all was quiet and peaceful at the Twilight, until the emergence of a true killer, an assassin to his very marrow.' He turned and beckoned to Ranulf and Ap Ythel. 'Bring up the prisoner.'

PART SEVEN

He fears the stratagems of certain persons.

The two men left the room. The chamber lay still and silent, the only noise being the crackling fire. At last footsteps echoed along the corridor, along with the sound of a walking cane scraping the ground. Three men entered the chamber. Brother Ricard, hobbling on his walking cane, was escorted by Ap Ythel and Ranulf.

Corbett got to his feet, bowed towards the queen and strode towards the prisoner. Pushing the Black Robe back, he kicked the walking stick from Ricard's hand. He kicked it again, ignoring the exclamations of the others, until it lay well beyond the monk's reach.

'What is this?' Ricard rasped.

'Oh yes, what is this?' Corbett echoed, turning to confront the Black Robe. 'Ap Ythel, Ranulf, search him.'

The two men, helped by Malfeson, dragged the Benedictine forward. They pulled off his robe to expose a long woollen shirt as well as a wicked-looking dagger, needle thin but sharp and serrated on both sides. Corbett drew it from its sheath strapped against Ricard's right wrist, and held it up for all to see, turning it so it caught the light.

'See!' he exclaimed. 'Ostensibly a man of God, but one ready for war or murder!'

He ordered Ricard to be searched again, but no other weapon was found. Corbett took a cresset torch from its sconce and handed this to Ap Ythel as he pointed at the Black Robe's thickly bandaged left knee. 'That is also a pretence, a lie,' he declared in a ringing voice.

'I was injured on the—'

Corbett snapped his fingers at Ap Ythel. 'Burn his leg.'

The captain of archers pushed the torch against the bandaged knee while Ranulf and Malfeson held the monk fast.

'Very well, very well,' Ricard gasped. 'It is good,' he sighed noisily, 'no injury.'

'Next question,' Corbett declared. 'You are Sarasin's brother?'

'No.'

'Burn him again,' Corbett ordered.

Ap Ythel made to do so, and again Ricard gasped his protest.

'Not brother,' he yelled. 'But half-brother. The same father, but different mothers.' The monk shook his head. 'There's no crime in that.'

'Very well,' Corbett retorted, 'and you were a moving spirit, albeit a very well-concealed one, in Puddlicott's raid on the Crown Jewels here in Westminster some ten years ago?'

The Black Robe simply stood shaking his head. Corbett ordered him to be taken to a chair at the end of the table, where he would be tightly bound.

'Back to my indictment,' Corbett declared. 'You were a high-ranking member of Puddlicott's gang along with your half-brother who had taken the name Sarasin. Correct?' He shrugged. 'For all I know you may have been the true leader of that gang. After all, that is what has now emerged. You are the self-proclaimed Immortal and the leader of the rifflers. Sarasin was your principal henchman.'

'I object.' The Black Robe beat the table with his bound wrists. 'I claim benefit of clergy. I am a priest, a monk . . .'

'*Cucullus non facit monachum*,' Corbett retorted. 'The cowl doesn't make the monk. A piece of profound wisdom I will return to by and by.'

'I object,' Ricard bellowed. 'I *am* a monk.'

'I don't care if you are the Bishop of Rome,' Isabella interrupted. 'You will truthfully answer Sir Hugh's questions here and now. If not, I will order you to be taken down to a dungeon, where your screams will never be heard nor your claims and protestations listened to.' She laughed. 'After that, I will make sure that what is left of you is handed over to a church court. What is it to be, you spawn of the devil? Which path do you wish to take? You are going to die. All you have left to decide is how that will be arranged.'

Corbett hid his surprise at the vehemence in Isabella's voice, harsh and merciless. He smiled to himself. She truly was her father's daughter. Clear proof that the apple did not fall far from the tree.

'Well?' the queen demanded.

Ricard just sat, head down.

'Very well,' Isabella declared. 'Captain Ap Ythel—'

'I will answer your questions,' Ricard sneered. 'Saving my rights and those of Holy Mother Church.'

'You have no rights,' Isabella retorted. 'Either as a priest or as a man. You plotted my destruction and you will pay the price for that. Captain Ap Ythel, tie a cord tight around this demon's throat. Fashion a noose with a small rod piercing the knot. Every time I believe he is lying, tighten that knot. If he tells the truth, of course that is a different matter. We have plenty of time.'

She fell silent as Ap Ythel carried out her order, slapping Ricard hard as the monk tried to turn in protest. Corbett just sat and watched. He felt no sympathy for this Black Robe, a true son of Cain. He recalled Rachel and Rebekah, two loving, innocent souls; poor Magpie the hangman; and those archers being tossed into the freezing North Sea. No, he reckoned, the dead were clustering close. God's justice and that of the king had caught up with this most evil malefactor.

Ap Ythel finished tightening the knot, then turned and bowed towards the queen.

'Very well,' Corbett continued. 'Some of Puddlicott's gang were caught and dispatched into the dark. Others escaped. Sarasin fled abroad. He joined the king's array and fought in several battles. He would have enjoyed that. Sarasin loved killing. Anyway, he received a pardon and came back to London like a dog returned to its vomit. You, however, remained undetected. Not even a whisper against you.'

'That's because I was – I am – totally innocent.'

'Captain Ap Ythel,' Isabella shouted. The captain of archers paused as Corbett raised a hand.

'Let that go, your Grace, it is of little import.'

Ap Ythel glanced at the queen, who nodded as a sign that she agreed with Corbett.

'You certainly played the part of an innocent,' Corbett continued. 'You successfully escaped my scrutiny. Anyway, once Puddlicott and his coven were gone, you planned for the future. You had probably already developed ties with the Twilight of great benefit to you. I suspect you persuaded your abbot, along with Malling and Appleby, to set up a small chantry chapel there. A most pleasing proposal, to minister to the host of travellers who journeyed through or passed that delightful tavern. Of course, your abbot agreed. Appleby has also told me how Malling always thought it was an excellent idea that would enhance the reputation of his hostelry. Oh yes,' Corbett paused to sip from his tankard, 'it was a truly clever ploy. You had a chamber in the Twilight. You could now listen and learn from all the chatter and gossip along the river as well as in the city. At the same time, you belonged to the Benedictines at their great abbey of Westminster. Again, a marvellous vantage point to hear all about the doings of the men of power.'

'Very clever!' Isabella declared.

'So we have it,' Corbett went on. 'Brother Ricard, the holy Benedictine, hobbling about with his old wound yet still caring for the traveller, a source of solace for the afflicted. In truth you were a prince among rifflers who moved like a shadow against the wall. People believed that Sarasin was the riffler leader, but the truth is that you, Brother Ricard, issued the orders.' He wetted his lips. 'You had tasted the merry joy of plundering the royal treasury and stealing the Crown Jewels. You rejoiced in what you had achieved.'

'All brought to nothing,' Ranulf spoke up, 'because of my master. Many of your accomplices ended up dangling at the end of a rope on one of London's gibbets. You must have raged at the turn of events. You nourished and sustained a deep hatred for the Crown and its principal clerk, Sir Hugh Corbett.'

'I plead benefit of clergy,' Ricard repeated. 'In accordance with canon law as well as statutes published by Parliament, I demand to be handed over to my lord abbot for trial. I do not recognise this investigation.'

'Remember what I said,' Isabella retorted. 'Answer here or you will answer somewhere else.'

The Black Robe made no reply.

'You developed a passionate hatred,' Corbett continued, 'as my colleague has said. Brother Ricard, the gentle, loving Benedictine, hobbling between the Twilight and Westminster. In truth, you had clear oversight of the city, the river, the abbey, the court and of course Parliament. I suspect the rifflers' robberies and other crimes were all carried out under your close gaze. Then there was a change.' He paused. 'We can speak clearly here. The change was caused by Marguerite, Countess of Burgundy, who emerged from the shadows. She did business with Sarasin, but in truth, of course, she was negotiating with you. The countess wanted our queen abducted. I can only speculate on the why and the wherefore, but in truth, all Marguerite wanted was our royal princess removed. She offered, I suspect, a fortune that could not be ignored. At the same time, she provided a marvellous opportunity for you to wreak revenge on the English Crown for the destruction of Puddlicott and his coven. You directed Sarasin, who cultivated a friendship with Louis Rahmel, a squire of the Queen's household. He would provide details of both the time and place for a possible abduction.'

'Poor Rahmel.' Isabella spoke up as Corbett took a sip from his tankard.

'I suspect,' Corbett continued, 'that Rahmel visited the Twilight on the day of his death to see Malling's daughters. Now, we shall never really know what happened between Sarasin and our noble squire. However, Louis was no traitor. He must have become alarmed at Sarasin's questions and, above all, at what the riffler chieftain wanted. He resisted; there was a quarrel. Rahmel was murdered and Sarasin was executed. If I recall the events of that day, you, Brother Ricard, kept well out of the light. However, I am sure you watched and listened from the shadows and did what you could without raising suspicion. Your claim that Rahmel, as he lay dying, warned how Monseigneur Malfeson should not be trusted by the queen, was just an opportunity you seized, wasn't it, monk? A lie to muddy the waters. Sheer nonsense, nothing more than stirring the shit for the sake of the stink.'

'I am a cleric, a priest, a monk—'

'Ap Ythel!' Isabella shouted.

The captain of archers came swiftly up behind the prisoner and began to tighten the noose clasped around his throat. Ricard fought back, gagging and choking, until eventually he gasped, '*Concedo, concedo*. I concede.'

Ap Ythel looked at the queen. She nodded, and the noose was slackened. For a while there was silence, broken only by Ricard gasping and coughing. Corbett asked Ap Ythel to give the Black Robe a sip of some ale, then he returned to the attack.

'As I have said, during Sarasin's trial and execution, you kept deep in the shadows. You were a presence, but no more than any other spectator in that tavern.'

'I offered to shrive Sarasin,' the monk retorted. 'He refused.' He paused to cough. 'If,' he continued, 'Sarasin and I were such close allies, the mercy pew would have been an ideal place to whisper to each other.'

'No, no,' Corbett replied, 'that would have been too dangerous. Sarasin recognised that he was well and truly trapped. There was no way out, so why risk betraying his brother? In the end, however, the two of you did communicate, didn't you?'

'How?' Ricard spluttered.

'Sarasin was issuing threats to all those involved in his

imminent demise. He warned his captors about retribution, vengeance for his death. You are that retribution; you are that vengeance! You would ensure that your half-brother could strike from beyond the grave. Sarasin was confident about that. Two brothers, two killers. In the threats he issued at the Twilight, he was sowing the seeds of further murder and mayhem.'

Ricard just shook his head, not deigning to answer. He slumped down in his chair, lips moving soundlessly.

Corbett continued. 'And you certainly did exact a most hideous vengeance on all those involved in Sarasin's trial and execution, or at least those who had played a significant part. You abducted Manning's two daughters, threatening their father that he remain silent or worse would happen. In the end, it didn't matter. You sent that poor taverner the ring finger of each of his daughters. At the same time, you seized Magpie the executioner. All three, the two young ladies and the hangman, were drowned at Broken Wharf. Oh, by the way, you made a dreadful mistake on the morning their corpses were recovered.'

'What mistake?'

'You apparently knew that Broken Wharf was where they were murdered. Remember? But the only people who knew about the three deaths were myself, Ranulf and Ap Ythel's archers. I made careful examination and nobody else was informed. So how did you know?'

'Malling told me.'

Corbett laughed and shook his head. 'Clever, clever,' he murmured. 'Malling, of course, is no longer with us, though his spirit is. It watches, as do the others of those murdered at the Twilight. The death and destruction you meted out there was very easy to accomplish. You could move undetected, unchallenged around that tavern under the guise of the concerned, anxious priest: the man of God who hobbled about tutting under his breath, decrying the wickedness of the world. I do wonder if you had an accomplice.'

'An accomplice in what, Corbett?' The prisoner drew a deep breath. 'I am not—'

'You are a vicious killer and a true shape-shifter. You could enter a chamber as a Black Robe and abruptly pass into another persona, an assassin, black of heart and black of soul. You certainly did when you threatened Swinton and Poulter, yes?'

'Let me hear your allegation,' Ricard declared. 'Your indictment. Above all, show me your proof.'

'Oh, certainly. Both men were terrified, weren't they? Somehow you, in the guise of the Immortal, dispatched a chilling warning to them that you were on the hunt. True, I never saw such a warning; I have no tangible evidence for what I have just said.'

'Then remember that,' Ricard snarled. 'I certainly shall.'

'You sent similar threats to Malling. You not only abducted his two daughters, but terrified him and them. As he grew more fearful, he chattered about someone called the Immortal. I just wonder how you tipped him into the madness that turned him into a killer. A man, a father, bent on bloody revenge. But not on you, of course. You were the compassionate priest, but then, like Satan, you stopped being an angel of the light and became what you truly are: a man of blood.'

Corbett lapsed into silence, which grew deeper and more ominous. 'Oh yes,' he murmured, 'you certainly tipped poor Malling's wits. Using the abduction and abuse of his daughters to make that final wrench that shattered his soul. He became obsessed with the idea of revenge. Of course, you would whisper like Satan in his ear that the French clerks, both Rahmel and Malfeson, were the root cause of all that had happened. Poulter and Swinton were also easy to turn. As I said, some silent but deadly threat sent them scuttling to hide in their chambers at the Twilight. Like a hunting wolf you penned them in while at the same time pretending to be the caring, ever so solicitous monk; the dutiful priest. You played that role when you knocked on Swinton's door. He pulled back that eye hatch, never realising that you had already rested the small hand-held arbalest in such a way that the barb you released sped between the bars,' Corbett clapped his hands, 'straight into Swinton's face. The poor man staggered back, dead before he even hit the ground.'

'Clever,' Ranulf exclaimed, 'so very clever.'

'Poulter was next,' Corbett declared. 'You knocked on his door. Of course, he would know it was you, with your caring voice and the tap-tap of your cane on the floor. He opened that door and let in the wolf. What did you do then, Brother Wolf?' Ricard just glared down the table, breathing intensely, chest heaving as he was confronted with his crimes. 'I cannot say exactly how you terrified Poulter. Perhaps, once you were inside his chamber you revealed who you really were. The shock killed him, a mortal blow to the heart. He probably found it impossible to believe what he was seeing, what he was hearing. The venerable monk was in fact a vicious killer who had come to murder him. That would unsettle the wits of any man.

'Poulter of course was overweight, big bellied and fat. He just collapsed to the floor. You must have felt satisfied, Master Wolf, that you could kill in such a way. You also wanted to create a mystery. You took the chamber key, locked the door from the outside, then slipped the key back underneath it, deepening the uncertainty surrounding Poulter's death. You're a pick-lock, aren't you? A skill you used in your last attempt to murder me with those caltrops. Another mysterious visitation. Oh yes, you made it appear that the Immortal was a real, terrifying presence carrying out judgement against all those involved in your half-brother's execution.'

Corbett stared down at his indictment sheet before continuing. 'You gave matters another twist. By assuming the title of the Immortal, you could be hinting that you were in fact Sarasin, who had defied death. Of course, Sarasin was truly dead, rotting in his grave, while you, the demon monk, continued to shift from one guise to another. You destroyed Swinton and Poulter. You were responsible for Malling's death and those of his two daughters, not to forget the Magpie. You also murdered my prisoner, one of those who attacked

Ranulf. He was injured and brought back to the Twilight. I made an error placing him in that outhouse without a guard close to his door. Ah well, that was my mistake. I thought he was grievously wounded, unable to escape and, indeed, more terrified of the Immortal than of me. Anyway, you gained entrance to that garden—'

'How?' Ricard's tone was loud and arrogant. 'You did not place a guard because there was only one entrance to the garden, and that was closely watched by Stigand.'

'Wrong, monk! There were in fact two entrances. One through the buttery, the other that you helped create.'

'That's nonsense!'

'Captain Ap Ythel,' Corbett called out.

'Yes, Sir Hugh?'

'I asked you to investigate the curtain wall around the Twilight, yes?'

'Yes, Sir Hugh.'

'Tell us what you found.'

'In the far corner of the garden, where the two walls meet, the stonework had crumbled slightly. Easy to manipulate.'

'And?'

'It had been used to create roughly hewn gaps for both hand and foot grips, making it an easy climb from either within or without.'

'A climb that a man like Ricard, never mind his counterfeit injury, would not find too difficult?'

'Certainly.'

'You climbed that wall.' Corbett pointed at the prisoner. 'You entered that garden as the dreaded Immortal, then changed your guise to talk to the wounded, vulnerable prisoner. You offered to help and, to show who you were, you slipped a tau cross beneath the door. The prisoner was persuaded to open the door, and you took his head. You made one mistake. You forgot the cross. I have it here in my wallet. Your chambers at both the Twilight and the abbey will be searched. I am certain we will find similar crosses, yes?'

Ricard just shook his head.

'One thing I can say about you, demon monk,' Corbett continued, 'is you know how to hate. You were determined to avenge your half-brother's death, but you also wanted revenge on the Crown. It is, I believe, no coincidence that you plotted to steal that treasure chest from *The War-dog*, a casket that contained many of the treasures Puddlicott had filched. A studied and malicious insult against the Crown. I believe you and your half-brother plotted to take that for yourselves, with, perhaps, some payment to the Flemish and Frisians who provided help and support. We now know what truly happened. I suspect you played a crucial role in getting your own navigator onto that battle-boat, though as yet I don't know the details. I still need to question someone else. I believe your man simply presented himself as a skilled gubernator, and Ensign Malachi accepted him for what he claimed to be. *The War-dog* cast off. The navigator played his duplicitous game, and the battle-boat and its crew were hoisted onto *The Basilisk* and taken down river to *The Hirondelle*.'

'They are all dead, priest,' Ap Ythel shouted. 'Good

men and true, with families and loved ones they will never see again. Your doing—'

'Oh yes,' Corbett interrupted, 'you are responsible for so many deaths. You truly are a son of Cain, an evil killer to the very marrow of your soul. No one is safe from you, a ravenous wolf. If someone crosses you, they have to die. You slaughtered poor Madcap because he saw *The Basilisk* take *The War-dog* aboard: to his crazed mind, that was a great dragon swallowing its prey. You also killed the navigator who guided *The War-dog* to its doom. You slit his throat lest he prattle in some tavern or alehouse.'

'You are a liar.' Isabella's voice was strident with anger. 'You live the lie and you practise the lie. You pretend to be good and virtuous, but in fact you have a sewer for a soul.'

'Where is this leading?' Ricard exclaimed. 'I am a priest. I plead benefit of clergy. I demand to be tried in a church court. Above all, I want to see your proof for all this nonsense.'

'If you were tried in a church court,' Corbett retorted, 'this would be the indictment that would be levelled against you. But in a court, any court, you would be trapped, because, as her Grace has just said, you are a liar born and bred. You kill the truth.'

'You forget, Sir Hugh, how I saved your life when Walter Mappe attacked you in my chapel.'

'Ah yes, very subtle. Very subtle indeed. Most worthy of a fox like yourself. So, let us talk about Walter Mappe. He was a Judas man during the Puddlicott business. He turned king's approver against a number of those who broke into the royal treasury. He then fled, but returned claiming his innocence and wishing to be accepted by you. Of course, he never was, was he? Once a traitor, always a traitor. You had no love or regard for him. In your eyes, he was a thorough-going nuisance who deserved to be punished. At the same time, you had your grievance against me. I suspect you presented him with a way of regaining favour with yourself and your henchmen. And what was that way? Well, it was killing me.

'Now, I was preparing for mass in the tavern chapel when he attacked. You apparently heard a disturbance and came slithering in with your great clubbed walking stick. There were chairs, benches; these would have slowed Walter up, but not you. You literally smashed his brains in. Now,' Corbett spread his hands, 'I did wonder about how such a miscreant was able to enter the tavern – a place completely unfamiliar to him – find the chapel, enter the sacred place and wait to carry out his ambuscade on me. I mean, you noticed nothing amiss? Oh yes, Walter Mappe may well have wanted to take my life as proof of his loyalty to the Immortal, as well as reparation for past treacheries. You, however, were determined to punish a traitor, a proditor who had helped bring down Puddlicott and his ilk. Very cunning. Walter Mappe gets rid of me and you rid the world of Walter Mappe. Once you had done so, you would once again assume the mantle of the faithful monk.

'If Mappe had been successful, I am not sure what you

would have done. Probably still killed him, though too late to save my life. On the other hand, by openly saving me from him, you demonstrated your innocence as well as your support for the Crown. A monk who defends a king's man working hard to resolve the murders at the Twilight. The hero who, despite his walking cane, can still fight on the side of the angels.' Corbett waved a hand. 'You know how the song goes. Of course, the truth is different. You are as guilty as Judas in your festering malice towards me and mine.' He picked up a sheet of vellum and stared down at what was written there.

'And the Brethren?' Ranulf demanded. 'You hired them, didn't you? Listening to Sir Hugh, I now recall that I did not see you do anything during that assault. Oh, when it was all over, you came into the taproom full of concern. You declared how you had blessed the dead, worried about who had been killed and so on and so on. But in truth, you did nothing.'

'I agree.' Corbett nodded. 'The Brethren had been hired by the Immortal. They'd certainly have been informed about who should die. Mention could have been made not to touch the Black Robe, an individual highly protected by both Crown and Church. Someone special, as our prisoner keeps reminding us. Anyway, just in case a mistake was made, you probably barred and bolted yourself in your chamber. Eventually you could emerge shaken, but still brave, peddling some story that would enhance you and everything about you.'

'What proof? What real evidence for what you

allege?' Ricard strained against the ropes. 'Where are the documents? Where are the witnesses?' He paused, breathing in deeply. 'I have sat here and listened to all the charges—'

'Not all the charges, monk. There are more.'

'I suspect,' Ricard swallowed hard, 'they will be the same empty words with no real substance. True or false?' he mocked. 'Where is all this evidence? Let it be shown.'

Ranulf made to reply, but Corbett gestured at him not to. He then sat staring at the accused, while the silence in the room deepened. Eventually he pushed away his chair and stood watching the pools of light dance around the table.

'Listen,' he intoned like a preacher beginning his homily, 'listen now, false priest, false monk, false soul, false everything. The dead do gather. They seek justice, and so we come to accept the truth, that they really do speak to the living. In this case, poor Rachel Malling, who, though dead, bears powerful testimony against you. You abducted that girl from God knows where. How you did that is clouded in mystery. I still need to question someone else. Anyway, killer that you are, you also abducted her sister Rebekah, as well as the hangman Magpie. You had all three drowned at Broken Wharf, a ghastly, cruel death. However, when I searched Rachel's corpse, I discovered in the lining of her skirt a thin, pipe-like roll of rough parchment. Its very coarseness probably accounts for why it survived the river water. It had two ill-formed words scrawled on it. They looked as if they had been written in a great hurry. In doing so, Rachel had got the word *cucullus* mixed up with *calculus*, a Latin term in mathematics. The two words are similar, and she was in a desperate hurry to write her message.'

'Which was?' Ricard demanded.

'I am sure,' Corbett replied, 'Black Robe that you are, you would recognise the Latin tag I quoted earlier: *Cucullus non facit monachum* – the cowl doesn't make the monk. It is certainly proved by you, Ricard.'

'This is a farrago of lies,' the Benedictine retorted. 'Pure nonsense, scraps of information. The scribblings of an ill-educated tavern wench who certainly had no time for me or me for her.'

Turning to the queen, he strained against his bonds. 'Your Grace, I beg you. Am I to be condemned by such paltry, ill-formed allegations, which your husband's justiciars would dismiss in a matter of heartbeats?'

The queen looked at Corbett, who sat slouched, watching Ricard intently. 'Sir Hugh?'

'Yes, quite so, quite so.' Corbett pulled himself up on the chair. 'So let me begin at the beginning again. I am going to repeat myself because I want to emphasise what will send you to the scaffold. I have given you a foretaste, and the defence you offer is paltry. Those two young women, their courage and bravery, will see you hang.

'So, you, who arrogantly describe yourself as the Immortal, organised the abduction of Rachel and Rebekah from the Twilight. Your ruffians entered this tavern, mingling with other customers. Somehow or other they lured both young women back to their respective chambers, where they were threatened against any resistance. If one of them did offer opposition, it would mean the immediate execution of the other, not to mention their father. Now I believe they must have been confined in the tavern; that was the last place where Rachel would have had the opportunity of writing anything. I doubt very much whether their prison at Broken Wharf was furnished with any comforts, let alone a chancery tray. No, Rachel, locked up in her chamber, decided to leave a message written in Latin, which, if her illiterate captors glimpsed it, would mean nothing at all to them. You see, she had somehow made the most remarkable discovery: in a word, that you, Brother Ricard, were not what you claimed to be. I admit, your Grace, I have no proof for this, but remember, Rachel lived in that tavern. She would also have seen Rahmel and Sarasin meet and talk. Did our now sadly departed French clerk help her to reach that conclusion about the Black Robe residing there? Or was it just something that occurred during her abduction and that of her sister? I cannot say.'

'All of this is dependent on a stupid tavern wench. Do you believe her accusation?'

'No, no, listen, Black Robe. Rachel does not accuse you of being the Immortal or anyone else. She is simply alleging that you are not what you claim to be. A good starting point for justiciars such as myself. Oh yes, even though abducted and imprisoned, probably frightened to death, she remained calm and confident.

She began to write out that Latin tag while confined to her chamber. However, she did not get the opportunity to finish it. Her abductors, quietly threatening both her and her sister, took the two young women out of the tavern, ostensibly to travel to Faversham. In truth they were going to their deaths. They had to pay for laying evidence against Sarasin.'

'Oh, your Grace,' Ricard yelled. 'What is this? Nothing more than a half-finished Latin tag by a tavern slut who could barely write her own name.'

'Sir Hugh?'

Corbett caught the anxiety in the queen's voice. 'Your Grace,' he replied, 'I have not yet finished. Rachel began to write her message, but in fact she was copying what she had already written in her horn book.' He stared at Ricard, who now sat mouth gaping. 'Oh yes,' Corbett continued, 'Rachel was going to try to leave messages wherever she could. I went into her chamber and found her horn book peeking from beneath a coverlet. I opened it and read the last entry, which goes as follows.' He spread his hands as if he was a choir master waiting to bring a chant to its fullness. '*Cucullus non facit monachum et frater Ricard demonstrandum hujus veritatem* – doggerel Latin, but its message is very clear: "The cowl does not make the monk and Brother Ricard demonstrates the truth of this." There it is, Brother Ricard! Scribbled by that young woman as she was detained in her chamber waiting for her fate. She had the truth of it. She balanced her accusation carefully, but that makes it all the more convincing and compelling.'

Corbett took a sip from his tankard. 'Let us continue. You talk of proof, evidence against you, but in fact you have produced all the evidence we need.'

'Nonsense,' Ricard gasped. 'More nonsense. If this was a legitimate investigation—'

'It certainly is,' Corbett snapped. 'You, sir, were involved in a conspiracy. You were hired by a person we both know. In short, this conspiracy was part of a plot to seize and abduct our gracious queen. Yesterday evening, the Flemings left their war cog. They, together with their riffler allies, invaded the Twilight, determined to abduct Queen Isabella. In truth, they walked into a trap; a snare to capture the most cunning Immortal. The persons who actually processed into the taproom of the Twilight did not include her Grace the queen but a member of my household, namely Megotta the Moon-girl. This talented young woman can, in the blink of an eye, adopt the guise of a princess of the blood or the most foul-mouthed denizen of the slums.'

Corbett paused to take another drink. He then rose and walked towards the prisoner, wagging a finger in the Benedictine's face. 'Now I can enlighten you as to the trap I created. You see, I had informed everyone that Edward our king was to visit the Twilight. He was the person to be expected. However, I then changed my plan but informed only one person that the visitors would be the queen and her ladies. That person was you, false priest. Oh, I wrapped the changed plan in some pleasing, convincing manner that demonstrated how much I trusted you. In fact, this was a completely topsy-turvy world. You had no choice but to maintain a dignified silence about what I had secretly told you. At the same time, I was providing you with the means to bring your foul conspiracy to a most satisfactory conclusion. In fact, I was like a physician bringing a hideous abscess to a head.'

'All lies,' Ricard shouted. 'The change of plan became common knowledge along the quayside.'

'It did not. Your plot failed. If you had been successful, who knows what confusion would have swept both Crown and kingdom. Yes, monk?'

'Others knew,' Ricard insisted, shaking his head. 'Others knew.'

'True,' Corbett conceded. 'Two others did know. Edward the king and Queen Isabella. Only they knew the trap I was creating, and I swore both to silence on it.'

'My husband certainly approved.' Isabella spoke up. 'Even though he laughed at what was being proposed for Megotta and Ap Ythel's archers.'

'I dispatched Megotta and the archers to Westminster,' Corbett continued. 'Only then were they informed what would really happen. Their Graces acted as if they were preparing to leave Queenhithe. The change came at the very last moment, swift and silent. Oh yes, Megotta was surprised, as were the archers, but speed was insisted upon. Once they were ready, Megotta and her escort, suitably disguised, climbed into the royal barge. The king and his wife just as quickly retreated into the royal apartments to await the outcome.'

Corbett paused. 'Now listen carefully, monk. Megotta

and all her pretence left Westminster by barge. A short while later, Admiral Kynaston and a cohort of royal troops, all arraigned for battle, saw the enemy leave *The Basilisk*. He followed Megotta's barge across the Thames, pausing to board *The Basilisk*, which had, of course, been totally depleted of defenders. The crew who remained were given a stark choice. Surrender or be annihilated. They very quickly chose to surrender. *The Hirondelle* was no problem: a small vessel, bereft of protection, with two great English war cogs closing in. So taking both ships was easy enough.

'While others looked after *The Basilisk*, Kynaston led the rest of his force across the Thames to Queenhithe and closed the trap. He ringed the Twilight with a circle of steel that controlled all lanes, paths and trackways leading to and from the tavern.' Corbett rose and walked the full length of the table before returning to his own chair. 'Their Graces,' he continued, 'were safely and closely guarded at Westminster, while their enemy was well and truly trapped in the Twilight. There was no countryside to flee through or forest to hide in. No barge to take them away. What they had thought was a trap for our king and queen suddenly became the cause of their own downfall and capture. You must have discovered what was happening, so you assumed the role of a concerned Benedictine. Nevertheless, you'd witnessed the trap being sprung, the snare tightening on all sides, so you fled.' He cleared his throat. 'Captain Ap Ythel,' he called out, 'where did you find our prisoner?'

'As you said we would, Sir Hugh, in the enclave

behind the high altar in the abbey church. He claimed he was in sanctuary.'

'On what grounds?'

'Sir Hugh, he prattled a stream of nonsense, but he claimed that serious disturbances at the Twilight had put him in mortal fear of death. How he didn't truly know what was happening except that the place had been invaded by foreign soldiers. These in turn had been confronted by royal troops. He declared he was anxious not to be caught up in such a frenetic disturbance.'

'Good Lord.' Corbett pointed at Ricard. 'You had the impudence to seek sanctuary.'

'Yes, I did,' Ricard bellowed back. 'I am a monk of the Benedictine order, an ordained priest. I invoked my right of sanctuary and this was violated.'

'Ah,' Ranulf retorted, 'further proof of your guilt. Why take sanctuary? Why hide from Sir Hugh? Never mind the nonsense you told Ap Ythel. In truth, you were acknowledging your sinful ways even before they were exposed.'

'I was dragged out of sanctuary.'

'You are a criminal,' Isabella declared. 'You are now arrested, indicted and ready for judgement. Sir Hugh, I would like to thank your three henchmen for their work in trapping this hideous creature, a true horror of hell.'

Corbett glanced along the table. Ricard now sat head down, muttering to himself in a childish prattle. Corbett walked across to the buttery table and poured himself a goblet of wine. He offered the same to the queen, but she just shook her head and continued whispering to Ap Ythel, Malfeson and Ranulf, who knelt before her. Corbett placed his own goblet down and crossed to open the door. However, apart from Chanson and some of Ap Ythel's henchmen, the gallery lay empty and dark. He closed the door. Isabella asked him to stay for a while, gesturing at his three companions to remain. She finished her whispering, then gave each of them a purse. Then she sat back in her chair, drawing herself up.

'We are finished here,' she declared. 'And I am finished with that false priest. You may go.'

All three men rose, taking the prisoner and slipping out into the night. Once they were gone, Isabella beckoned Corbett to sit and pull his chair as close as possible to her.

'This is not finished. Not really, Sir Hugh.' She paused as an owl nesting in the ancient oak outside the chamber began its mournful lament to the night. 'Strange,' she murmured, 'my mother, Joanne of Navarre, maintained that when you hear the owl's hymn to the dark, something highly unpleasant is being fashioned close by. Do you think that's true, Hugh?'

'You know it is, your Grace. We have just discovered the true source of the malicious mystery that confronted you and all those devoted to you.' He lowered his voice to just above a whisper. 'Marguerite, Countess of Burgundy, is the root cause of this evil. We can only speculate on why. Perhaps a deep-felt jealousy of your Grace, of who you are and what you do. Or is it a profound fear that none of your brothers will produce a healthy male child to succeed your father? Yes,' he continued, 'she and your other two sisters-in-law may be terrified at the prospects collapsing around them. Your brothers Louis, Philip and Charles are married to three high-born ladies who have not produced a son. Time is passing. Opportunities are dying. You, your Grace, are what they would desperately like to be.'

'Marguerite does not help herself.' Isabella picked up a perfumed cloth from a tray to dab her brow and cheeks. 'Then there are the Squires of the Glove and what they signify.'

'Yes, your Grace, one more malignant root to turn the situation into a fully blossomed horror. In heaven's name,' Corbett breathed, 'three princesses of the blood. Three women who could be the mother of the next French king entertaining pompous squires in some dirty, derelict tower overlooking the Seine. When your father discovers their sin, and he certainly will, he will be beside himself with rage. The Squires of the Glove will be torn apart on some scaffold. Your sisters-in-law could well suffer the same fate, or at least be immured in some desolate convent for the rest of their lives. Such a root has to be dug out so that nothing remains of this poisonous flower, be it branch, twig, fruit or leaf.'

'True,' Isabella whispered. 'For a short while I shall stay clear of it, though I shall be watching most closely. My sisters-in-law will eventually make a mistake. My father always believes in not hanging certain people because they do such a good job themselves. Time will pass and, at the right moment, in the right place, I shall, with the help of Malfeson, close the trap.'

Corbett nodded as he sat back in his chair. Somewhere deep in the palace a bell tolled. A door opened, then slammed shut.

'And the Templars, your Grace? You do recognise that there will be hideous consequences for what has been inflicted upon them. In my view they are more sinned against than sinned. They simply took the wrong path: their vision became blurred, but they were good men, totally innocent of the hateful allegations levelled against them.' Corbett spoke carefully, measuring his words. He had decided not to tell anyone else about Cartaphilus. He had said enough without complicating matters further. He was sure he didn't have to convince Isabella about the real damage her father had done.

'Hugh,' Isabella crossed herself, 'I know what you are saying. I agree with you. I have informed my beloved father of such, but he is iron willed on that issue. Jacques de Molay and other Templar leaders will end up being burnt alive on some island in the Seine. The fate of the Templars truly frightens me. One of the reasons my father dissolved the order and confiscated their wealth was because of the huge dowry I was to bring to my marriage to my dear husband Edward. A dowry,' she added bitterly, 'soaked in blood.' She then smiled wanly. 'But let it be, let it be.'

'And Brother Ricard?'

'You mean Brother Snake.' Isabella shrugged. 'Your three henchmen, Ap Ythel in particular, have their orders.'

Corbett turned and stared across at the shuttered lancet window. Outside, the darkness was deepening.

'A haunt of ghosts' was how he had once described the palace and abbey of Westminster. The hosting place of a legion of spirits. The souls of men and women who'd died there, killed or executed, watched and waited. He knew that another such ghost would be joining that host, to hang between heaven and earth till all sins were purged.

The purging had already begun in the cellars beneath the palace. A labyrinth of narrow, twisting galleries that snaked past cells and dungeons. Ap Ythel and his two companions had opened one of these. They had lit torches, fastening them into the sconces or thrusting them into gaps between the brickwork. The fluttering flames illuminated the macabre preparations for Ricard's death. Ap Ythel had found a stool and placed this in the centre of the cell. He had looped one end of a coarse rope around a ceiling beam, while the other end formed a noose, which he had placed over Ricard's head. The prisoner, hands now tied firmly behind his back, tottered on the stool, gasping and moaning. Ranulf and Malfeson had helped with proceedings and now stood in the doorway, studying their handiwork. At last, everything was ready. Ap Ythel approached the condemned man, staring up into his face.

'It won't be swift,' he declared in his echoing sing-song voice. 'I remember Malachi and his men tossed naked into the sea. Oh no, priest, it will not be a swift death. Now listen. Her Grace gave me one message for you, and it's this. Go down to hell, and when you do, tell the Lord Satan that she sent you there.'

'Please.' Ricard gasped and gagged as he rocked on the stool. 'I can give you wealth, money and good coin, both silver and gold.'

'You mean the profits of your wicked ways?'

'For a swift and easy death.' The prisoner's voice had risen to a scream. 'Gold and silver,' he rasped.

Ranulf shouted at him to stay silent. The prisoner yelled back, and Ranulf, in a fit of temper, kicked the stool away. Ricard was left doing a frenetic dance in the air as he fought to get back on the stool, anything to relieve the noose tightening slowly around his throat. The sound of his death struggle created a macabre scene, as he gasped and gargled, legs flailing, making the shadows dance even more. Abruptly Ap Ythel darted forward, dagger out. He slashed the hanging rope and Ricard collapsed in a heap onto the ground. Ignoring the shouts of his companions, the captain of archers loosened the noose so the prisoner could cough and splutter as he strained to breathe freely.

'Why?' Malfeson demanded.

Ranulf walked towards Ap Ythel and placed a hand on his shoulder. 'Malfeson asked a question. Why, my friend?'

'Listen,' Ap Ythel replied, 'if I had not cut him down, our villain would have been well on his way to hell by now.' He breathed in noisily. 'He is responsible for the callous murder of Malachi and six other good men, who left loved ones back in the valleys. Malachi and his cohort signed indentures for the Crown so that they could earn money to send back to their families. They cannot do that any more.'

'Ah, I see,' Ranulf replied. 'Our purged priest mentioned treasure.'

'I spoke the truth,' Ricard rasped from where he lay on the floor, hands still tied, face all bruised by the fall from the stool.

'If you are speaking the truth, it's the only time you have done so,' Corbett declared as he walked into the cell. 'Her Grace the queen intimated that God's justice and that of the king was being carried out close by.' He crouched beside Ricard, then glanced up at Ap Ythel. 'You cut him down, yes?'

'I did.' Ap Ythel squatted down on the other side of the prisoner. 'Listen.' He poked Ricard. 'What are you offering in exchange for a swift death?'

'I have treasures buried out in God's Acre here. Good leather panniers bulging with coin.'

Ap Ythel rose to his feet. 'As I informed my comrades, Sir Hugh, Malachi and his stalwarts have kin back in Wales; families desperately in need of money. We should use the wealth this priest has boasted about and send it to them. It will bring some comfort and relief to a host of mourning families. Quite simply a business arrangement. We've almost strangled him. He is being punished. He hands over his treasure and we dispatch him to hell.'

'I agree,' Ranulf declared.

'As do I,' Malfeson added.

'Then so be it.' Corbett nodded. 'Gentlemen, bring the prisoner.'

They left the cell, Ranulf and Ap Ythel gripping Ricard, his wrists still tightly bound. They took him along the corridor, up the steps and into God's Acre. The darkness had deepened while the harsh cold still held everything fast. Here and there they could glimpse lantern- or candlelight peeping through shutters or beneath doorways. Ranulf, dagger drawn, forced the prisoner to show them the way. He led them along a narrow, pebble-hard trackway that cut across the cemetery. Here the deceased monks of Westminster lay shrouded in their graves, waiting to be wakened by the blast of Archangel Michael's trumpet. That last moment of time when the elements would melt and Christ would appear. This, however, did not concern Corbett and his henchmen. They were fully determined to seize the treasure that would bring some justice, as well as execute a criminal who had caused such heart-rending misery.

Corbett stared up at the sky, now cloud free so the stars sparkled like diamonds on a cushion. Glancing around, he realised they were trudging towards the crypt, a grim, forbidding place almost buried under the great chapter house. Abruptly they paused. Ricard mumbled and pointed across to an ancient table tomb. He said he needed his hands untied. Corbett agreed to this, then watched as the Black Robe, cursing quietly, knelt by the side of the tomb. He used a fallen branch to prise loose a block of stone in the side, just above the ground. The stone was neatly cut: it created a slab that could easily be slid in and out, yet, when closed, it was completely hidden from view. Corbett crouched and stared through the gap. He recalled how a leading member of Puddlicott's coven had been a skilled master mason: his help to the robbers in cutting their way through the stony walls of the fortified crypt had been crucial.

'I wager,' he turned, peering at the Black Robe, 'the mason who cut this stone is no longer with us.'

'I cannot say, Sir Hugh.'

Corbett caught a tinge of the Black Robe's former arrogance.

'Let us see what we have,' he demanded. 'Show us now.'

Ricard reached forward and began to pull through the gap a pannier of the best leather, bulging with clinking coin. He then drew out four more. Ap Ythel dropped to his knees and crawled under the tomb. He cast about for a while, then slowly edged out.

'There is no more,' he gasped. 'Sir Hugh, we have everything he had hidden away here.'

'And rest assured,' Corbett replied, 'I shall personally seek royal approval for what we have done here as well as what we intend to do elsewhere.' He stared up at the sky. 'Dawn will break soon enough,' he murmured, 'and we must be gone. I have other urgent business to attend to.' He paused. 'Oh yes, my friends, we are not finished, not yet, with the work of the so-called Immortal.'

'What do you mean?'

'You will see soon enough, Ranulf. There are specific questions I must lay before a certain individual. I expect him to tell the truth, and only then will I be satisfied. Ap Ythel, I will need you and some of your archers. Malfeson, I thank you for your help, but as far as you are concerned, matters are settled. The queen will now need your support and counsel. I am sure,' he added drily, 'we shall meet again.' He pointed at the Black Robe still kneeling beside the tomb. 'Now we must be gone and so must he.' He noticed how Ranulf had slipped, sword drawn, behind the prisoner.

'You promised . . .' Ricard's voice was strident.

Corbett raised his hand. Ranulf now had his sword up, moving like some deadly dancer. Corbett dropped his hand. Ranulf, with all the speed of a master swordsman, swung his weapon, and the razor-edged blade hissed through the air to take Ricard's head in one clean cut. The severed head bounced away. The blood-spurting torso turned slightly, then toppled over to crash against the ground.

'Mortal enough,' Corbett whispered, crossing himself.

He readjusted his war belt and pulled his cloak tightly around him. He had been so immersed in what had happened, he'd hardly noticed the night air or the freezing cold. Now, however, the masque was over, and he felt the chill close in. He declared that they must return to the palace for a while. Ranulf would help carry the panniers, which Ap Ythel would hold all sealed until the king gave his approval. Then he gestured at the blood-soaked remains of his opponent.

'Bury these where the criminal kept his treasure: that's where his heart was, so that's where his corpse can lie till the end of time.'

PART EIGHT

The memory of a man should be condemned
when his body was condemned.

egotta the Moon-girl squatted in a cobwebbed corner of the taproom at the Tabard tavern, which was not at all as luxurious as the Twilight only a brief walk away. Nonetheless, she felt secure here after the frantic excitement of the last few days. She would never forget what had happened at Westminster.

'Where I,' she whispered to the darkness, 'was transformed from a whore to a princess and then to a queen.'

Megotta had not heard from Corbett or his henchmen, but she lived in hope. What she had learnt was that some great disturbance had occurred at the Twilight, the Tower and Westminster. She knew that the truth would soon seep out, or at least one version of it. The street heralds, the announcers of the alleyways, along with a host of others, would soon be spreading the gossip and fanning the rumours. Megotta, however, realised that the only people who knew the truth were Corbett and his coterie. She just wondered where they were. She also wondered if she should eat and drink at the Tabard or move back to the Twilight. But there again, Corbett had asked her to stay well away from that tavern, as much as possible. Nevertheless, she would love a hearty meal.

She was about to get up when the Tabard's great tomcat slid out of the shadows with a squealing, squeaking rat caught firmly between its jaws. The cat slipped in front of Megotta and shook its head as if the rat was some great trophy, before continuing on into the dark. Megotta felt she was about to gag. She swallowed quickly and rubbed her belly. 'I think I will wait,' she murmured to herself.

'Good morrow, mistress.' She startled as she stared up at the dark-faced stranger who had slipped into the taproom as silently and swiftly as any hunting cat. 'Mistress Megotta, is it not?'

She nodded, her hand going beneath her cloak to grip the bone handle of her stabbing dirk.

'No need for that, Megotta,' the stranger soothed. 'No need at all.' He held his hands up, palms facing outwards in a gesture of peace. Megotta nodded and withdrew her hand, and the stranger pulled across a stool so he could sit as close as possible.

Megotta remained impassive, staring at this dark-skinned man with the proud face of a hunting falcon. He was dressed soberly, but she noticed how his cloak, jerkin and hose were of the purest wool, while his leathers, be it his sword belt or boots, were of the best Cordova. He was delicate in his movements as he made himself comfortable and paid for the two stoups of ale the snotty-nosed slattern brought across. Once she had served them, he lifted his tankard.

'All hail, Megotta,' he declared, 'moon-girl and close bosom friend of Lord Hugh Corbett. Oh yes, you are the moon-girl, the mummer who can shift from one guise to another.'

'I would like to return your salutation,' Megotta retorted tartly, 'and unless I can do so swiftly, I am going to leave.'

'No, no,' the stranger replied. 'Let me introduce myself. I am Cartaphilus.'

'And?'

'I wander the face of the earth.'

'Along with millions of others. So?'

The stranger chuckled. 'I am of the Temple, and what I tell you will be of great interest to Sir Hugh.'

Megotta relaxed. This stranger undoubtedly meant well and, if Corbett was involved, then that was all to the good. 'If you have a message,' she spoke her thoughts, 'why don't you deliver it yourself? I mean, Westminster or the Twilight tavern are only a short distance away.'

'Two reasons, my friend. I am a Templar. Corbett is the king's own officer. My order is proscribed, which means so am I.'

'I doubt if Corbett would lift a hand against you,' Megotta retorted, 'and you know that.'

'You are correct.' The stranger grinned. 'I am safe with him,' he declared, 'but that's not my way. I prefer to keep to the shadows in my wanderings. Anyway, I am all packed and ready for the morning tide, and I have someone waiting to accompany me.'

'Where to? Where are you going?'

'That is part of my message. It's best if I am not seen with Corbett. So, what I tell you is only so he may become aware of what is happening. Listen now.' Cartaphilus edged a little closer. 'As you know, the Templar order is destroyed. Jacques de Molay, our Grand Master, along with other senior officers will be executed, murdered. Probably burnt alive over a slow fire on some island in the Seine.' He half smiled. 'Not far from the Tour de Nesle and all the dreadful secrets that place holds. De Molay, before the flames consume him, will curse the French Crown. He will also summon the two men responsible for the destruction of our order, Philip of France and Pope Clement V.'

'Summon them where? De Molay is a prisoner. How can he summon anybody? What authority or power does he wield?'

'Oh no, de Molay is not concerned with human justice; his taste for that is bitter in the extreme.' Cartaphilus crossed himself. 'As Grand Master of the Templar order, he will summon Philip of France and Pope Clement to appear with him before God's tribunal within a year and a day of his death.'

'Will this happen?'

'The curse has been released and the consequences are already emerging.' Cartaphilus shrugged. 'It has been published like any proclamation, and I, Cartaphilus, will tend it as carefully as I would a precious plant.'

'You say already emerging?'

'Oh yes. Take Philip's three sons, degenerates who spread their seed like mongrel dogs. As you may well know, there are philtres, potions and powders that can turn a man into a stallion in bed, and there are potions, philtres and powders that can render the opposite. Louis, Philip and Charles, the three princes of the blood, unbeknown to them are consuming such powders. They will never beget a living boy.'

'Are you sure of this?' Megotta demanded.

'As I have said, it has already begun. We Templars have our followers in all the palaces. They cook in kitchens, serve wine at banquets, and no one is the wiser. Oh yes, Megotta, matters will take a more urgent turn. Philip and Clement will go, and Philip's three sons will follow soon afterwards. The Capetian line will die out. Once that happens, Edward of England, or at least his mother on his behalf, will enter the tournament. She will lay claim to the crown of France and, in doing so, de Molay's curse will gather strength.'

'Is Malfeson part of this?'

'Malfeson is who he is, a royal clerk totally infatuated with his mistress. I will return to him.'

'And Queen Isabella and King Edward, are they caught up in this curse?'

'Of course, though they are guilty in a different way. Isabella's dowry was raised through Templar blood. Someone must answer for that. Edward her husband, albeit reluctantly, joined the attack on our order. All that bloodshed, all that abuse and degradation must be atoned for. Think of a thunderstorm; it grumbles in the distance but then it sweeps in and the rain pours down. However, with this storm, it will be blood.'

'So what is Corbett to do or not do?'

'He acted honourably, Megotta. He defended our order. We shall remember that.'

'But he serves both king and queen. He has pledged fealty, he is sworn to defend them.'

'Oh yes, we recognise that.' Cartaphilus sipped from his tankard. 'We watch and we wait. I know what happened at the Twilight. How the king's enemies were frustrated.'

'And?'

'I concede,' Cartaphilus replied, 'that what happened at that tavern was a faithful royal clerk protecting his liege lords. However, I tell you this, Megotta, there really is no need for us to intervene in England as we have in France. Edward and Isabella? Well, I have studied them closely. They will inflict hideous wounds on each other. Edward is no warrior general like his father. I strongly suspect his foray into Scotland will end in disaster. At home, he has made it very clear that he has not forgotten the capture and execution of his "beloved brother" Peter Gaveston, his dearest, darling favourite. You know that. I am sure Corbett has referred to it. Edward of England will never forgive his great earls for Gaveston's death, so there will be more bloodshed.'

'And Sir Hugh?'

'Oh, he will try to counsel both king and queen,

but . . .' Cartaphilus shrugged. 'Megotta, I am not a soothsayer, a fortune-teller. I simply watch how events unfold and I deduce possible conclusions. It's simple enough.'

'So why have you come to tell me this?'

'Well, we owe Corbett a debt. He has a right to know that a storm is coming. Finally,' he grinned, 'you are a mummer, a very good one. You remember lines. You deliver speeches and, in doing so, you are the best of messengers.'

'And Malfeson? You mentioned him then brushed him aside.'

'Megotta, you have me wrong. I have one last message to deliver, and it involves Malfeson. However, it's best if you hear this from another witness.'

'What witness?'

'Stay here.'

Cartaphilus rose and crossed the empty taproom to the main door. Megotta heard him speak, then he came back accompanied by a Franciscan nun garbed in the earth-brown robe of her order. She had a tired, lined face, but she also had that serene look of one who kept herself detached from the world. She accepted Cartaphilus's offer of a stoup of ale and a platter of honey-smeared croutons. She then sat down on the stool Megotta fetched for her. She made herself comfortable and turned to Cartaphilus.

'So this is Megotta, the mummers' girl, yes?'

'The very same.'

The nun smiled and proffered her bony, vein-streaked

hand for the moon-girl to clasp. Megotta lifted it to her lips and kissed it as tenderly as she could.

'This is Sister Hildegarde from the Convent of the Friar Minoresses close to Cripplegate. She has something to tell you.'

'But first may I break my fast?' asked the nun.

Sister Hildegarde pecked at her food like some bright-eyed spring sparrow. Once finished, she pushed the platter away and stared at Megotta.

'I understand you are a very skilled mummer. That you have participated in all the great miracle plays that reflect the liturgy of our Church.'

'That is correct, Sister.'

Hildegarde leant forward, pulling back the voluminous sleeves of her gown. 'Well let me tell you, Megotta, about a masque I was involved in many years ago. Now listen. I am English born but my mother was French. I had, thank God, a gift for languages. As a young woman, I realised I had a vocation to follow the rule of St Francis, so I joined the Minoresses. I soon became involved in physick; God be thanked for my talent. I was pleased and proud to be apprenticed to Mathilde of Westminster, who was renowned as a skilled physician. Now our house decided to help the Convent of Saint-Sulpice, just beyond the gate of Saint-Denis in Paris. Mother Mathilde and I journeyed there. We became members of the community. Oh, we had the best of times! I truly loved Mathilde. She was funny, humble, yet ever so skilled: her reputation as a healer became well known. Excuse me a moment.' Hildegarde took a few generous sips of her morning ale and sat back smacking her lips. 'To be brief,' she continued, 'one Sunday evening, in the year of Our Lord 1295, Mathilde and I were summoned to the Louvre Palace. Well, not so much summoned as taken there by armed men, hooded, visored and all buckled for battle.'

'Who were they?'

'Oh, we didn't know. We didn't see their faces; we weren't given names, but their tabards displayed the royal arms of France.' She paused, staring hard at Megotta. 'I haven't forgotten what happened.' Her smile widened. 'I could have been an excellent mummer.'

'Very true,' Megotta retorted, fascinated by this little nun who must have a mysterious tale to tell.

'Mathilde and I were taken to what was called La Salle Secrète, the Secret Room, deep in the bowels of the Louvre Palace.'

'Very close to the Chambre Noire,' Cartaphilus interjected.

'The room was well furnished,' Hildegarde continued, 'and the reason for our presence – as Katerina, one of the ladies-in-waiting declared – was that a young noblewoman was due to give birth to a baby, but this had become plagued by complications. Mathilde pulled back the curtains of the four-poster bed and set to work. She soon had matters under control. The mother, Lady Isolda, gave birth to a lusty bawling baby boy, who, as soon as he was washed and swaddled, was taken away by the same armed men who had brought us there.

Apparently they had been waiting outside for the birth of the child.

'That was when it happened.' Hildegarde's eyes welled with tears. 'The armed men, before they left, gave us a gift to celebrate: a carafe of what was described as "the best wine from the royal cellars". Once they'd gone, I served the wine for Mathilde, the Lady Katerina and the mother of the child, openly rejoicing in the birth of a sturdy baby boy. I did not drink any myself; I very rarely do. We then prepared to leave but, as we did, the Lady Isolda began to complain of belly pains. I also became deeply alarmed as I heard chilling screaming and squealing from rats that had apparently tasted some of the wine I had accidentally spilled while pouring it.

'Matters quickly descended into a nightmare. I knew I had to get Mathilde, also complaining of belly pains, out of that palace. In the end, we were almost thrust through the gate and left to our own devices. By the time we reached Saint-Sulpice, Mother Mathilde was in a dreadful state. We took her to the infirmary. I did what I could, but it was futile. She died just before daybreak. We received similar news regarding Lady Isolda and the Lady Katerina. Our abbess demanded that I tell her what happened. I did so. I was terrified. For some unknown reason, somebody wanted the Lady Isolda dead, as well as the women who had witnessed the birth of that baby boy.'

Hildegarde pointed at Megotta. 'You will ask me why that should be. Over the years, both myself and my order have made careful enquiries. I believe that the boy child I helped bring into the world was a by-blow of King Philip of France. On the one hand, he would welcome a son. However, on the other, by removing the women who had witnessed the child's birth, no one could use the boy in any move against him or the French Crown. Such a solution would satisfy Philip. Moreover, he is a dyed-in-the-wool prude who would feel acutely embarrassed at having to own up to fathering a child outside marriage.

'Time passed. Matters became more relaxed. We eventually discovered that the boy had been raised well and had proved himself most able both in the chancery and out on the tournament field.'

'And his name?'

'Guillaume Malfeson.'

'Ah,' Megotta exclaimed, 'a man now so active in matters politic. A high-ranking clerk in the Chambre Noire, or so I've learnt.' She leant over and gently stroked the nun's hand. 'And what about you, Sister?'

'At the time, as I said, I was terrified, and so was the lady abbess on my behalf. She wanted me out of France, so she cast about to find a safe and secure way. Eventually she discovered that English envoys had arrived in Paris led by Henry of Lincoln, the present king's kinsman. He was accompanied by a group of English Templars, as well as a young clerk called Hugh Corbett.'

Megotta clapped her hands in surprise.

'Oh yes! Corbett and those Templars sheltered me

until I was safely on a cog bound for Dover.' The nun pressed her hands together as if in prayer.

'Corbett didn't know the full story,' Cartaphilus added. 'Anyway, Hildegarde returned to England. Once there, she began to make her enquiries about the child. Now during her journey from France, she had made herself most agreeable to the Templar contingent. A deep friendship flourished. My order was only too willing to help. She called on the Templars in Paris to assist her, and thus I became involved.'

'At the same time,' Hildegarde continued, 'I begged the Templars to keep an eye on Malfeson's safety. They did more than that, didn't you, my brother?' She leant over and tapped Cartaphilus on the shoulder.

'Yes, yes, we did. Little wonder he secretly joined the order. Over the years, Philip had grown more mellow about his bastard son, and he was very supportive. I suspect he wanted a spy deep in our ranks.' Cartaphilus laughed. 'In fact, the opposite happened. Malfeson gave us early warning about Philip's secret plans. It's a tragedy we did not heed his words. Philip of France is utterly ruthless; his destruction of our order proves that. Little wonder rumours abound that he even poisoned his wife, Joanna of Navarre, the mother of his four children.'

'And why have you chosen to share this information with me?' Megotta demanded.

'Well, first, you are English and can be easily protected against Philip's malice should he decide you have no right to such information. But there are other reasons.' He turned to the nun. 'Hildegarde?'

Sister Hildegarde dug beneath her robe and drew out a scroll of parchment. 'What I have told you is written here. All sworn, signed and sealed by myself. This is the truth. In telling it, I make reparation for three murders perpetrated some years ago. I wish you to hand this to Corbett and, at the appropriate time, he can pass it to Malfeson. By doing this, we testify to the truth that what is written here is not a figment of someone's disordered imagination. Oh no! It is the true confession of a fully professed nun that has been handed to an English royal clerk to be given to a French royal clerk. Such a transfer emphasises the document's provenance. It is also further punishment for Philip of France. When Malfeson reads this account, and one day he surely will, there is no doubt that he will sever all ties with the man who murdered his mother.'

'And you, Sister?' Megotta asked. 'What will you do?'

It was Cartaphilus who replied. 'Sister Hildegarde will join me in crossing the Narrow Seas. I will leave her at Saint-Sulpice before journeying south.'

'I want to visit Mathilde's grave. I want to lay flowers there.' Hildegarde blinked, then smiled. 'Brother,' she turned to Cartaphilus, 'it is time we were gone.'

Corbett sat up straight, leaning into the cushioned back-rest of a bench in the great buttery at the Twilight. He rolled up the scroll Sister Hildegarde had given Megotta, then handed it to Ranulf sitting opposite him.

'Will you give it to Malfeson?' asked Ranulf.

'In time, in time,' Corbett replied. 'As scripture says,

there's a time under heaven for everything. Let us first deal with the business in hand. All matters come to an end. Everything breaks down eventually and drains away. Now . . .'

He paused at a knock at the door. A pale-faced, anxious-looking Appleby almost crept into the buttery. He wiped his hands against the long leather apron that covered him from neck to toe.

'Sir Hugh, you said you needed to see me.'

'Yes, yes, I do.' Corbett waved him to sit next to Ranulf. Appleby did so, sliding onto the high-backed cushioned bench.

'Do you want anything to eat or drink?'

He mumbled his refusal.

'Have you heard the news?'

'Sir Hugh, I know what happened here at the Twilight.'

'Yes, you would, but there's more. The so-called Immortal is no longer immortal. He has been caught, questioned, condemned and executed last night. He was no less a person than the so-called priest Brother Ricard, Benedictine monk of Westminster Abbey.' Corbett paused. Appleby's agitation was most obvious. 'Oh yes,' the royal clerk continued, 'the news will indeed affect you! So, Master Appleby, let us clear up any doubt on this issue. I have a number of questions for you. First, when I reflect on the trial and execution of Sarasin, I cannot recall any involvement by yourself. I mean, you are steward of the Twilight, its co-owner, yet you were as silent and secretive as a ghost.'

'I . . . I, er, I was,' Appleby stammered. 'I was not involved. I was a mere spectator.'

'But you must have served Sarasin and Rahmel many times. You must have listened to their conversations. That's what a good taverner does. Knowledge is power. You must have been curious? I mean, a riffler lord consorting with a French royal clerk. You served them wine and food on many occasions.'

'Well, no, not really. Malling did that mostly.'

'And when Malling was absent? Please tell me. Or if you won't, I could take you to the taproom and ask what others saw and heard, eh?'

'True, Sir Hugh, I did serve both men occasionally.'

'Of course you did. Indeed, Rahmel informed Malfeson that one of the reasons Sarasin frequented the Twilight was that he had a friend there to protect his back. Master Appleby, I put it to you that you were not only Sarasin's friend, but his accomplice as well.'

'That was not me.' Appleby's face was all flustered, his forehead sweat soaked.

'Oh, I disagree,' Corbett murmured. 'But let's move on to the dire occurrences at the Twilight after Sarasin's execution. Now, we know that Brother Ricard only pretended to have an injury. In fact, at the Twilight he moved swiftly from room to room during his murderous foray. He killed both Poulter and Swinton, and also abducted Malling's daughters, Rebekah and Rachel. So where were you when all this was happening? Didn't you sense, see or hear anything untoward? Didn't you glimpse Ricard slipping along the galleries or going up and down the stairs? Weren't you concerned about events? Do you know something, Appleby? I don't believe you are a murderer but, of course, Ricard had to be protected by an accomplice. Somebody had to stand watch. Someone had to make sure that your master, the Immortal, could move silently and swiftly, dealing out death and punishment to his enemies.'

'Sir Hugh, you forget, I sent for you.'

'Oh yes, you certainly did, but only when Ricard had finished his murderous foray. Poulter and Swinton were dead, Rebekah and Rachel imprisoned in their chambers and then abducted, leaving their father to teeter on the edge of madness. Let's reflect on that.' Corbett wetted his lips. 'Henry Malling was your friend, your business partner, an old comrade. Didn't you go to his aid? You claimed you didn't have authority to force entry into this chamber or that.' He shook his head. 'Absolute nonsense. I accepted that at the time, but not now. I mean, when I arrived at the Twilight after you had sent for me, you had apparently done nothing but try the two chamber doors, yes? And weren't you worried about the continued absence of Rebekah and Rachel, Malling's adored daughters? Did you try to comfort their father? Did you send for a leech? You know a very skilled one, I believe. Master Thirston. He would have been ideal in soothing Malling's disturbed humours. Well, did you do any of these things?' Corbett shook his head. 'No, you didn't. Very well, did you organise a search for Malling's daughters?'

'I understood that the two girls had left for Faversham.'

'Oh, that was just a farrago of nonsense. It was obvious they hadn't. I am sure if you gathered the tavern people here, they would bear witness that the first reports that the two young women had gone to Faversham originated, Master Appleby, from you! Anyway, we know they didn't go to Faversham, and so did you.'

'I was very confused by all that was happening.'

'Oh come, Master Appleby, don't act the maiden in distress. Did you organise a search for Rebekah and Rachel? Did you send out tavern servants?'

'Yes, I did.'

'Why did you do that if you thought the two girls had gone to Faversham? Whom did you send?'

'I dispatched Stigand.'

'I thought you might say that; after all, he is in no position to confirm it. Did you send anyone with him? You must have done. The cook, or that legion of spit boys you employ. Well, did you?'

'I forget, I . . .' Appleby's voice trailed away.

'Ah well, let us move on to Master Malling himself. You remember how he died and who was where when it happened? I was conferring with Ranulf and Malfeson. I had asked you to look after poor Malling. Did you? Did you check on him every so often, scrutinise him, have words with him? Did you see him tip into madness, a killing madness as he issued bloodthirsty threats against French clerks? Did you see him arm himself with dagger and cleaver? No? Why not?'

Appleby just stared at Corbett bleary eyed.

'Now let's move to the assassin, Walter Mappe. He

329

made his way up the stairs to kill me while I was praying. Again, I emphasise, you are the steward of the Twilight. Nevertheless, you saw or heard nothing of this complete stranger creeping through your tavern. True, Mappe may have received assistance from your leader, the so-called Immortal, but your role in this, or rather the lack of it, is truly puzzling.'

'You are now,' Appleby blurted, 'accusing me of being involved in an attempt on your life.'

'Oh, much more than that, Master Appleby, much more than that. Other matters are also clouded in mystery. Let's talk about the curtain wall of this tavern. My good friend Ap Ythel carefully checked that wall and found roughly cut gaps that provide secure foot-holds and hand grips for anyone to use either entering the garden or leaving it. We scrutinised that wall. Why didn't you? Surely as a steward you'd carry out such checks, especially if someone else was apparently coming in and out of the garden, be it some felon bent on murdering my prisoner, or the Brethren who killed poor Stigand.'

'I . . . I didn't know, I didn't realise . . .'

'Listen, Master Appleby. The so-called Immortal came and went so secretly, so mysteriously because of that wall. Indeed, I am sure that somewhere in that garden is his purple clothing, worn to reflect his authority. All of this lies stowed away in some cleverly hidden chest so that he could change into whatever he wished. One of my many informants saw our so-called Immortal beneath the tavern sign. He went to discover more. Of course, by then, the Immortal had disappeared, not into the dark, but up those roughly hewn steps into the garden, where he could hide or transform himself back into the humble Benedictine monk! Any comment? No? Then I shall press on, because that curtain wall is an important part of the mosaic of murder that I am now trying to complete. The steps hewn into it resolve the mystery of the murder of the prisoner I lodged in the outhouse. The Immortal simply used these steps to enter and to leave. I cannot prove how the Brethren, that cohort of assassins, actually entered the Twilight. However, I strongly suspect that they too came over the curtain wall.

'Now the story peddled by you was that the assassins knocked on the door while Stigand was on guard. Yes? He opened it, and one of the assassins loosed the bolt that killed him. Now that is a nonsense. Stigand would never have opened the door to a knock, especially at a time when the tavern was seemingly under attack, a severe disturbance in the dead of night. No, no. He was probably murdered by one of the Brethren who lodged at the tavern. The killer then opened the garden door so his comrades could slip in with their cache of weapons. They also ensured that they could use that gateway to escape if matters turned against them, as they did.'

'I was not party to Stigand's murder,' Appleton protested. 'I wouldn't have hurt him.'

'I am sure that's true,' Corbett replied. 'I am certain you did no ill, but I am equally certain that you did

331

no good. Now, let us return to a most sorry chapter in this murderous tale.' He leant against the table, staring at Appleby, who was now on the verge of tears. 'Let us talk,' he declared, 'about *The War-dog*.' Appleby moaned quietly as he put his face in his hands. 'Let me be succinct. Ensign Malachi and six archers, along with a battle-boat and a heavy treasure chest, just disappeared off the face of God's earth. I now know what happened. I also know that the navigator was crucial to the boat's disappearance that night. So, who hired this navigator?'

'Well, in truth, it was Malachi.'

'But who recommended him to the ensign? Who had the status and authority at the Twilight to do that, eh?' Corbett paused, jabbing a finger at Appleby. 'And please don't tell me that it was Malling. No, Master Appleby. It was you.'

The tavern steward just stared blankly back. Corbett steeled himself. The lie he was about to tell was necessary. 'Master Appleby, I have questioned the so-called Immortal. He claimed you had a decisive role in all of this. You appointed the navigator to Ensign Malachi's troop. You know you did. Are you going to deny it? Are you going to make matters worse for yourself? Were you responsible for that navigator, yes or no?'

'Yes,' Appleby sobbed. 'Yes, I was, and all you have said is true. I am not going to contest it.' He sprang to his feet, knocking away Ranulf's restraining hand. 'I need to go to the jakes closet,' he said. 'I need to go now.'

'Ranulf, go with him.'

A short while later, both men reappeared. Appleby slumped down onto the bench.

'Master Appleby, you could hang for this. You could suffer even worse because it is treason.'

Appleby stared at a point above Corbett's head. 'You don't know what it was like,' he began slowly. 'I am a taverner. I love cooking, choosing fine wines, making sure my customers feel better about themselves. I am also a former Templar, vulnerable to all sorts of allegations and accusations. The Immortal threatened all of this. He demanded that I cooperate with him or he would personally bury my wife and three children out on the mudflats along the Thames. Sir Hugh, you now know he was more than capable of that.'

'Did you know that the Immortal was Brother Ricard?'

'No, I didn't. All I knew was that he threatened me as he did Malling. We had no choice but to agree.' Appleby lifted his hands from beneath the table. 'So if you are going to arrest me, then do so now.'

'No, no, Master Appleby. Let me come swiftly to the point. What you did was wrong, but like others in the Templar order, you are more sinned against than sinning. I am going to issue letters of pardon for any crimes you have committed.' Appleby gaped in astonishment. 'I don't want your life and I certainly don't want your death,' Corbett continued. 'You are a good man, so listen carefully. You will manage the Twilight on behalf of the Crown. You will make a good profit and ensure the Exchequer gets its portion as you do yours. In return, you will make this a watching post. You will listen to the chatter along the river, in the city and in Westminster. You will pass such information to me. You will be honest and direct, and then, Master Appleby, you will be my friend and a most loyal subject of our king. You look surprised? For God's sake, man, I don't want you to hang, so just do what I ask.'

Appleby nodded, almost beside himself with relief, rubbing his face in his hands, wiping the sweat from his brow.

'So, my friend,' Corbett declared, 'let's have that lovely beef stew you are so skilled at, with a dish of vegetables and the best Bordeaux you can muster.'

Appleby left. Corbett and Ranulf sat for a while in silence.

'A merry end,' Ranulf murmured, 'to a truly murderous tale.'

'No, Ranulf, the tale is not yet complete, but when it is, believe me, it will be anything but merry!'

AUTHOR'S NOTE

Historical fiction, where possible, should try to reflect historical fact. Of course, sometimes that is not possible. Nevertheless, strands of my story are reflected in what actually happened. Plots to abduct Queen Isabella seem fairly preposterous, but in fact they did occur. Isabella herself accused her great enemy, Hugh Despenser, of leaving her vulnerable to abduction by the Scots in 1312 during a clash between the English king and his Scottish enemy Robert the Bruce. In 1320, a Yorkshire knight, Edmund Darel, was arrested for attempting to abduct the queen a year earlier and hand her over to the Scots. Finally, in 1325, when Isabella was in exile, attempts to abduct her from the French court forced her to seek refuge elsewhere.

The Templar order was destroyed. Philip IV wreaked savage punishment on what was once a formidable fighting force. Its Grand Master, Jacques de Molay, and other leading Templars were barbarously executed, burnt to death on islands in the Seine. Of course, historians regard the 'Templar curse' as something best left to fiction writers. However, even the most critical observer would have to concede that those involved in the dissolution of the Templars faced the most sinister and eerie fate. Pope Clement V did die within the same twelve months, as Jacques de Molay prophesied, struck down by a violent dysentery; his corpse, left in a church before burial, was consumed by a fire that broke out during the night. Philip IV fell suddenly ill while hunting and was struck dumb; his council believed he had sustained a stroke. He never recovered to utter even one word. Philip's principal advisers also suffered. Enguerrand de Marigny was hanged early in the reign of Philip's successor, Louis X. Guillaume de Nogaret went mad, wandering around babbling nonsense and sticking his tongue out at passers-by. None of Philip's three sons begot an heir and, in 1328, the crown of France passed to the house of Valois. This was immediately challenged by Edward of England, and the seeds of the cruel and vicious Hundred Years war were sown.

In England, Edward II and Isabella became estranged, which led to Edward's deposition, imprisonment and execution. Isabella was forced into retirement, and died in something akin to the odour of sanctity at Castle Rising in Norfolk in 1358. The Tour de Nesle scandal did occur. Isabella played a leading role in this, sending letters to her father and being closeted with him in a number of meetings. All this ended with the d'Aunay brothers being torn apart on a public scaffold and their lovers, the three princesses, being consigned to either convents or castles. It was indeed a time of great turbulence, which greatly affected the royal families of Europe – and that is fact, not fiction!

Finally, the Wandering Jew is one of those delightfully mysterious tales that can provoke great interest and comment. If you wish to read more, I recommend Gustav Doré's elegant essay on this phenomenon, and then you can judge for yourselves!

Pax et bonum!

Paul C. Doherty

PAUL DOHERTY

THE MASTER HISTORIAN HAS CAST HIS MAGICAL SPELL OVER ALL PERIODS OF HISTORY IN OVER 100 NOVELS

They are all now available in ebook, from his fabulous series

Hugh Corbett Medieval Mysteries
Sorrowful Mysteries of Brother Athelstan
Sir Roger Shallot Tudor Mysteries
Kathryn Swinbrooke Series
Nicholas Segalla Series
Mysteries of Alexander the Great
The Templar Mysteries
Matthew Jankyn Series
Canterbury Tales of Murder and Mystery
The Egyptian Mysteries
Mahu (The Akhenaten-Trilogy)
Mathilde of Westminster Series
Political Intrigue in Ancient Rome Series

to the standalones and trilogies that have made his name

The Death of a King	The Haunting
Prince Drakulya	The Soul Slayer
The Lord Count Drakulya	The Plague Laws
The Fate of Princes	The Love Knot
Dove Amongst the Hawks	Of Love and War
The Masked Man	The Loving Cup
The Rose Demon	The Last of Days

LIVE HISTORY
VISIT WWW.HEADLINE.CO.UK OR
WWW.PAULCDOHERTY.COM TO FIND OUT MORE

HEADLINE

RAISING READERS
Books Build Bright Futures

Dear Reader,

We'd love your attention for one more page to tell you about the crisis in children's reading, and what we can all do.

Studies have shown that reading for fun is the **single biggest predictor of a child's future life chances** – more than family circumstance, parents' educational background or income. It improves academic results, mental health, wealth, communication skills, ambition and happiness.[1]

The number of children reading for fun is in rapid decline. Young people have a lot of competition for their time. In 2024, 1 in 10 children and young people in the UK aged 5 to 18 did not own a single book at home.[2]

Hachette works extensively with schools, libraries and literacy charities, but here are some ways we can all raise more readers:

- Reading to children for just 10 minutes a day makes a difference
- Don't give up if children aren't regular readers – there will be books for them!
- Visit bookshops and libraries to get recommendations
- Encourage them to listen to audiobooks
- Support school libraries
- Give books as gifts

There's a lot more information about how to encourage children to read on our website: **www.RaisingReaders.co.uk**

Thank you for reading.

hachette
UK

---

[1] OECD, '21st-Century Readers: Developing Literacy Skills in a Digital World', 2021, https://www.oecd.org/en/publications/21st-century-readers_a83d84cb-en.html

[2] National Literacy Trust, 'Book Ownership in 2024', November 2024, https://literacytrust.org.uk/research-services/research-reports/book-ownership-in-2024